The
Stone House
Secret

Debra Burroughs

Lake House Books
Boise, Idaho

First eBook Edition: 2014
First Paperback Edition: 2014

THE STONE HOUSE SECRET by Debra Burroughs,
1st ed. p.cm.

Visit My Blog: www.DebraBurroughsBooks.com

Contact Me: Debra@DebraBurroughs.com

ISBN-10: 1505349982
ISBN-13: 978-1505349986

DEDICATION

This book is dedicated to my amazing husband, Tim,
who loves me and encourages me every day to
do what I love – writing.

TABLE OF CONTENTS

ACKNOWLEDGMENTS

I would like to acknowledge my awesome Beta Readers, Cathy Tomlinson, Janet Lewis, and Buffy Drewett, who inspire me and help me with their words of encouragement and critique.

I want to also acknowledge my brilliant Editor, Lisa Dawn Martinez.

CHAPTER 1

"THE COUNCILMAN APOLOGIZED for the scandal," Jenessa muttered under her breath, "and any embarrassment he caused his family and the town." Her lithe fingers flew over her computer keyboard as she finished up another story for the Hidden Valley Herald. She hit the period key with a flourish. "The end."

Sitting in her tiny cubicle at the small-town newspaper, with her article finally done, she rolled her shoulders to work out a kink, then scrubbed her fingers through her long hair. With a wisp of a sigh, she leaned back in her chair, closed her eyes, and let her mind happily drift to visions of the tall, dark, and delicious Detective Michael Baxter. Dreamy thoughts of their impending date floated in and out of her mind, anticipation building at the pleasure of it. At six o'clock, he would be whisking her away for a romantic night out.

After peeking down at her watch one more time, she closed her eyes again and leaned her head back.

Michael's face filled her imagination—his strong angular jaw, his warm brown eyes, and that enticing mouth that smiled at her like she was the only woman he ever wanted. Only two more hours and he'd be standing on her doorstep, all six feet four inches of his heart-fluttering manliness.

"Jenessa!" her editor bellowed as he stepped into her workspace.

The sharpness of his voice startled her, making her eyes fly open as she almost fell out of her chair. She grabbed for her desk and regained her balance, and composure—hopefully, before he detected any sign of embarrassment. "Yes, Charles," she turned toward him and forced a little smile on her face, "what can I do for you?"

"I just received a tip on a breaking story and I need you to get out to Whitfield College. There's been a shooting."

"At the college? How bad is it?" Horrific thoughts of the tragic massacre at Virginia Tech and other schools around the country popped into her mind. "Any casualties?"

"That's why I'm sending you out there—to find out what's happened. Now get me something I can run in the morning paper."

"Sure thing, Charles." *There goes my date with Michael.* She'd have to phone him on the way to Whitfield and reschedule. On second thought, he'd probably be at the crime scene as well. Being one of only two detectives on the small Hidden Valley police force, he and his partner would certainly have been called out to investigate.

Ah, the small town life.

Her return to Hidden Valley was taking some getting used to, even though she had been back in town for a few months already. Before her return, Jenessa had been an investigative reporter on a large Sacramento newspaper, where she was used to a high crime-rate and people working at the newspaper until all hours of the night to get breaking news out in the morning edition—not to mention dealing with a large police force and numerous different detectives.

At times she missed the adrenalin rush of covering a compelling, hard-hitting story and having her byline on the front page of a major newspaper, but since her parents died and she inherited their upscale home in Hidden Valley, she had decided to move back and reconnect with her family and friends.

Jenessa fumbled around in her purse for her car keys but came up empty handed. She thought for a moment. Where could they be? "Shoot! I forgot my car is in the shop, Charles," Jenessa lamented, glancing down at her watch again. "They said it wouldn't be done until five o'clock. I guess I could call a cab or—"

"No need." Logan Alexander poked his head over Charles's shoulder.

"Logan." She did her best to hide her surprise and the rush of warmth that heated her cheeks. Funny what an ex-boyfriend could still do to you.

Although, Jenessa had to admit to herself, he was more than just any ex-boyfriend. Logan Alexander was a gorgeous specimen of a man, over six feet tall with wavy blond hair and deep blue eyes the color of the Aegean Sea. She had fallen madly, deeply, in love with him—in

3

high school. Now, at twenty-nine, the sight of him still brought back a flood of memories.

"What are you doing here?" she asked.

He flashed his charming, confident smile at her, every pearly white in perfect alignment. "Just meeting with Charles and checking on one of our businesses."

Logan's father, Grey Alexander, owned the newspaper, a bank, and a real estate office, among other enterprises in Hidden Valley. Logan had been temporarily put in charge of the family empire while his father was away and unable to oversee things for a while. "I'm happy to give you a ride over to the college." A mischievous gleam shone in his azure eyes.

That was the last thing she needed. Since her return to Hidden Valley, Logan had made repeated ovations to her, trying to rekindle what they'd once had. But, to his dismay, she had begun to date Detective Michael Baxter, an old friend from their high school days, and things were moving along quite well with him.

What would the handsome detective think if he saw her at the crime scene, climbing out of Logan's snazzy, red BMW convertible?

Logan had made it clear he was not going to give up trying to win her back. He wanted her in his life again and it seemed he saw Michael as nothing more than a temporary bump in the road.

Handsome, successful, rich—what more could a girl want? Well...trustworthy, maybe? The past she shared with Logan was a huge stumbling block, at least for her, to their ever getting back together.

"I think that's a fine idea, Logan," Charles said, giving the young man a light clap on the back.

"Then it's settled." Logan grinned. "Jenessa, your chariot awaits." He stepped aside and swept his hand toward the door.

None too pleased, she clutched her handbag to her chest and quickly slipped past him, hearing his footsteps following her down the hall.

"I'm gone for the day," she called out to Alice, the elderly receptionist, as they stopped by her desk. "Call my cell if you need me."

"Good-bye, Alice," Logan said with a wink.

"Good day, Mr. Alexander," Alice said sweetly, wearing a girlish grin, as Jenessa and Logan turned and walked to the entrance door. "You two make such an attractive couple."

"He's just giving me a lift," Jenessa tossed back over her shoulder. Something told her she was probably going to regret taking it.

~*~

It was a sunny and mild September afternoon. Gold and orange leaves floated down from the trees as they drove down Broadway Avenue, toward the college. Logan attempted to make small talk. In her peripheral vision, she could see him glancing at her from time to time, but Jenessa kept her replies short and her eyes from meeting his, afraid any encouragement would give him the wrong idea.

She had loved him once and it had ended disastrously. She was determined not to make that mistake again, but, unfortunately, the sizzling spark she felt when he touched her, or whenever she looked into his devilishly alluring eyes, told her she had not totally gotten him out of her heart.

As Jenessa stared out the side window, she remembered the summer before her senior year of high school, the summer Logan was leaving for college. They'd been teenagers in love, and one evening at his family's lake house they'd given in to their passion for each other. It was the only time they had slept together, but one time was all it took for her to become pregnant.

They'd decided to break the news to both sets of parents at the same time. They were well acquainted—Jenessa's father was Grey Alexander's attorney. So they gathered their folks together in the Alexanders' living room to explain the situation. His parents were livid, Jenessa's were humiliated.

After what seemed like hours of arguing and tears, it was decided that the best thing for all concerned was for Logan to go to college as planned, and for Jenessa to be sent away until she had the baby and gave it up for adoption. Then she could go on with her life, her father had said. Logan agreed with them—that giving up the baby was best—which had broken her heart.

She had left Hidden Valley soon after that night and did not return for twelve long years. At seventeen she had given birth to a healthy baby boy. She'd held the newborn for a few minutes, cradled him against her chest. Then, the woman from the adoption agency said it was time. With unstoppable tears and unspeakable pain shredding her heart, she kissed his tiny cheek and handed her son over, knowing he would soon be placed with his new mother.

Her arms had felt sadly empty, as had her heart, and

THE STONE HOUSE SECRET

no amount of time had diminished those feelings. Jenessa had longed for that child every day since.

Logan put a hand on her arm. "Jenessa."

She flinched. "What?"

"Where did you go? You seemed like you were a million miles away."

"Lost in thought, I guess." She rubbed her arms at a sudden chill.

They sped down the long driveway that was the entrance to the college, flanked on each side of the roadway by majestic old maple trees that were beginning to turn gold, orange, and crimson as autumn was upon them.

Logan said something, but Jenessa couldn't say what, for her mind was still somewhere else.

Finally his words made it through. "Looks like we're here."

Her gaze slid from the side window to the scene ahead. Several police cars were strategically positioned to block off traffic, their red-and-blue lights flashing, yellow crime scene tape strung between cars and trees to create a perimeter. She spotted Michael with his back to her, standing beside his silver-haired partner, Detective George Provenza.

"This is far enough, Logan," she instructed, not wanting to draw Michael's attention to her getting out of Logan's car. "Just pull over and let me out."

"I can get you up closer," he offered as he slowed.

"No. This is good." She opened the door while the car was still moving, hoping it would force him to halt.

"All right already, but at least wait until I come to a stop."

The second he did, she spit out a quick thanks and bolted from the car, slamming the door harder than she'd planned. The sound from the door caused Michael to turn and her heart dropped to her stomach—this was the very thing she was trying to avoid. Even from thirty feet away, she detected Michael's eyebrows wrinkle in irritation.

Jenessa shrugged and sheepishly approached him, but a young uniformed officer stepped in front of her. She pulled up short and stopped, recognizing the man. "Hello, Luke. Can I get through to talk to the detectives?"

"Sorry, but Detective Provenza ordered me not to let anyone through."

Luke was Michael's cousin. He had recently moved to Hidden Valley, having secured a job on the police force. From almost the first day he'd arrived in town, Luke and her sister, Sara, were inseparable.

Jenessa looked past him, to Michael, but he and Provenza had turned away again. "Michael!" she called out, waving her hand in the air, trying to get his attention once more, hoping to gain permission to pass.

As Michael and Provenza both turned at the sound of his name, they revealed a striking redheaded woman, middle aged, seated on a bench. Another woman, about the same age, with honey-blond hair, sat beside her with her arm laced around the shoulders of the first.

"Aunt Renee?" Seeing her aunt there—the second woman—threw Jenessa off a bit. "Are you all right?" she called out.

When Michael motioned for her to approach, with a stern look on his face, the young officer stepped aside.

"Sorry, Jenessa, just following orders," Luke said.

Jenessa gave him a nod and swept past him, dashing to her aunt's side. "Are you all right? Were you involved in the shooting?"

"No, I'm fine, sweetheart," her aunt replied. "But my friend here, she was the one shot at. She phoned me right after she called nine-one-one."

Jenessa's attention moved to the redheaded woman.

"This is my friend Professor Daphne Stone," Aunt Renee introduced.

The woman rose. "Dr. Stone," she corrected, extending a weak hand. She was tall and slim, and fairly attractive if it hadn't been for the nervous lines around her mouth and eyes. Her dark, auburn hair was thick and hung in loosely layered waves above her shoulders, her fair skin making a striking contrast to her deep emerald eyes.

Framed by her open collar was a small, unusual birthmark in the shape of a bowtie at the base of her throat. Dr. Stone must have noticed Jenessa looking at it, for she quickly gathered her collar together with her other hand.

Jenessa lifted her gaze to meet the woman's and shook her hand firmly but gently. "Yes, my aunt has mentioned you, Dr. Stone. My name is Jenessa Jones. I'm a reporter for the Hidden Valley Herald. Do you mind if I ask you a few questions?" Jenessa's eyes moved from Dr. Stone to Michael, raising her brows at him, seeking his approval.

Michael stepped beside Jenessa, his hand resting lightly on the small of her back. "We've already taken her statement," he said, "so, if she's willing…"

"Another time maybe," Daphne Stone replied flatly with a slight wave of her hand, sitting back down. "I'm too upset right now. I just want to go home."

"I understand, but I was hoping for just a few quick questions. My editor is expecting my story for the morning paper."

"Jenessa," her aunt chided.

"Just a few."

Daphne gave her a pensive look, as if she was considering the request, then turned to her friend. "It's all right, Renee, as long as she keeps it short." The woman raised her deep green eyes to Jenessa. "I really don't know much. I was walking to my car and heard a loud crash, my back window exploded." Daphne's trembling hand fluttered to her collarbone. "Then I called nine-one-one."

"I think that's enough for now," Aunt Renee interrupted. "Let's get you home, Daphne."

"I appreciate what time you were able to give me, Dr. Stone," Jenessa continued. "I'll interview the detectives to get the rest of the story." She turned her attention toward Michael. "Right, Detective Baxter?"

"Sure. Let's step over by my car, Miss Jones," he gestured to the vehicle, which was only a few feet away, "and I'll be more than happy to answer your questions." Michael leaned in near Jenessa's ear and whispered, "And we'll talk about Logan later."

As he spoke, his breath was warm on her skin and his aftershave was musky—an unexpected wave of excitement swept over her body. Her gaze met his for a moment and she gave a slight nod. "Later."

Would he believe her when she said that being with

Logan in his car meant nothing? The truth was it was Michael she wanted to be with, not Logan, yet circumstances seemed to make that unclear at times. His obvious jealousy could be endearing, but Logan's repeated attempts to get between her and Michael were getting old, and Michael's patience with it seemed to be wearing thin.

"That's my wife! Daphne!" someone hollered.

Jenessa and Michael turned to see a man sprinting past the young officer, toward them. He was nice looking in a sophisticated, scholarly sort of way, neatly trimmed brown hair, maybe early forties, wearing a navy blue blazer and tan slacks. "I just heard about the shooting. Are you okay, darling?" With his arms outstretched, his hazel eyes searched the woman's face.

Daphne rose and stepped into his embrace for a brief hug, their gaze not meeting. "I'm fine, Drew." She took a small step back and straightened. "If, in fact, the shooter was actually aiming at me then, fortunately, he missed his target."

Surprise flashed in Drew's eyes for a second. He put a hand on Daphne's arm. "You think someone was aiming at you? But why?"

"I don't really know." Daphne seemed to recoil a bit from her husband's touch, then she sat back down on the bench. The atmosphere became oddly cool and uncomfortable. Was something going on between these two?

Aunt Renee glanced away. Did she know what it was?

Detective Provenza cleared his throat as he studied the man. "And you are?"

"This is my husband, Drew Stone." Daphne gave a slight hand gesture toward him. "He's a professor here as well."

Michael rejoined the conversation. "The shooter took out the rear window of your wife's car, so we have to consider the fact that she may have been his intended target."

"But why on earth would someone—"

Provenza put his hand on Mr. Stone's arm and cut him off. "Why don't we step over here by the building to talk?"

"But my wife—" Drew Stone pulled his arm back, allowing the detective to escort him the few steps to the abutting brick building, while Michael followed. "What did you want to talk to me about?"

Jenessa strained to hear their conversation.

"Where were you in the last hour, Professor Stone?" Had Michael noticed the chilly interaction between the couple too?

"I was in my office, working, of course."

"Can anyone substantiate that?" Detective Provenza said, following Michael's line of questioning.

"Yes, my secretary and the student I was meeting with." His eyes grew round. "You can't think I had anything to do with this."

"We have to ask, Mr. Stone," Provenza replied. "We'll need their names to follow up."

"Of course." Drew patted his jacket as though looking for something to write on.

Jenessa brought her attention back to Daphne as the woman leaned over and whispered something to Aunt Renee.

What did she say? Whatever it was, Aunt Renee nodded in agreement.

Jenessa glanced over her shoulder at the men as Drew pulled a small notepad and pen from his jacket pocket. After scribbling a few things on the page, he ripped the paper off and handed it to Provenza.

"That's all for now," Provenza said. "We may have more questions later though."

"Fine. Just give me a call." Drew's eyes narrowed a bit. "Can I get back to my wife?"

"Sure," Provenza responded.

As the men headed back toward where Daphne and Aunt Renee were sitting, Drew questioned the detectives. "Do you know where the shot came from?"

"Not yet." Provenza shook his head. "When the CSI unit shows up, they'll figure it out."

"When will that be?" Drew asked.

Michael pitched his chin toward the driveway. "Looks like they're finally here."

As Michael and Detective Provenza peeled away to meet the arriving CSI team, Jenessa's focus returned to Daphne. "Can we set a time tomorrow for a short interview, Dr. Stone? I have a few more questions."

Aunt Renee draped a protective arm around Daphne, casting Jenessa a look that said, "Not now."

"Interview?" Drew asked, his brows knitting together.

"Yes. I work for the Hidden Valley Herald, and I want to ask your wife a few questions," Jenessa replied, then turned her attention back to Daphne. "Would nine am be good?"

"Are you sure you're up for that?" Drew asked his

wife.

Daphne stood, as if in defiance of her husband's doting. "Yes, nine would be fine. Why don't we do it over the phone? Just give me a call."

"I think it's time we get you home, darling." Drew took his wife's hand and began to lead her away.

"Renee has my number," she called over her shoulder.

Aunt Renee recited Daphne's number to Jenessa, and she made note of it. Then Aunt Renee's gaze followed the Stones across the parking lot.

"Trouble in paradise?" Jenessa muttered.

CHAPTER 2

"WHAT DO YOU MEAN, JENESSA?" Aunt Renee stood from the bench at Whitfield College. "Are you asking if there's something going on between Drew and Daphne? Some sort of trouble?"

"You saw how cool she was to him. She's one of your best friends. Don't tell me you don't know what's going on with those two."

"That's none of your concern."

"What were you two whispering about?"

"Jenessa, that's enough," Aunt Renee scolded. "Anything I say to you would just be gossip. I won't do that to her. You should know that." She began to stalk away.

Jenessa sprinted to catch up to her. "I'm sorry, but it's my job to dig for information."

Aunt Renee stopped and turned to face her niece. "Not everything is for public consumption, my dear. I'm sure it has nothing to do with this terrible incident that happened today."

"Do you think there might be someone who would want to kill your friend? Maybe someone who has an axe to grind because of a bad grade or something?"

"I can't imagine who. It was probably some random shooter, like that DC sniper a few years back."

The thought of it made Jenessa suck in a quick breath. "That would be frightening if that were true. Someone taking shots at innocent people for no good reason. I can't imagine that happening in sleepy little Hidden Valley."

"It's equally as frightening for me to think someone is trying to murder my friend." Her hand went to her chest, her eyes growing tense and glassy. "I hope Michael and George catch whoever did this before he tries again." She turned and walked away.

"Wait, Aunt Renee!" Jenessa went after her. "I need a ride to the auto shop."

~*~

Around five thirty Jenessa picked up her deep blue Mercedes SLK Roadster from Eurosport Auto Repair then zipped through town, heading for home. Her father had died a few months ago and had left her this little gem of a sports car in his Will, along with the family home, a lovely English Tudor on a quiet tree-lined street. He'd said, in the Will, that he hoped these things would bring her back to Hidden Valley permanently. Only time would tell if his wish would come true.

As she cruised down quaint Main Street, she pulled to the curb in front of The Sweet Spot for a quick coffee and a chance to visit for a few minutes with her best friend, Ramey. Several years ago, Ramey and Jenessa's mother opened the coffee shop and bakery—before her mother was tragically killed. Now it was run by Ramey and Jenessa's younger sister, Sara.

There was a crispness in the evening air as Jenessa approached the entrance. The glass door and the expansive windows of The Sweet Spot Café were artfully bordered with painted autumn leaves and pumpkins. Sara, who ran the business end, had balked at the cost, Ramey had said, but it had become a tradition, and Ramey won out in the end.

As Jenessa put her hand on the car door to open it, her cell phone began to ring. She dug it out of her purse, checked the caller ID, and smiled to herself as she answered. "Hello, Detective Baxter."

"Hello, Miss Jones," he replied in kind.

"Are we still on for dinner tonight?" she asked with a small ray of hope.

"Sorry, I'm still at the college with Detective Provenza. When we're done here, I've got a pile of paperwork to do."

Disappointed, she worked to keep a hopeful cheer in her voice. "I understand. But, if it's not too late when you're done, why don't you stop by? I'm sure I could round up a bite to eat for you."

"I'll need to pick up Jake. He's at my folks."

Jake was Michael's five-year-old son, who just started kindergarten. Michael had married a young woman named Josie while they were still in college. She was a drama major and had great aspirations of becoming an actress, until she became pregnant with

Jake and dropped out. After Michael graduated, he moved his little family back to Hidden Valley and joined the police force. Unfortunately, Josie didn't take to the small-town life, or motherhood. She left a couple of years later to try her luck in Hollywood.

Jenessa had become very fond of Jake over the past few months, while her relationship with Michael had been blossoming. He seemed to fill an empty spot in her heart—the spot left by the baby boy she had given up.

"Oh, I'm sure he'll be fast asleep by the time you're finished working," she said, hoping he would pick up on the gentle nudge to stop by and see her. "Why don't you ask your mom to keep him overnight and you can pick him up in the morning? Wouldn't that be better than waking him up to take him home?"

"Better for whom?" he replied with a hint of mischief.

A smile tickled her lips at his inference. "Okay, back to business," she said. "So, I'm working on my article about what happened at the college this afternoon. What can you tell me about the shooting?"

Michael outlined the facts of the case, as much as he was allowed to disclose. They believed it was a single shooter and only one shot was fired. The CSI team had deduced where the shot originated, but he couldn't give out that information. They dug the bullet out of Dr. Stone's car and sent it in for ballistics testing. She had been walking to her vehicle and the shot came as she was about to unlock the door. Either the shooter missed, which was lucky for Dr. Stone, or it was a warning shot and missed her on purpose.

"A warning shot? Warning her about what?"

"We haven't been able to determine that yet. Dr. Stone claimed she really couldn't tell us anything."

"I appreciate the info, Michael. I've got to get busy and turn this story in before Charles starts hounding me for it."

"You're very welcome. Maybe I'll see you later tonight."

"I hope so." Jenessa was a little surprised Michael made no mention of her getting out of Logan's vehicle. Perhaps he was saving that topic for their face-to-face.

Jenessa climbed out of her car and pushed through the glass door, the familiar tiny brass bells announcing her entrance. Ramey looked up from behind the cash register and a big smile lit up her face. Her long red curls were piled on top of her head, and her bright blue eyes twinkled at seeing her friend.

"Hey, Jenessa," she greeted. "What are you up to?"

"I'm running on empty, Ramey," Jenessa dragged herself to the counter, "and I need a quick pick-me-up. What have you got?"

"Not much, I'm afraid. It is almost closing time." Ramey motioned toward the glass case. "As you can see, we're pretty empty."

"Ah, don't tell me that."

"But," Ramey said with an encouraging lilt, "I set aside a few of those pumpkin chocolate chip cookies you like."

"Yum!" Jenessa licked her lips for emphasis. "How about one of those and a cup of coffee to go?"

"Sounds like you need fortification." Ramey took a little paper sheet and retrieved a few cookies for her. "I'd better make it more than one."

"I've got a story to put to bed pretty soon. There was a shooting at Whitfield College this afternoon. Did you hear?"

"Oh my gosh, no." Ramey's smile twisted into a worried expression. "Was anyone hurt?"

"Fortunately not, but one of Aunt Renee's good friends was almost shot. Do you know Dr. Daphne Stone?"

Ramey slipped the handful of cookies into a small paper bag. "Oh yes. She's married to that hot professor Aunt Renee used to date."

"What?" Now that was news. "When was that?"

"A long time ago. Right after you left Hidden Valley, before Aunt Renee married her third husband."

"How come I didn't know about it?"

"Well...you weren't exactly in touch with your family back then."

Ramey was right. After Jenessa had left town, she was so angry with her mom and dad for sending her away to have the baby that she severed ties in Hidden Valley for a while. Then it was off to college in Sacramento and throwing herself into her studies. Although she eventually made amends with her mother, her father was a different story entirely.

"Touché," Jenessa quipped dryly. "Now, how about that coffee?"

~*~

Sitting at her dad's antique desk in what had been his home office, Jenessa opened her laptop, took another cookie from the bag, and got busy with her article. There

20

wasn't much to go on, but she pulled together what she could, polished the story to make it interesting, and emailed it to her editor right under the deadline.

A couple of hours later, her doorbell rang. She dashed to answer it, a ripple of excitement spreading through her body at the prospect of spending time with Michael. She swung the door open wide, ready to favor him with an impassioned kiss.

"Hello, Jenessa."

Her heart sank. "Oh. Hello, Logan."

CHAPTER 3

"SORRY TO STOP BY SO LATE, but I saw your lights on," Logan said. "May I come in? It's a little cold out here."

With the door standing open, the chilly evening breeze blew into the house. "All right." She stepped back to let him pass, but she kept her feet firmly planted in the entry. "I was expecting someone else, so we'll need to keep this short."

"Michael?" The word was colored with resignation.

"Why are you stopping by, Logan?" she pressed, avoiding his question.

"I wanted to give you a heads-up."

That didn't sound good. "About what?"

"My father is expecting to be released from jail soon. I thought you should know."

The news hit her like a punch in the gut. "I don't understand. I thought he got two years. It's only been two months."

"He did, but his high-priced lawyers have been

fighting it ever since he was sentenced. I got a call from Dad this evening saying that he thinks they've found a loophole, and he expects that he'll be released with time served."

The thought that Grey Alexander would be free to make her life miserable again was unconscionable. She believed it was his formidable power and coercion that made her parents send her away and give up the baby.

After having recently returned to town, she went to work for the Herald. Even though Grey owned the paper, he'd fought her at every turn when she'd investigated the story of Lucy St. John's suspicious death.

Jenessa had been instrumental in his arrest. But now, to think he would be free to exact his revenge on her for her part in it, it was upsetting. She drew a deep breath, trying to steady her nerves, but it proved a futile effort. She put her hand out to him. "I appreciate your telling me."

He enveloped it in his. "You're shaking."

"Just a little cold," she tried to cover.

The doorbell rang. Her back stiffened. *Michael.*

Jenessa reached for the doorknob. "I'll have to talk to you about this tomorrow," she said, not looking at him.

"Anytime. Just give me a call." He moved toward her and tucked a couple of fingers under her chin, gently raising her face to meet his gaze.

He wasn't going to try to kiss her, was he? Mesmerized, her heart pounded, she couldn't move.

The doorbell rang again.

Logan's deep blue eyes held concern as he ignored the door and studied her face. "Don't worry, Jen. I'll let you know if I hear anything else." He moved his hand away.

Relieved, she nodded and turned away to pull the door open.

"Hey there, Michael," Logan said casually, as he stepped through the arched doorway and vanished into the night.

Michael's gaze caught Jenessa's. Irritation flashed through his eyes, then his brows knit with curiosity. As he stepped into the house, she flew into his arms and buried her face in his chest. "What's wrong?" he asked, his arms encircling her.

"Grey Alexander," she muttered, avoiding the unexpected moment she had just had with Logan.

"I don't understand."

Grey Alexander was the most powerful man in Hidden Valley—and Logan's father. He was used to getting whatever he wanted and trampled anyone who stood in his way. Both she and her dad had suffered under his tyranny. She had fought to fortify her backbone when she'd been forced to stand up to the man—and had succeeded—yet even now his very name turned her spine to jelly.

Michael kissed the top of her head. "Let's go sit down and we can talk." With his arm around her waist, he led her into the living room. With her hand enfolded in his, they sat together on the sofa. "Now, what's going on? Why was Logan here?" His jaw seemed to tighten when he spoke the name.

Jenessa reported what Logan had shared about his father. "I can't believe Grey will be back in Hidden Valley so soon."

"It doesn't sound to me like it's for certain, more like only a possibility. Besides, you handled him once, you can do it again."

His supportive words helped to soothe her frazzled spirit. He was right, she had stood up to the mighty Grey Alexander several times, and, in the end, she had come out the victor. She caressed Michael's cheek and gave him a kiss. "Thank you for that."

In quick response, his arms slid around her, pulling her into another kiss, longer and deeper. When their lips parted, he smiled. "The pleasure was all mine."

She relaxed and leaned her head against his chest, snuggling her face in the crook of his neck. "I'm glad you decided to drop by. I hope your parents didn't mind keeping Jake overnight."

"No, tomorrow's Saturday, so they were happy to do it."

"How's Jake liking kindergarten?"

"Oh, I almost forgot to tell you."

She sat up. "What?"

"Jake's birthday is next week and we always throw a party at Mom and Dad's. Jake wanted me to be sure to invite you."

"That's sweet. I'd love to come."

Michael's voice turned serious. "He thinks the world of you, you know."

"I know." Thinking about little Jake warmed her heart. "He's a sweet kid." But it was more than that.

"If this thing we're doing here doesn't work out," Michael held her gaze, a serious tenor coloring his voice, "he'll be absolutely heartbroken."

She nodded that she understood, not sure how else

to respond. Jenessa knew Michael was concerned about bringing her into Jake's life too soon—they had talked about it early on in their relationship—but with each passing day, her connection to Michael and Jake grew. It was too soon to talk about marriage, in her estimation, but was he fishing for some sort of commitment from her? Maybe it was time to change the subject.

"You want something to eat? I have sandwich fixings and Ramey gave me a small bag full of pumpkin chocolate chip cookies." She began to get up.

Michael grabbed her hand. "Not so fast." He tugged her back down to the sofa.

Now what?

"Tell me, why were you getting out of Logan's car this afternoon?"

~*~

A few days later, Jenessa was standing in line at The Sweet Spot for her afternoon energy jolt. "Mocha cappuccino, please," she said, giving her order to Ramey and handing her a five.

"It'll be just a minute," Ramey said. "Rosa is taking over for me while I get a batch of cupcakes ready for the mayor."

The fortyish, dark-haired woman stepped to the register.

"Something going on at city hall I should know about?" Jenessa asked as Ramey backed away.

"No, they're for his grandson's birthday party. Double devil's fudge with blue buttercream frosting and chunks of Snickers on top." Ramey pushed the kitchen door partially open and paused. "See you later."

Jenessa moved to the side to wait for her order. The tinkling bells on the door drew her attention to a beautiful young brunette with dazzling violet eyes entering the shop. With having been gone from Hidden Valley for the last twelve years, certainly there were people who'd moved in since Jenessa had left, but she'd been back for months and didn't recall ever seeing this striking female.

The beauty went to the counter and placed her order, then stepped to the side, near Jenessa, to wait. The woman's gaze floated out through the large decorated storefront windows to the view of Main Street.

Jenessa's curiosity got the better of her and she struck up a conversation. "Don't you just love the changing of the seasons? Fall is my favorite time of year. What about you?"

"Yes, I love the fall, but the leaves here don't seem to change as much as they do back east, where I went to college," the young woman replied. "Even so, this place is more charming than I remembered."

"So you're not from around here?" Jenessa asked.

"I used to be, but I've been gone for a while."

That's why she didn't know her. "What brings you back to town?"

"I'm here to see family, try to reconnect."

Jenessa could totally relate. "My name is Jenessa," she began, just as her phone started to ring in her purse. Pulling it out, she saw it was her boss. "Sorry, I have to take this."

"Hello," she answered as she pushed the door open and stepped outside.

"Hey, this is Charles. I've got another story for you—and this one's a real doozie."

At the prospect of a big story, the fine hairs on the back of her neck stood to attention. "What's going on?"

"It's Professor Stone—"

"The husband?" she interrupted.

"No, the wife. She was just found dead in her office at the college. Get over there and see what you can find out."

Jenessa peeked back inside the café and saw her coffee was up. She'd grab it first, then rush to the college. "I'm on it!"

Finding out more about the mysterious beauty with the violet eyes would have to wait.

CHAPTER 4

JENESSA RACED ACROSS TOWN to Whitfield College, keeping one eye on her rearview mirror for any cops who could catch her speeding. She had gotten more tickets than she thought possible in the last three months, driving the powerful machine she had inherited. With a juicy story waiting for her, now was not the time to get pulled over.

She swung the sports car into a campus parking space and asked a few students for directions to Dr. Stone's office. Once inside the right building, she approached the door to the professor's office, which was buzzing with activity. Down the hall a short way, beyond Dr. Stone's door, Detective Provenza was speaking to an attractive young woman with a blond bob, mid-twenties. The woman dabbed her eyes with tissue, her delicate shoulders hunched and shuddering. Maybe a student of Dr. Stone's?

Jenessa stepped to the open doorway of the dead woman's office, but a uniformed officer blocked her entry.

"Sorry, ma'am. Only law enforcement personnel are permitted," he said.

Jenessa poked her head in between the officer and the door frame and waved to Michael. He finished what he was saying to another uniform and came to the door. Michael put a hand on the shoulder of the officer on guard and he moved to the side.

"Can I get a statement, Detective?" she asked.

"I guess the word is out already," Michael said. "Looks like a heart attack, but we can't be sure until we get her body autopsied."

Jenessa's phone began to ring and she checked the caller ID. It was Ramey. Bad timing. She hit *ignore* and stuffed it back in her purse. "Any reason to think it was anything other than a typical heart attack?"

"No reason. That's probably what it was, but we can't give you a statement saying definitively that's what she died of until it's confirmed by the ME."

Jenessa glanced down the hall and pitched her chin in Provenza's direction. "Who's that woman George is talking to?"

"That's the professor's assistant, or, at least, she was," Michael said. "She's the one who found Dr. Stone and called it in."

Michael's statement brought back memories. Her own father had recently died from a heart attack while in the middle of dictating a letter to his secretary. The woman was inconsolable for hours, she had been told.

"She looks pretty upset," Jenessa noted. Maybe this one would calm down enough to talk to her.

Even though a heart attack was not the juicy story

Jenessa had expected, with the attempted assassination just a few days ago, she could at least make it into an interesting twist of fate. Maybe she could get some background information from Aunt Renee as well.

Her breath caught. *Aunt Renee!* She'd have to phone her as soon as she was done here, before her aunt heard the tragic news from someone else. Aunt Renee wouldn't likely see it on the TV—Jenessa hadn't noticed any television news crews on site when she'd walked in. Perhaps they had already heard it was a simple heart attack and had decided to pass on sending a crew. But news traveled fast with this town's lightning-speed grapevine, so she couldn't put off calling her aunt for long.

Detective Provenza joined them. "Hello, Miss Jones."

"Do you mind if I step inside the office, George?"

"That's Detective, young lady. How many times do I—"

"Sorry," she spit out quickly. "You're right, Detective, but do you mind?"

"I guess it'd be all right, as long as you don't touch anything. You keep an eye on her, Baxter."

Jenessa pulled a small notepad and pen from her bulky purse and stepped into the office, Provenza right behind her. The room was spacious and paneled in light oak. A large mahogany desk sat at one end, behind it were floor-to-ceiling bookcases crammed full of books. "Was the assistant able to tell you anything?"

"No," George replied with a shake of his head, "except that she brought her boss some papers to look over and found her like this." He motioned toward the professor, seated in her leather chair, slumped forward on her desk. "She said she immediately called nine-one-one."

"What's the assistant's name?" she asked.

Detective Provenza looked down at his notes. "Ashley Brandon."

"Thanks, Geor—Detective." Jenessa stepped to the desk and readied her pad and pen. From a few feet away, her gaze drifted over it, making note of the details. Scattered atop the desk, around the woman's lifeless arms, were a tall stack of papers, a micro-recorder, several pens in a neat row, and a bottle of juice with a small amount puddled in the bottom of it. Had her late father's desk looked like this when he'd suddenly died?

The image of her dead father prompted her to spin away and return to Michael and Provenza, who had been talking to the medical examiner across the room. She joined them just as the ME peeled away to inspect the deceased.

"What about the husband?" Jenessa asked. "I'm assuming you've informed him."

"Tried to, but he's not in his office," Michael replied. "We called his cell phone, but it goes to voicemail."

"The schedule doesn't show he's teaching a class this afternoon," Provenza added, sticking his hands in the pockets of his slacks, "but he must be somewhere he has his phone off."

"Like the gym maybe?" Jenessa asked.

"We've left several messages that it's urgent he calls us," Michael said. "We tried the home number too, but no answer."

An irritating jingling noise emanated from Provenza's pants. From the sound of it, he was fidgeting with the keys in one pocket, something her father did when he was bored or nervous. "Looks like we'll have to try going to the house in person to let him know."

The three-person crime scene investigation unit spilled through the door, carrying their equipment, and then headed toward the ME. Provenza went to join them.

It was time for Jenessa to make a speedy exit and let her aunt know what had happened. "Michael, I'm going to get out of your hair." She stuck her notepad and pen away. "Will I see you tonight?"

"I can't say how long I'll be tied up here, and then the paperwork." He leaned closer and lowered his voice. "Can I call you if I get free early enough?" His fingers slyly brushed against hers as if he didn't want anyone else to notice.

His touch warmed her, sending a little tingle dancing up her arm. "I'd like that." A smile spread across her lips and she gave his hand a light squeeze before she walked away.

Once out in the hallway, Jenessa paused to check her phone messages.

"She was a great lady," the assistant said tearfully, standing near Jenessa, gazing toward the office doorway.

Seizing the opportunity, Jenessa stuck her phone back in her bag and pulled out her pad and pen. "What can you tell me about her?"

The young woman turned and rested her back against the wall and ran her fingers under her eyes to clear away the tears. "Dr. Stone was the smartest woman I've ever known." Her attention turned to Jenessa. "She had a wonderful husband and a job she loved."

Daphne Stone's life sounded too perfect.

"Your name is Ashley, right?"

The young woman nodded.

"Was there anyone she didn't get along with, Ashley? Anyone who might want her dead?"

"I can't think of anyone," Ashley slowly shook her head as she replied, then her eyes rounded momentarily. "Wait. What?" She blinked a few times. "Why are you asking that? Dr. Stone had a heart attack."

"Oh, just a reporter's suspicious nature, I guess."

"Well," Ashley paused, "there was someone who tried to shoot her last week. You must have heard about that."

"I did."

"But I can't see how that would have anything to do with her having a heart attack."

"No, likely not." Jenessa stuck her pad and pen back in her bulky handbag. "It was probably just what it looks like." She lightly touched Ashley's arm. "Thanks for talking with me. I'm so sorry for your loss."

~*~

Jenessa peeled out of the college parking lot and headed back to the newspaper to write her article, making a phone call to her aunt as she drove. Hopefully her aunt hadn't heard about her friend's death some other way. "Aunt Renee, I'm afraid I have some very bad news. You might want to sit down."

"I'm already sitting. What is it, dear?"

"I'm so sorry to have to tell you this over the phone,

but your friend Daphne had a heart attack today. She passed away in her office."

"Daphne? Oh, dear God," Aunt Renee gasped, her voice trembling. "Are you certain?"

"Yes. I saw her for myself."

The line went silent, only muffled sobs drifted through.

After a long while, Aunt Renee spoke. "I don't understand how this could happen. She's not that old, and she was in good health. Are you sure it was a heart attack?"

"It appears so, but the medical examiner is going to do a routine autopsy to be certain."

"Poor Daphne," Aunt Renee muttered, her voice cracking with emotion.

Jenessa's phone beeped that she had another call coming in. It was Ramey again, but she couldn't take it. She hit *ignore* once more.

"It's such a shock, Jenessa," Aunt Renee squeaked out. "I, I…"

"I'm on my way over. I don't want you to be alone right now." She kept her aunt on the line until she pulled into her driveway.

CHAPTER 5

"SO WHAT'S THE BIG NEWS, DOC?" Detective Provenza asked as he and Michael entered the morgue. "You said on the phone you had something important for us."

Dr. Yamamoto, the medical examiner, looked up from the woman's body he was working on and pulled the sheet up to cover her opened chest. "Thanks for coming so quickly, Detectives."

Michael stepped to the table. Daphne Stone's body was so pale, ghostly. "That's interesting."

Provenza came up beside him. "What's interesting?"

"That birthmark at the base of her throat. It looks like a little bowtie."

"Huh," Provenza grunted. "Never seen anything like that."

Dr. Yamamoto moved to his desk and picked up a chart. "I ran a panel of tests on Dr. Stone to be sure certain of the cause of death. Tyramine showed up, which raised a red flag in my mind."

"Tyramine?" Michael repeated.

The ME continued. "That's right. It's usually harmless, but in certain instances it can wreak all kinds of havoc with drug interactions."

"So maybe it wasn't a heart attack?" Provenza asked. "Or something triggered one?"

"It appears Dr. Stone was taking Phenelzine, an MAO inhibitor used to treat depression. The drug has powerful contra-indicators—you know, interactions."

"That sounds serious," Provenza remarked.

"It is," the ME went on. "In this case, they're drug interactions that can kill. MAO inhibitors become lethal when they interact with anything fermented—wine, beer, certain kinds of cheeses, etcetera—even the smallest amount can set off a hypertensive crisis."

"Do you think she ingested any of those substances?" Michael asked.

"The contents of her stomach included vinegar."

Michael cut a look at Detective Provenza, then his gaze returned to the doctor. "Vinegar is fermented, right?"

"Yes, and that's what could have done it."

"If she knew she couldn't ingest anything fermented, why would she do that?" Provenza asked.

Before the ME had a chance to answer, Michael asked a question. "So besides vinegar in her stomach, was there anything else?"

"No, nothing else that would have vinegar in it or on it—no salad or pickles or anything. The only other thing I found was cranberry juice."

Provenza turned to Michael. "Are you thinking what I'm thinking?"

Michael nodded. "Murder."

"That's why I called you here, fellas," the ME said. "I believe the cranberry juice might have been strong enough to mask the vinegar. And based on the rates of fatal MAO interactions, my best guess is that it narrows down the time she must have taken it to between four and six hours before she died."

~*~

Seconds after Jenessa rang her aunt's doorbell, the large black door to the stately red-brick Georgian opened.

"Aunt Renee." It was all Jenessa could say as she looked into her aunt's red, teary eyes. She stepped through the doorway and threw her arms around her aunt, who sobbed into her shoulder.

Aunt Renee stepped back, shaking her head. The words "I can't believe she's gone," slipped out through trembling lips.

Jenessa draped an arm around her aunt and guided her down the hall to the family room. "Why don't we sit for a while?"

They sat close on the floral sofa and Aunt Renee dabbed her eyes with a cotton handkerchief. No words passed between them for a minute or two.

"Daphne's husband is probably happy, now that she's out of the way." Aunt Renee stared blankly out through the wall of small-paned windows, toward the sparkling blue pool.

"What do you mean?"

"He was having an affair."

"Did Daphne know?"

Her aunt turned to face her. "Yes, but she didn't know with whom."

"Why didn't she leave him?" Jenessa questioned.

"That's what I asked, but she said she couldn't."

"Why not?"

"She wouldn't tell me, but it drove her into a depression. She was seeing a therapist about it." Aunt Renee took a deep breath and sighed. "I figured Drew must have had something he was holding over her head."

"Like what?"

"I wish I knew, dear girl." Aunt Renee shook her head sadly. "Now he can have his mistress and all of Daphne's money."

"Did she have a lot?" *Millions, maybe?*

"I don't know for sure, but I know she makes more than he does, being head of the psychology department. And she's done some lecturing around the country, not to mention she regularly saw a few patients on the side."

"So, not millions."

"Oh, heaven's no," Aunt Renee breathed a laugh, "but I'm sure she's squirreled away a tidy sum—she was pretty tight with her money."

"And she had a small practice as a psychologist too? Busy lady. Do you know where she went to college? What degrees she held?"

"I don't know that she ever said." Aunt Renee's eyes misted at the thought. "Why do you ask?"

"I'd like to write a piece on her life," Jenessa replied. "She seemed like an interesting woman."

"She was. Such a shame she had to die so young."

"How old was she?"

"Forty-six." Aunt Renee paused and looked down at the wadded up handkerchief in her hands. "I just had coffee with her yesterday." A light came into her eyes. "Now that I think of it, Daphne did seem troubled about something."

"Troubled?" Something inside her reporter's mind perked up. "Something besides her husband's affair?"

"She didn't elaborate, so I didn't press. She said she wanted to talk more, but she had to rush off to a doctor's appointment—her therapist, I assume. She said she'd call me about having lunch soon."

"Maybe whatever it was bothered her so much, it brought on the heart attack," Jenessa proposed.

"Perhaps." Aunt Renee wiped her nose. "I need a cup of tea." She rose from the sofa and started toward the kitchen. She paused at the breakfast bar and turned back. "Would you like some, dear?"

"No thanks." Jenessa stood too. "I need to get back to my office and start writing my article for the morning paper."

Aunt Renee began filling a tea kettle with water. "Sorry I couldn't give you more information on Daphne's life."

"No worries, I'll search the internet. I'm sure I can find enough info to do her justice. I'd give her husband a jingle, but it's probably not a good idea, this close to her passing."

Aunt Renee carried the kettle to the stove and turned on the burner. "Please don't print a word about Drew's affair in your story," she pleaded, turning toward

Jenessa for her agreement.

"Oh no, of course not." Jenessa stepped to her aunt, put her arm about her shoulders, and gave her a little hug. "But I can't help wondering what he was holding over her head."

~*~

Michael's cell phone started to ring and he pulled it out of his jacket pocket. "Hello, Jenessa." He shot a quick look at his partner, who was giving him a disapproving frown. "I can't talk right now. We're walking up to the Stone house to give the husband the bad news. I'll have to call you back."

"Just checking to see if we're on for tonight."

"I have a feeling it's going to be a late night."

Provenza motioned with his thumb toward the Stone's front door.

"I've really got to go. I'll call you if I get free early." Michael clicked off the call before Jenessa could respond, picking up on his senior partner's impatience. "Sorry about that."

"Get your head back in the game, Baxter," Provenza growled as they marched up the walkway. "This part is never easy."

They had looked for Drew Stone at the college, but his assistant informed them he had gone home early due to illness. Phoning him was an option, but not one they wanted to pursue. Detective Provenza was old school and insisted they make the notification in person—it was the honorable thing to do. So, here they stood, ringing the doorbell, having to tell the husband that his wife was dead.

Not only dead, but murdered.

The door opened and Drew stood there in a dark blue jogging suit, holding a small dog. He didn't look sick. "Hello, can I help you?" Something sparked in his eyes. "I know you two, from the shooting incident with my wife. I already told you I had nothing to do with that."

"That's not why we're here," Provenza said flatly. "Can we come in?"

Drew nodded and moved to the side. The detectives stepped in and followed him to the living room. He gestured toward the sofa. "Have a seat, gentlemen. Just let me put this dog in the backyard."

The detectives sat and waited.

"Now, what's this about?" Drew asked as he came back into the room and claimed a chair.

Detective Provenza cleared his throat. "I'm sorry to have to tell you this, but your wife passed away this afternoon, in her office."

"Daphne?" The husband's eyes grew wide at the news. "What happened?"

Michael studied his facial expression. "She appeared to have a heart attack. Dropped dead at her desk."

Drew shot up out of his chair. "Oh my god." He raked a hand through his hair and paced nervously. "A heart attack? But she was always so healthy." He stopped and faced the detectives, his eyes moist. "I guess you never know when your time is up."

Michael stood. "I said she *appeared* to have a heart attack." Was Drew genuinely surprised by Daphne's sudden death, or was he acting? After all, he was a professor of English literature and drama.

"Appeared?" Drew repeated. "What does that mean?"

"Have a seat, both of you, and let's talk about it," Provenza said. He leaned forward, his forearms resting on his knees. Once the men sat down, he continued. "She was found by her assistant, Ashley, who phoned nine-one-one. Initially, the paramedics thought it was a heart attack, but when the medical examiner ran some tests, he found that she had been poisoned."

Drew's eyes rounded again as he fell, with a huff, back against the chair. "Murder?"

"That's what it looks like, Mr. Stone." Michael couldn't get a good read on the man. "I hate to ask at a time like this, but were there any problems between you and your wife?"

Drew bolted out of his chair again. "You think I did it?"

Provenza cut a sideways glance at Michael. "Sorry, Mr. Stone, but we have to ask. Everyone is a suspect until we clear them."

The husband's lips grew tight and thin, his glare like a laser. "I loved Daphne. Our marriage was fine." His voice broke a little and the large vein in his neck pulsed as he spoke. "We had rocky times now and then, like any couple, but we were committed to each other. I would never do anything to hurt her."

Both Michael and Provenza stood, ready to leave.

"We are sorry for your loss, Mr. Stone. We'll let you know how our investigation is going," Provenza said. "If you think of anything that could help us find her killer, no matter how small or insignificant it might seem, give us a call." He pulled a white business card out of his coat pocket and handed it to the man. "There's our numbers."

Drew escorted them to the door and opened it. "Tell me you'll find whoever did this to my wife."

"We'll do our best," Provenza replied as he and Michael stepped outside.

~*~

"Hello, boys," Jenessa greeted, leaning against their unmarked police car, which was parked half a block down the street from the Stone house. After briefly speaking to Michael on the phone, she had the brilliant idea that she'd wait for them to finish up their meeting with the husband to see if he had anything to say about Daphne that she could use in her article.

"What are you doing here?" Michael asked, a friendly smile spreading on his lips, seeming surprised, though pleased, to see her.

"She's looking for a story, of course," Detective Provenza groaned.

CHAPTER 6

JENESSA PUSHED AWAY from the police car's fender. "I won't lie, George, I was hoping I could get a few more details for my story."

"That's Detective, young lady," Provenza groaned.

Jenessa seemed to ignore his correction. "A run-of-the-mill heart attack isn't all that exciting, but if I had an angle, an interesting nugget, maybe I could turn it into a real human-interest story. Now that would make my editor happy. You guys have anything you can share?"

Michael glanced at Provenza, and Jenessa seemed to pick up on the silent communication between them. "What are you boys not telling me?" The focus of her pale green eyes drifted from one man to the other. "Michael? George?"

Provenza nodded his approval at Michael.

"Turns out," Michael said, "this has actually become a murder investigation."

"Murder?" Her face lit up at the prospect of a juicy

story hiding in there somewhere. "Spill. Don't leave anything out."

Michael repeated what the ME had told them about the vinegar in Dr. Stone's stomach interacting with Phenelzine, which is taken for depression, meaning it was not likely an accident.

"Depression?" Jenessa muttered, pushing a hand through her dark tresses. "I found out today that the woman was seeing a therapist because her husband was having an affair."

"Who did you hear that from?" Provenza demanded.

"You know I can't reveal my sources, Detective."

"Drew Stone just got through telling us their marriage was fine," Michael huffed, "how they were totally committed to each other."

"He was obviously lying." She crossed her arms and leaned back against the cruiser, her long hair shining in the evening sun that had begun to set behind her. "I wonder what else he's lying about."

"We'd better go back and ask him a few more questions," Michael said to his partner.

Provenza nodded. Leaving Jenessa standing there, the detectives trudged back to the front door to further question the husband.

"Forget something?" Drew asked when he saw Michael and George on his front porch again.

"Actually yes," Provenza said. "Mind if we come in again?"

"I guess not." Drew moved to the side and the detectives entered his home. "Make yourselves comfortable."

Michael and George took a seat on the couch again, but Drew chose to stand.

"Where were you this morning, Mr. Stone?" Michael asked.

The husband's eyes flared. "You actually think I killed my wife?"

"We have to ask," Detective Provenza said. "This morning between eight and noon?"

"Let's see," his gaze drifted up and to the right as he dug into his memory. "I left here about eight thirty to teach a nine o'clock class, which went 'til eleven. I wasn't feeling well, so I came home after that."

"You don't look sick," Provenza said, eyeing the man.

"I'm feeling better."

"Do you have cranberry juice in the house?" Michael asked.

"Of course. My wife keeps a bottle in the refrigerator. She drinks it every day."

"What about vinegar?"

"Probably. Why do you ask?"

Michael pitched Provenza a knowing look, then returned his attention to the husband.

Provenza leaned forward. "Do you mind if we take the bottle and have it analyzed?"

The husband's brow furrowed. "Why?"

"Your wife was poisoned," Provenza replied. "Cranberry juice and vinegar."

The man's eyes popped wide for a moment, then narrowed suspiciously. "Don't you need a warrant for that?"

"Not if you hand it over willingly," Michael said.

51

"Otherwise, I'm happy to stay here with you while my partner goes and gets one. Your choice."

"I think I need to call my lawyer."

~*~

Jenessa went back to the newspaper to write her story while the detectives continued their investigation. She stuck her head in her editor's office to bring him up to speed on the story.

"Busy, Charles?"

He looked up from his computer. "Always." He motioned for her to come in. "What have you got?"

"It turns out Dr. Daphne Stone was murdered."

"Now we'll have a real story," he said. "Don't get me wrong, I am sorry she's dead, but a murder sells newspapers far more than a heart attack."

"I don't have much in the way of details yet," Jenessa came to stand across the desk from him, "but I do have enough to put a short story together."

Perched on the credenza behind him, and visible to the right of his chair, sat a photo of Charles and his son, Charlie. The boy's sandy-blond hair and green eyes made her think of the son she had given up. He would be about Charlie's age now and she wondered if that was what he might have looked like. The boy's father, Logan Alexander, was blond and blue eyed, whereas Jenessa had deep brown hair and pale green eyes. Between the two of them, their little boy might have turned out to look a lot like Charlie. A stab of regret stung in her chest.

"Jenessa?"

Apparently Charles had been talking to her, but she hadn't heard a word. Her attention had been totally focused on the picture of the boy. She pulled her focus away from the photograph and looked her editor in the eye. "Sorry, my mind was somewhere else."

"Focus, Jenessa." He shook his head at her. "I was just saying I want you to stay on this story and see what you can dig up. Get me what you have by six thirty and I'll run it on the front page of tomorrow's paper."

"I'm on it, Boss." She headed for the door, then paused and turned back. "By the way, I heard a nasty rumor that Grey Alexander might be let out of jail early." Just saying the words sent a chill up her spine.

"Where'd you hear that?"

"Logan."

"See what else you can find out about that story. The whole town will want to know."

"Sure thing." Her gaze drifted to the picture again. "Nice photo of you and your kid. How old is he?"

"Eleven, last May."

Eleven? May? That's when she had given her baby away.

"Handsome young man," she said as she went through the door.

"Takes after his old man," she heard Charles say as she wandered down the hall.

After sitting in her cubicle writing the article, and spending some time polishing it, she hit the *send* button on her computer and it was off to her editor. Would Michael be finished working soon? They hadn't been able to spend any alone time for the last few days and she longed to see him. With a fresh murder investigation, it wasn't likely he'd be ready to go home this early, though.

Ramey. She had almost forgotten. Her friend had left three voicemails and Jenessa hadn't called her back yet. Now that the story was put to bed, she checked her messages. "Call me back," was all she left the first two times. The third message said she had something juicy to tell her, so she gave Ramey a jingle.

After four rings, her friend's cell phone went to voicemail. Jenessa left a brief message, hoping whatever she had called about wasn't too important. They'd have to connect later.

Jenessa stuck the phone in her handbag and quickly stood from her desk. As she spun toward the opening of her cubicle, she ran smack into the solid chest of a well-dressed man who smelled of intoxicating musk and sandalwood. His hands flew out to catch her.

She tilted her head up in surprise, her back tensing when she found herself looking into Logan's engaging eyes.

A roguish smile spread on his lips. "Going somewhere?"

"Yes, home." She took a small step back.

"Want to grab a quick dinner?"

"With you?" She already knew what he meant, but she was trying to make a point. His pursuit of her had to stop. "I think you know my answer. I'm dating Michael. I wish you would accept that."

One side of his mouth tugged up. "You can't blame a guy for trying, Jenessa."

Can't I?

"Logan," she shook her head slowly, "there are

54

plenty of other girls in this valley to choose from. You should invite one of them out to dinner."

"Like who?" he bit back with a frown.

"Well," she searched her mind for an answer, "I saw a stunning young woman at The Sweet Spot today. I think she's new in town. She'd be perfect for you, if she's not already taken."

"But she's not you, Jenessa."

"I'm off the market, Logan—you know that. You have got to move on, for your sake and mine." She squeezed past him in the doorway, trying to end the uncomfortable conversation, but he grabbed her arm as she slipped by and turned her to face him.

"I won't make you any promises," he said, his uncertain gaze locking on hers, "but I'll try."

He released her arm, looking so sad, so resigned, she almost felt sorry for him. Almost. But this was Logan Alexander she was talking about. He was used to getting whatever he wanted, not settling for anything less—like father, like son—but this time he would not be getting his way.

She rushed toward the building's entrance, not wanting to give Logan the chance to make any more advances. Once settled in her sports car, she phoned Michael, anxious to hear his voice, hoping he would be off duty by now. Disappointed that it went to voicemail, she called the police station.

"Sorry, Jenessa, but Michael left about an hour ago. I believe he said he was headed home," the receptionist said.

"Thanks, Ruby." Maybe he hadn't answered because he was on another call or away from his phone.

Her stomach growled, reminding her she'd missed lunch. Picking up a pizza and surprising Michael and Jake with dinner sounded like a stellar idea. She loved watching little Jake devour a big slice of pepperoni pizza, leaving a sloppy ring of sauce surrounding his satisfied smile.

She phoned in her order and swung by Romano's Pizzeria to pick it up. The scent of red sauce and pepperoni filled her Roadster, and her stomach grumbled again in response.

When she reached Michael's house, his car was parked in the narrow driveway as she pulled to the curb out front. The sun had already gone down and solar garden lights illuminated the walkway to the front door of the 1940s bungalow.

She rang the doorbell and waited, anticipating wide grins from her two favorite guys. The door swung open and Jenessa's breath caught in her throat.

Instead of Michael and Jake, standing in the doorway was a beautiful young woman with long dark, tousled tresses, wearing one of Michael's NYU t-shirts and not much else that she could see—it was the stunning brunette from the coffee shop. "Hello. Can I help you?"

"Uh…uh…pizza," was all Jenessa could manage to squeeze out as she held out the box. Her mind was spinning with a thousand different questions, but only one of them made it to her lips. "Michael?" she squeaked out.

"Oh, Michael ordered the pizza?" She looked over her shoulder, then back to Jenessa. "He's in the shower, but I'm his wife. Let me grab my wallet. How much?"

The sound of Jake's young voice came wafting over the air, "Mommy, Mommy! Come see!"

Jenessa's heart dropped to her stomach. She handed over the pizza and waved a hand in the air as she stepped off the porch and hurried back down the walk. "On the house."

By the time she reached her car, her breath was returning, but her cheeks were on fire.

His wife?

She slid behind the wheel and started the car. Her cell phone rang and she answered.

"Hey, Jen, this is Ramey."

Jenessa took a deep breath and blew it out. "You're never going to believe who I just saw."

"Josie Baxter," Ramey replied.

"How did you know?"

"That's why I've been trying to call you. She was in The Sweet Spot this morning. I thought you should know. Do you think Michael knows yet?"

Jenessa looked toward his house. "Yeah, I'm pretty sure he does." The question was, how long had he known?

She drove home, so shaken by the sight of that woman at Michael's house that she barely recalled how she came to be parked in her own driveway. Her phone rang again. Caller ID showed it was Michael this time. She hit the *ignore* button, too upset to speak with him. If she didn't cool down first, she would likely say something they'd both regret.

How could he not tell her?

CHAPTER 7

SO, THE LOVELY NEW BRUNETTE in town was Michael's ex-wife. Jenessa played the surprising scene over in her mind as she kicked her flats off in the foyer and dropped her purse on the entry table. Why did that woman say she was his wife? Had Jenessa been so shocked by the sight of her that she'd missed hearing the word ex?

And what was she doing in his house, looking like she'd just tumbled out of a sexy romp in bed, while he was in the shower? Jake was there...but had he been there the whole time? Was Michael even actually in the shower?

She shook her head. This was crazy.

Jenessa stomped down the hall to the kitchen. Having just given away dinner, now she'd have to forage for something else to satisfy her grumbling stomach. Double fudge-chunk ice cream was always good for what ailed her. The frozen delight might help cool her temper too.

The phone rang again. Michael. She hit *ignore*, turned the thing off, and reached for the tub of ice cream.

~*~

After a fitful night of tossing and turning, the bright morning light spilling into Jenessa's bedroom signaled it was time to get up. She felt around on the nightstand for her phone. Bleary-eyed, she checked for messages. Eleven. She rubbed her eyes and looked again. Yep, eleven. Ten from Michael and one from Ramey.

Rather than calling Ramey back, she'd head for The Sweet Spot for breakfast and meet up with her friend in person. As for Michael, well, she still wasn't ready to call him back. With the case having turned into a murder, she was sure to run into him in the course of her story investigation. Perhaps by then she'd be ready to talk to him. Right now she just wanted a cup of coffee and one of Ramey's delicious cinnamon rolls before tackling the world.

~*~

When she arrived at The Sweet Spot, Ramey was standing behind the glass bakery case helping a lady choose a cake. She looked up when the brass bells tinkled as Jenessa swept through the door.

"Hey, Jenessa. I'll be right with you," she greeted with a smile before returning to her customer.

Jenessa took her place in the short line to order. The bells rang again and she heard the animated voice of a familiar little boy. She swung around, thinking it was Jake with his dad, but his little hand was snugly folded into his mother's.

It would have been awkward to avoid them at this point, so with hands on her knees, Jenessa bent down to Jake's level. "Good morning, young man."

Jake smiled broadly. "Hi."

Against all she was feeling, she stood erect, plastered a cordial smile on her face, and stuck out her hand in a friendly gesture. "Hello, I'm Jenessa."

The woman took her hand and returned her smile. "Josie."

"I think we met yesterday, right here," Jenessa said, giving Josie's hand a good shake, "but I had to dash out and take an important phone call." Why did she add the word important? Who was she trying to impress?

"I think you're right," Josie replied pleasantly. Then her head cocked slightly and her mysterious-colored eyes narrowed for a brief second. "Aren't you the one that delivered the pizza last night?"

Jenessa's back muscles seized and her mouth went dry as cotton. "Well, yes, I, uh…"

"Next person!" Rosa called from behind the cash register.

I love you, Rosa.

"Sorry," Jenessa blushed, "looks like I'm up." She spun toward the counter and spit out her order, her gaze trying to catch Ramey's in hopes she would save her from having to face Josie again.

Ramey had just finished with the woman's cake order and must have seen Josie, and the dilemma in which her friend found herself. "Jenessa, why don't you step over here and I'll take care of you."

Relief washed over her at Ramey's rescue. How embarrassing!

"Cinnamon roll?" Ramey pulled one from the case and put it on a small plate. "I see you've met Michael's ex," she said, keeping her voice low as she handed it over.

Jenessa gratefully took the roll. "You could say that."

"What did Michael say?"

"I haven't talked to him yet."

"Why not?"

"He's tried calling me a few times, but I needed some time to get over the shock of seeing her at his house last night."

"What? You saw her at his house last night?"

"Shhh, keep your voice down."

Ramey leaned over the bakery case and whispered, "Don't let it drag on too long. Talk to him. I'm sure he has a good explanation for having her there."

"But you didn't see her, Ramey. She answered the door looking like she'd just gotten out of bed."

"Maybe she was taking a nap," Ramey suggested in her innocent way.

Jenessa paused and raised a questioning brow. "Not that kind of getting out of bed."

Ramey's bright blue eyes expanded. "Oh." Her gaze flew to Josie, who was placing her order with Rosa, and just as quickly returned to Jenessa. "I'm sure you're wrong. Michael's over the moon for you and you know it."

"I keep trying to remind myself of that fact, but you

didn't see her, standing there in one of Michael's favorite t-shirts and nothing else—at least from what I could tell."

"She probably had short shorts on, you just couldn't see 'em." Ramey tended to perpetually give people the benefit of the doubt.

"I guess that's possible," Jenessa grumbled. Her gaze drifted in Josie's direction momentarily, seeing her take Jake by the hand and lead him to a table.

"Take my advice. Talk to Michael," Ramey urged, drawing Jenessa's attention back, "before you blow this thing all out of proportion in that crazy suspicious mind of yours."

"Crazy?" Jenessa frowned at her. "How would you feel if you dropped by Charles's house and his past wife answered the door?"

"I'd be freaked out," Ramey gasped.

"Exactly."

Ramey grimaced. "The woman Charles was married to is dead."

~*~

Jenessa might as well get it over with. Talking to Michael was unavoidable. The story of Dr. Stone's murder was too important for her to let her personal life get in the way of doing a thorough job of reporting on it. And, like Ramey had said, she'd better talk to him and find out what was going on before her mind continued to awfulize the situation.

Sure, *awfulize* wasn't really a word, but it seemed an apt way to describe the way someone's mind could make something more awful than it actually was. Perhaps that's what she was doing here. Maybe hearing his side would calm her fears about their relationship moving forward.

She said her good-byes to Ramey and walked a few blocks to the headquarters of the Hidden Valley Police Department.

"Hey, Ruby," Jenessa greeted as she strolled to the front desk of the station. "Is Detective Baxter in?"

"Let me try his extension." The receptionist made a quick call while Jenessa waited, half hoping he was out. "He's on a phone call," the woman said as she hung up the receiver, "but he said to send you on back."

Ruby buzzed her in and Jenessa found her way back to the office Michael shared with his partner, George Provenza. George was sitting with his feet propped up on his desk, tossing a worn baseball in the air.

"Hello, George."

His feet flew off the desk and he caught the ball as he pulled up straight. "That's Detective Provenza, Miss Jones," he said with a bit of irritation. "What can we do for you?"

"Actually, I'm here about the Daphne Stone murder case. Got anything I can report?"

Michael sat at a desk that faced his partner's. He hung up his phone. "I'm afraid there's not much to tell you yet. We have a few leads, checking into some things."

Jenessa met his gaze. "Playing it close to the vest, are we, Michael?"

George stood. "This is an ongoing murder investigation. We can't share the details with the press."

"That never stopped you before, George." There had been a few other times when she had helped him and he had given her an exclusive story.

At her use of his first name, his brows wrinkled. She knew he didn't like it when she called him that, but she liked to remind him they could be friends and help each other out. "You scratch my back, I'll scratch yours. You know how it works."

"They'll be no scratching each other's backs," Michael said. "I thought this might be a social call. I've tried phoning you and—"

"So what have you got to trade?" Provenza interrupted.

"Unfortunately, not much at the moment," she replied. "However, my aunt was good friends with Dr. Stone, and she had a relationship with Drew Stone a while back, so if I probe a little, I'm sure I could come up with something."

"You're saying Renee Giraldy was romantically involved with the murder victim's husband?" Detective Provenza asked, pitching a quick glance at his partner before bringing his attention back to her.

Had Jenessa said too much, gone too far in trying to get information from the detectives for her story? Why would they ask that about Aunt Renee? "A long time ago. I'm not exactly sure when. Why do you ask?"

Provenza cut a sideways glance toward Michael again, who said nothing. Then his gaze slowly returned to Jenessa. "Just seems a little curious, that's all."

That didn't sound like it was all.

Michael stood and took Jenessa lightly by the arm. "We need to talk," he said, opening the door and escorting her into a conference room across the hall.

"About Aunt Renee?" she asked as they entered the room.

Michael closed the door. "No, about us." He looked into her eyes, as if searching for something. "Why haven't you been taking my calls?"

"Why don't you ask your wife?" She cringed. That came out more sharply that she had meant.

"My wife?" His face twisted into a confused frown. "You mean my ex-wife?" He rubbed a hand over his forehead. "Is that what this is about?"

"I showed up at your house last night with a pizza and she answered the door wearing nothing but one of your old t-shirts, looking all sexy and…well, I don't know what. She said she was your wife and that you were in the shower."

He let out a hollow laugh and shook his head. "First of all, let me be clear. Josie is my ex-wife and there is nothing going on between us. Nothing." He gently put his hand under her chin and lifted it to give her a soft slow kiss.

His lips were warm and moist and she started to melt into it, but caught herself. She pulled back, "Whoa there, cowboy," putting a hand on his chest to establish space between them. "Don't think you can distract me from the topic at hand. What about her lack of clothing?"

"Yes, Josie was wearing one of my old t-shirts, but she had a bathing suit on under it. She had picked Jake up from my parents' house earlier and took him swimming."

"A swimsuit?" That was better than the conclusion she had jumped to.

Michael went on to explain that he had stopped by his folks' place to pick up Jake and learned Josie had shown up, asking to take Jake swimming. She'd told them she had Michael's permission, but they insisted on calling him to verify. He had been on the phone when they called and hadn't been able to call them back right away because of being knee deep in the murder investigation. Jake begged them to let her take him to the community swimming pool and they eventually gave in.

"And the shower?" she asked, raising her brows.

"I did take a shower, grabbed a couple slices of pizza, and came back to the office to work a few more hours on the investigation."

"Pizza?" Jenessa huffed, again feeling the humiliation of that night. "Pizza *I* brought for *us*."

"I'm sorry." Michael slipped his arms around her. "I didn't know."

"So where's she staying?"

His expression turned sheepish. "Uh, well…in Jake's room."

Jenessa pulled out of his embrace. "Why?"

"She said she couldn't afford a hotel. She wanted to spend time with Jake. When I insisted she find somewhere else to stay, Jake began crying and pleading with me to let her stay with us."

"No." She shook her head with resolve. "You put her up in a hotel or a motel, a halfway house or a dog house—I don't care—just not at your house."

"It's only for a week. Jake's birthday is coming up and—"

"A whole week? Are you serious?"

"She always comes for Jake's birthday. After that,

she'll be gone."

"And does she always stay at your house when she comes?"

"Well, no, she usually stays in a hotel, but she claims she's down on her luck and—"

"What about your parents? Can't she stay with them?"

"No. They despise her after what she did, leaving Jake and me."

"Then you pay for her to stay in a hotel."

"That's like eight hundred dollars for a week."

"Don't they offer weekly rates?"

"Maybe, but—"

"I'll even help you pay for it," Jenessa offered. Anything to get that voluptuous, conniving woman out of Michael's house.

"It would break Jake's heart. I can't do that to him. You should have seen him, big fat crocodile tears streaming down his little cheeks when I told her she had to go."

"Then let him go stay a few nights at the hotel with her."

"I don't feel good about that, disrupting his routine when he's just starting school. No."

The vivid image of that sweet little boy crying for his mother melted her heart. She wrapped her fingers around Michael's hand. "Does she know about us?"

He shrugged. "I told her I was seeing someone, but I didn't say who. The less she knows the better."

Jenessa wondered, though, if Jake had already spilled the beans.

CHAPTER 8

WHILE MICHAEL AND GEORGE followed up on leads, the details of which they refused to share with her, Jenessa had an interview with a soon-to-be bride and groom for their photo and short story in the weekend social section of the paper. Though Jenessa was first to be assigned the important stories, it was still part of her job description to cover local weddings and social events in this small town.

After that appointment, she had a meeting scheduled with her attorney, Ian McCaffrey, something of a personal nature. He had been her late father's law partner.

His assistant ushered her into his office.

Mr. McCaffrey stood from behind his massive mahogany desk and came around to offer her his hand. He was wearing an expensive navy blue Brioni suit and his full head of gray hair was perfectly coiffed with every strand in place. "So good to see you again,

Jenessa."

She firmly shook his hand and took a seat across the desk from him, anxious to get down to business. "I think you know why I'm here, why I asked for this meeting."

"I already told you I can't give you any information on your baby's adoption," he replied, sitting back in his black leather chair with a resolved look in his eyes. "Total confidentiality was one of the specific terms of the adoption."

"At whose insistence?"

"Well," he cleared his throat, "I can't really say."

"My father's? Logan's father's?"

He steepled his fingers and tapped them against his lips, but said nothing.

"I'm going to find out, Ian, with your help or without it."

"Just leave it be, Jenessa, for the boy's sake. He's in a good family and he's happy. Isn't that what you want for him?"

Jenessa leaned forward. "How do you know he's happy?" Had he seen him? Was he living in Hidden Valley?

"Well, I, I..." Mr. McCaffrey stammered and looked away for a moment. He slowly brought his gaze back, compassion filling his eyes. "Just trust me on this. Your contacting him would only disrupt his life. Please, take my advice—move on, find a husband, and have more children...just leave this one alone."

Tears began to form and she blinked them back. "It's not that easy." She didn't want to disrupt the boy's life, she just wanted to know where he was, that the people raising him were good to him. Couldn't she at least see him from a distance?

Is he Charlie McAllister?

"I would never have to tell him I'm his biological mother. I just want to see him."

The verbal sparring went on for several more minutes, each side passionately pleading their case. Finally, Mr. McCaffrey admitted he could see her side and he felt for her, but divulging any information that led back to the child could provoke a lawsuit against him, or worse—it could mean disbarment.

"Not if there was a way you could help me that no one could trace back to you," she suggested.

"What way is that exactly?"

"I don't know. You're the brilliant attorney. I'm sure you could figure it out if you put your mind to it."

He studied her for a moment. "I'm not promising you anything, young lady, but let me think on it."

~*~

Encouraged, Jenessa went home to work on her story about Dr. Daphne Stone's murder. She sat at her desk and opened her laptop to type in some notes. What did she know so far? Not much.

She knew Dr. Stone was seeing a therapist and was taking anti-depression medication because she was distraught over her husband cheating on her. She didn't know who with, but, according to Aunt Renee, Daphne had confided in her that she suspected it was with a blonde, that she had found golden hairs on his clothes. Aunt Renee had begged Jenessa not to write anything about the affair—but it might not only be pertinent to the story, it might be pivotal.

Jenessa knew that her aunt and Drew Stone had been lovers at one time—well, maybe lovers was too strong a word—they had dated.

What else? Drew Stone had lied to the police about the state of their marriage. Why? To protect the blonde?

Aunt Renee had blond hair. *Was it possible…?*

~*~

Michael wadded up a piece of paper from his desk and pitched it into the trash can across the room. "Score!"

"Hey, look at this," Detective Provenza exclaimed, staring at his desktop computer.

Michael skirted the desk and leaned down to see. "What do you have?"

"That warrant came through for Dr. Stone's financials, and you'll never guess what I found. Looks like she recently changed her Will from her husband as the beneficiary to—" George ran his index finger along the line of text.

"Renee Giraldy?" Michael pulled up straight.

George scrubbed his fingers through his thick gray hair. "What do you make of that?"

"Jenessa mentioned she heard Drew Stone was having an affair. That would be a good enough reason to cut him off." Michael stepped back to his own desk. "Find anything else interesting in her financials?"

"Hold your horses, young man. I'm working on it."

The phone rang on George's desk. "This is Detective Provenza." He covered the receiver and whispered to Michael, "Dr. Yamamoto."

George paused and listened. "Oh really. That's very interesting, Doc."

"What is it?" Michael asked after George hung up.

"The ME said testing on the bottle of cranberry juice from the house came back clean, no other substances found in it, so she must have drank from another bottle."

"She probably poured it into a smaller bottle to take with her—or someone did it for her. Didn't we see a small bottle on her desk the day she died?" Michael asked.

"We did. I hope it didn't end up in the trash when they thought her death was just a heart attack."

"CSI would know better than that, wouldn't they?"

"I hope so, but there was something else. The doc also took fingerprints off the bottle we gave him."

"Really?" Michael raised his brows in question. "Whose fingerprints?"

"Daphne's, Drew's, and Renee Giraldy's."

"How do you know they're Renee's? Are they on file?"

"Yeah, they're in the system. Apparently she was a real estate agent years ago, so she had to submit them when she got her license," Provenza replied.

"I didn't know that."

"I wonder what else we don't know about our friend Renee Giraldy."

~*~

Detective Provenza stood beside Michael on Renee

Giraldy's porch and rang her doorbell. "I really hate doing this. She's such a nice lady."

"What about me? Jenessa won't be happy with me for serving a search warrant on her aunt," Michael added, reluctantly waiting for the door to open.

"We have to follow the leads wherever they go," George replied. "She'll just have to understand."

"Not likely." Michael grimaced.

"The warrant for her financials should be in by the time we get back to the station."

The door swung open and Renee greeted them with a friendly smile. "Hello, fellas. What brings you to my door?"

"I'm sorry to have to tell you this, ma'am—" Provenza began to say.

"Ma'am? That sounds so official, George."

"It is official, I'm afraid. We have a warrant to search your house." He handed the document to her.

"My house?" She took the warrant and her free hand flew to her chest. Her green eyes grew big. "Why on earth would you want to search my house?"

Two uniformed officers joined the detectives.

"Sorry, Renee, but we're not at liberty to discuss it. It has to do with Dr. Stone's murder," Michael said, wishing he didn't have to do this.

"Her murder? I thought she had a heart attack."

"That's what we initially thought," Michael replied, "but it turns out it was murder." Obviously, Jenessa hadn't filled her in yet.

"Anyone else in the house?" Provenza asked.

"My niece Sara and our friend Ramey. They're fixing dinner."

"Stay here," Provenza ordered her, then he and Michael marched down the main hall to the kitchen, which was located at the back of the large home. Michael had been there several times for family dinners and knew the way well.

"Hello, Michael, George," Sara greeted.

"Are you guys hungry?" Ramey asked brightly. "There's plenty."

"We're here in an official capacity," Michael replied with a solemn tone.

"I see," Sara said, her gaze traveling to the additional officers joining them.

"What's going on?" Ramey asked, also appearing to notice the other uniforms.

"We're exercising a search warrant, ladies." Michael glanced around the kitchen. "You'll have to go wait out front with your aunt."

"Oh, Michael, you can't be serious," Sara snapped. "This is ridiculous."

"Out front, please," Detective Provenza repeated, motioning down the hall toward the front door. "Now."

Sara turned the stove off and followed Ramey out. "There has to be some kind of mistake."

Michael watched them stomp off down the hall until they were all the way out of the house. "Now let's see what we can find," he told the officers. "Anything to do with Daphne or Drew Stone, and any possible motive for her murder. Let's take Mrs. Giraldy's laptop and see if she researched anything about drug interactions."

"Here's a bottle of balsamic vinegar next to the stove. It looks like the expensive kind," Provenza noted. "The lab probably can't tell one from the other, but let's bag it just in case." He opened the refrigerator and looked inside. "No cranberry juice, but she could have used the one at the Stone's house. After all, her prints were on it."

"Do you hear yourself?" Michael asked George, with disgust, keeping his voice down so the officers would not overhear. "This is Renee Giraldy we're talking about."

"I know it's hard, son, she's my friend too, but we have to treat her like anybody else, like we don't know her personally at all."

George was right, but Michael wasn't sure he could do that.

"Now bag that vinegar and let's keep moving," George ordered.

The front door closed hard, drawing their attention to the hallway.

Jenessa stomped toward them with anger written all over her face. "What the heck do you think you're doing?"

CHAPTER 9

"WHY ON EARTH ARE YOU searching my aunt's house?" Jenessa's voice rose with more than just concerned curiosity as she headed for Michael. "You can't possibly think she had anything to do with Daphne Stone's murder."

Detective Provenza stepped in front of her. "Don't take another step, young lady. You can't be in here. We have a legal warrant to search these premises. Don't make me arrest you for getting in the way of us doing our job."

"But, Michael?"

"He's right, we have a warrant." Michael shrugged apologetically. "I'm sorry, but you'll have to wait outside with the others."

"I want to know what evidence you have that's specifically pointing you to Aunt Renee."

"We can't divulge that info at this point," Provenza said. "Now get going."

"Michael?" She looked to him, giving him her most pleading gaze, hoping he'd toss her even a morsel of information.

"Please," Michael replied, the word heavy with angst, "don't make this any harder than it already is."

Jenessa paused and thought about his request. Though he was right, it was hard to see them poking through her aunt's home looking for evidence that she had murdered her friend. She spun on her heels and stalked out, slamming the door so hard behind her that the windows rattled.

~*~

"So, what did you find out?" Aunt Renee impatiently asked, standing on the lawn with Sara and Ramey huddled around her, waiting.

"Zilch," Jenessa replied as she approached them, feeling like she had failed her aunt somehow. "They have a warrant, so they have the legal right to search your house."

"But why?" Ramey pleaded. "What were the grounds for the warrant?"

Jenessa shrugged, throwing out her hands, palms up.

"I don't get it," Aunt Renee muttered as she shook her head slowly. "What on earth would make them think I had anything to do with Daphne's death? She was one of my best friends, for Pete's sake." There was an unfamiliar look of fear darkening her eyes.

"They must have some reason to suspect," Sara added. "A judge wouldn't give them a warrant without a valid reason, would he?"

"Sara!" Ramey chided.

"No, no, that's okay," Aunt Renee said. "Sara has a good point. They must have discovered something that makes it seem like I might be involved. But I can assure you girls, I had nothing to do with it."

Ramey draped an arm protectively around Aunt Renee's shoulders. "We know you didn't."

Sara turned to her sister. "Did you ask Michael for a reason?"

"Or Detective Provenza?" Ramey chimed in.

Jenessa nodded. "But they wouldn't say." She took both of her aunt's hands in hers. "I promise you, Aunt Renee, one way or another, I'll find out."

"I appreciate that, dear girl."

"By the way, Jenessa," Ramey said, "did you ever talk to Michael about his ex-wife showing up in town?"

All eyes were suddenly on her.

"You mean Josie?" Aunt Renee asked with interest.

"Well, I did talk to—" Jenessa started to speak, but before she could finish her sentence, the front door opened and the men filed out, drawing all their attention toward them.

Michael and Provenza marched over to the young women clustered defensively around their aunt.

"Renee Giraldy," Detective Provenza said, standing before her, without any hint that he knew her personally, "we need you to come down to the station and answer some questions."

"What sort of questions?" Jenessa asked. "Are you accusing her of murder?"

"Please don't try to get in the middle of this, Jen."

Michael motioned toward the police car, "Mrs. Giraldy?"

As Provenza took her by the arm and began to lead her away, Jenessa stepped in front of them. "Wait."

"What is it now?" Provenza moaned.

Jenessa leaned over to her aunt's ear and whispered, "I'll call Ian McCaffrey, have him meet you at the police station. Don't say a word until he gets there."

She stepped back and nodded to Provenza to proceed, her heart thumping nervously for her aunt.

~*~

"Where were you yesterday between eight am and noon?" Detective Provenza asked Renee. He and Michael were seated across the table from her in the starkly lit conference room. Provenza had a manila file sitting in front of him.

She folded her hands on the table. "I think I had better wait for my attorney."

"If you're innocent, Renee, you won't mind helping us find your friend's killer by answering our questions," he said. "After all, we're friends."

She huffed. "Is that what you call us?"

"Now, don't be like that," George went on. "You have to know we take no pleasure in doing this. But we have some questions that need answers—from you."

"Since this is a murder investigation," Michael jumped in, "we've already read you your rights, so you could keep quiet and wait for your attorney. But if you had nothing to do with Dr. Stone's death, and you choose to waive those rights, answering our questions would help us a great deal in finding out who did kill her."

Renee set a steely glare on Michael. "Nice try, but like I said, I'm not going to answer your questions until my lawyer gets here."

Just then the door opened and Ian McCaffrey filled the doorway with his commanding presence. "I need a few minutes with my client, Detectives," his deep voice boomed as he stepped into the room.

Provenza and Michael exchanged an exasperated knowing glance, then stood and marched out of the room, taking the file with them. They regrouped in the hallway, speculating while they waited, wondering if they'd get any answers out of her at all, now that her attorney was in there. With what evidence and information they had so far, it wasn't enough to make an arrest—at least not yet.

Michael had to admit he was glad of that and suspected George was as well. But if Renee did do it, or helped in some way, no matter who she was to him or how it would affect his budding relationship with Jenessa, Renee would have to be held accountable for her crime.

After a few minutes, the door opened and Mr. McCaffrey invited them back in. Taking their seats opposite him and the suspect, the questions began again.

"Did Daphne Stone know that you were having an affair with her husband?" Detective Provenza asked, setting the file down.

"I'm not having an affair with Drew," Renee answered emphatically, her expression saying she was surprised and insulted by the accusation.

"Have you ever had an affair with Drew Stone?" Provenza went on.

Renee's gaze lifted to her attorney and he nodded for her to answer. "Years ago, before he married Daphne, Drew and I had a brief relationship."

"Who broke it off?" Michael asked.

"It was mutual and we remained friends. Why do you ask?"

"We have reason to believe Daphne suspected him of currently having an affair with a blonde," Provenza stated.

"And you think because I'm a blonde that I started up with him again?"

"You can't deny that it is a plausible possibility," Michael said.

"Is that all you have?" she snapped.

"No, actually," Provenza opened the file. "In digging into your financial information, we find that you are having some money troubles."

A wave of surprise washed over her face, colored with embarrassment.

"What does that have to do with this?" Mr. McCaffrey asked.

"I made some bad investments," Renee said, "and the remodel of my house ended up costing much more than anticipated. I hope you won't make my financial situation public, gentlemen."

"We can't promise—" Provenza started.

The attorney slapped his hand down on the table. "You haven't answered my question, Detectives. What does that have to do with anything?"

"I'm sure you already know this," Provenza said,

looking at Renee, "but Dr. Stone changed her Will in the last few days. She cut her husband out and named you as the new beneficiary of her estate. With you being such good friends, she probably told you she was going to do it, no?"

"What?" Renee gasped. "I had no idea."

"You think my client killed her good friend to get at her money?"

Provenza shrugged, but did not reply.

"Think about it from our perspective, McCaffrey," Michael said. "Your client gets Dr. Stone's money and her husband. I'm afraid the District Attorney will think that's pretty good motive for murder." Michael folded his arms across his chest and leaned back in his chair.

"But Michael—" she started to counter.

"Don't say anything," her lawyer advised, putting a hand on her forearm to stop her.

"Your client knew her friend was on medication for depression," Provenza added, "and her—"

"But I didn't know," Renee cut in, but the detective continued.

"—her fingerprints were found on Dr. Stone's bottle of cranberry juice, which the ME believes is how the fatal dose of vinegar was administered, causing a lethal drug interaction."

"Don't talk about me like I'm not here, George," Renee said. "You know me. You know I'm not capable of doing what you're saying. I swear I didn't know about her medication." She searched his face for a response, but he gave none. "You don't believe me, do you?"

"We can't ignore what we've discovered," Provenza finally responded, his eyes meeting hers. "The

DA will think we're giving you preferential treatment if we do, and he'll get our captain to assign this case to someone else who will be even tougher on you than we are." He paused to let his words sink in, glancing briefly at her attorney before coming back to her. "Let me talk to you as a friend, Renee. If you are innocent, tell us all you know so we can find the real killer."

She leaned over to her attorney and whispered something into his ear. He nodded to her.

"Well?" Provenza's mouth twisted in question.

"Let me make one thing perfectly clear, gentlemen," she began, her determined gaze moving from George to Michael, "I did not murder Daphne Stone, and I had no idea she had changed her Will to leave her money to me. That being said, she did confess to me that she had suspected her husband of having an affair for months. She had discovered blond hairs on his clothes and the scent of a perfume that wasn't hers. I knew she was seeing a therapist, but I had no idea she was on an antidepressant."

"Why were your fingerprints on the bottle of cranberry juice in her refrigerator?" Provenza asked.

"Well, let me think." She paused momentarily. "I did have dinner at her house a few days before she died. I helped her cook, so I'm sure I was in and out of the refrigerator several times grabbing ingredients," she said. "Wait," a light flashed through her expression, "I do remember moving the bottle of cranberry juice out of the way and wondering if she had a urinary tract infection."

"Why would you wonder that?" Michael asked.

"Cranberry juice helps you get rid of it, Michael.

Everyone knows that."

"I didn't," Michael replied.

"I wondered if that's why she had a doctor's appointment a week or so ago," Renee went on. "We were having coffee at The Sweet Spot and she said she had something important she wanted to talk to me about, but she had to dash off for a doctor's appointment. I could tell from her expression she was upset about something. That's when she asked if I could come to dinner, we'd talk about it then, she said. I had thought her appointment was with her therapist, but when I saw the cranberry juice I thought maybe it was with her regular doctor."

"Did she talk to you at dinner about whatever it was that was bothering her?" Provenza asked.

"She was about to, but Drew walked in and she clammed up."

"What do you think it was?" Michael inquired.

"I thought she wanted to talk about her marriage problems, but maybe it was about changing her Will." She shook her head sadly. "Now we'll never know."

"And you never talked to her again after that?" Michael asked.

"Well, we made plans to have lunch the day she died, but I got a message from her assistant that morning saying she couldn't make it and would have to reschedule. I figured she'd call me later, but she never did." Tears welled in her eyes. "Later that afternoon I found out she was dead."

"I'm sorry, Renee, but I have to ask," George said, "where were you the morning Dr. Stone died?"

"I was at a meeting for the Hidden Valley Garden

Club from nine until almost eleven, then I went home."

Ian McCaffrey stood. "My client has answered all of your questions, Detective. Unless you're planning on arresting her, I think it's time for me to take her home."

Renee rose as well. "I don't know who killed Daphne, but it wasn't me. Find out who would benefit the most from her death, then you'll find your killer."

"Unfortunately, Mrs. Giraldy," Michael said, "that appears to be you."

CHAPTER 10

JENESSA, SARA, AND RAMEY were anxiously waiting in the reception area of the police station when Michael escorted Aunt Renee and her attorney out of the secured area. The girls hurried to her as soon as she came through the door.

"Are you all right?" Ramey gushed.

Jenessa shot Michael a searing look as she put her arm protectively around her aunt. "Let's get you home."

"I'm sorry, Renee," Michael said. "I hope you understand, we're just doing our job."

Renee nodded with a weary expression. "Just make sure you find whoever did it."

"Jenessa," Michael lightly touched her arm, "can I talk to you for a minute?"

She cast him a questioning glance, wondering whether or not she should listen to what he had to say. Her anger was telling her no, keep moving, but her affection for him demanded she give him a few minutes.

"All right," she replied before turning to her aunt and the others. "You all go on ahead and wait for me at the car. I'll only be a minute."

Aunt Renee squeezed her hand, appearing to notice the conflict in Jenessa's eyes. "Give him the benefit of the doubt."

"But, Aunt Renee…"

Her aunt leaned in, keeping her voice low. "He's a good man, Jenessa. You'll regret it if you drive him away over this. He's only doing his job."

Michael held out his hand and raised his eyebrows a little, inviting Jenessa to steal away with him for a moment. She reluctantly slipped her hand into his and let him lead her down the hall to an empty office. He pushed the door open for her and flipped the light on. She stepped inside. What would he offer to make the insufferable situation with her aunt tolerable?

At the sound of the door closing, she spun around to face him. "What did you want to say?" Her tone was cool, trying to contain her anger.

With one stride, he was inches from her. "I know you're mad, but we had to follow the lead."

She nodded, her gaze drifting to the side, too angry to speak. Yes, it was his job, her head knew that, but her heart ached for her aunt. Her eyes lifted and held his.

"I've missed you, Jenessa." His gaze drifted over her face as his fingertips ran gently down her arms until he took hold of her hands.

"I've missed you too, Michael, but my aunt…"

"You have to believe me—Provenza and I hated having to search her house and bring her down here for questioning, but there was evidence that pointed to her.

We had to get answers or we wouldn't be doing our job. The captain would be raking us over the coals right now for going easy on her because of our personal relationship. This is a murder investigation we're talking about, not a measly little traffic ticket."

Jenessa bit her tongue, restraining herself from volleying back with a terse retort. She pressed her lips together and silently looked him in the eye.

"Say something." He squeezed her hands as he said it, his voice pleading for a response.

She nodded. "I understand. I don't like it, but I do understand."

A bit of a smile curled on his lips and a hopefulness lit his eyes. "Now about us…"

She was listening.

"Are we okay?" he asked.

"We're okay," she replied, but the words seemed flat, even to her own ears.

He leaned down and kissed her, not seeming to pick up on the lack of enthusiasm in her voice, but apparently the lack of passion on her lips did not escape his notice. "Are you sure?"

"Is your ex-wife still staying at your house?"

"She is. I offered to pay for a hotel, but she refused my offer, said she wanted to spend all the time she could with Jake while she's here."

"But he's in school now."

"Only until three," Michael said. "Josie's been cleaning the house and doing the laundry while he's gone, which has been pretty nice."

"Does she cook for you, too?"

"Uh, yeah," he answered hesitantly.

"Cooking, cleaning, like a good little wife." Jenessa pulled her arms out of his grasp. "What else is she doing, Michael?"

"What are you getting at?"

"Where's she sleeping?" She asked with a raise of one brow.

"I already told you, in Jake's room," he answered firmly. "You can't think she's sleeping with me."

"Bet she'd like to." Angry tears began to form behind her eyes, but she refused to let them come. She drew in a deep breath and blinked hard.

"She's not back in my life, it's not like that. She's just visiting for Jake's birthday."

"But you told me she never comes this far in advance. She's never asked to stay with you before, not to mention the fact that she's low on money." Did he really not see what was happening here?

"Well, yeah, I did say all those things, but she'll be gone as soon as Jake's party is over. I'm sure of it. She doesn't want this small-town life. She made that pretty clear when she left me and Jake."

"Things change, Michael. People change."

"What about us?"

"I thought, as a couple, we were progressing nicely, and I adore spending time with Jake, but having Josie here, playing the sexy little homemaker in your house, is putting a serious cramp in our relationship."

"I think you're reading way more into this than you should." He put his arms tenderly around her and drew her to his chest. "It's you I want to be with, Jenessa. And I know Jake loves you."

And what about Michael? Did he love her too? Was

Jenessa ready to say that she was in love with him?

With her head resting against his chest, the strong steady beat of his heart was soothing to her raw nerves. Maybe she was reading more into Josie's actions than was truly there—or maybe she was not. What was that ex-wife really up to?

~*~

Jenessa rode with Aunt Renee and the girls back to the house to finish the dinner they had started, if it was still salvageable.

"Did you clear the air with Michael?" Aunt Renee asked as she unlocked the front door. "Everything okay?"

"As far as what happened to you is concerned, yes," Jenessa replied. "As far as his ex-wife staying at his house is concerned? Not by a long shot."

"She's staying at his house?" Aunt Renee gasped. "No one told me that."

"Me either!" Sara and Ramey cried out in unison.

"Well, let's get inside and you can tell us all about it," Aunt Renee said.

Jenessa groaned.

They filed back to the kitchen and began assessing what was able to be saved for their dinner and what was not. Jenessa took a stool at the breakfast bar while Sara and Ramey finished making the meal.

Aunt Renee put a kettle on the stove for tea. "I hope you made it absolutely clear to Michael that his ex-wife could not stay at his house. From my experience, things happen when an attractive man and woman stay under the same roof, things they hadn't planned, if you get my drift."

"Don't worry, I told him exactly how I felt," Jenessa said, "also that I suspected she was trying to weasel her way back into his life."

"What did he say?" Ramey asked as she tossed the salad.

"He said it wasn't like that. She's sleeping in Jake's room—there are two twin beds in there—and that she just wants to spend more time with her son while she's in town."

"And she can't spend time with her son while she sleeps in a hotel room?" Sara asked with irritation. "Sis, she can spend all afternoon and evening with Jake, she doesn't have to sleep at the house too."

"I made all those points with Michael. He promised to try to get her out."

"Like Yoda says in Star Wars," Ramey interjected, "no try, just do."

CHAPTER 11

WHILE JENESSA AND HER FAMILY ate dinner, Aunt Renee recounted the interrogation she had endured at the police station. Within her aunt's narrative, Jenessa gleaned a few tidbits of information she could use as she built the story of the murder investigation.

"I knew Daphne was upset over her husband's infidelity, but I had no idea she was so depressed that she was on medication," Aunt Renee said, pushing her food aimlessly around on her plate.

"How could you know?" Ramey laid a sympathetic hand on Aunt Renee's arm. "Don't go blaming yourself for any of this."

"I should have known something was up, though." Tears glistened in her light green eyes. "The last few days she seemed even more depressed than ever. I wish I knew what she'd wanted to talk to me about." Her eyes lowered to the napkin she was smoothing in her lap.

"Perhaps she wanted to tell you about how she was

changing her Will to leave her money to you," Sara suggested.

"Or maybe Drew found out about the Will and had threatened her somehow," Jenessa said.

Aunt Renee's eyes had cleared when she lifted them to reply. "She did say he was holding something over her."

"Like what?" Jenessa asked, her attention piqued.

"I don't know, but it sounded like something serious." Aunt Renee took a long sip of her tea. "I told the detectives they should be looking at someone else, not me."

According to Aunt Renee, Drew likely knew Daphne suspected he was having an affair, but could Jenessa confirm it? Getting rid of the old wife in favor of a new love, not to mention getting his hands on her money before she cut him off, that would certainly make for a salacious and riveting exposé, but Jenessa couldn't help but wonder if that's all there was to it. Yes, it would probably be enough to get a conviction if the DA had the proof he needed, but Jenessa was after a plump, juicy story, one with a shocking twist, if one existed.

Could the shooting at the college be connected to Daphne's murder?

Perhaps if she questioned Aunt Renee more in depth, privately of course, maybe she could find a thread to start tugging on that would unravel an entire web of secrets and deceit. On the other hand, maybe it was simply her own wild imagination, coupled with her experience as an investigative reporter, that was hoping to uncover a more compelling story. She'd never know, though, unless she did the hard work, continued to dig deeper, and battled to peel back the layers to expose the ugly truth of what really may have happened to Dr. Daphne Stone. Now that had the makings of a great story.

~*~

Early the next morning, Michael and Detective Provenza were back in their office working the case, poring through Daphne Stone's phone records, emails, and financial accounts, looking for anything that would give them a clue as to who would have wanted her dead. Having all but ruled out Renee Giraldy, Drew Stone was their next best suspect.

With Daphne having suspected him of having an affair, according to Renee, and the fact that he did not know he had been written out of his wife's Will, they were able to get a warrant approved to search the husband's records as well.

"Hey, look at this," Michael said. "Three phone calls on the mister's phone to the same number late at night. You think it was the girlfriend?"

"Let's see," Provenza replied. "What's the number?"

Michael read it off and Provenza slowly typed it into the computer.

"Hmm, not the girlfriend unless her name is Buck Baird," George quipped. "Let's check out Mr. Baird and see if he has anything to do with this case." He entered the man's name into a search program and Buck Baird's photo and history popped up on the screen. "Got him."

Michael hurried around the desks and peered over

Provenza's shoulder to check the computer screen. "Five nine, slender build, brown hair, hazel eyes. Says he served time for assault. He's out on parole and his last known employer is Whitfield College where he works as a maintenance man."

"Why would the school's ex-con maintenance man be getting calls from the professor late at night?" Provenza wondered out loud.

"Good question. Why don't we go pay Mr. Baird a visit?" Michael suggested.

"Hello, boys," came a sexy female voice from the open doorway, quickly drawing both men's attention. The woman was holding a pink bakery box in one hand and a cardboard carrier with a couple of coffees in the other. "Mind if I come in?"

Provenza looked at Michael with a puzzled expression, his mouth gaping open. Michael tried his best to avoid his partner's gaze. "Yeah, come in."

"Sorry to bother you men, but I recalled you like a coffee and a pastry in the middle of the morning, Michael." Her violet eyes followed him as he took a seat behind his desk. "Aren't you going to introduce us?" she asked him, her gaze landing on Provenza.

"George, this is my ex-wife, Josie. Josie, Detective George Provenza."

"A pleasure to meet you." George stood with a grin and took the coffees from her.

"How did you get back here?" Michael asked, irritated that someone let her through without his permission.

"Ruby buzzed me through. She remembered me from a few years ago, and it didn't hurt I brought her a mocha latté. It's not hard to bribe a small-town receptionist, Michael."

"Got a lot of experience with that, do you?" George asked sarcastically, cutting his partner a sideways glare.

Josie ignored his comment and sauntered over to Michael, setting the box of pastries on his desk before bending over to plant a soft kiss on his cheek.

Someone cleared their throat from the doorway.

"Jenessa." Michael shot up out of his chair, wiping his cheek. He was certain there would be a smudge of deep pink lipstick smeared from Josie's lush full lips—lips that would give Angelina Jolie's a run for their money.

Josie slowly turned toward the door and smiled. "Hello, Jenessa," she greeted. "It's nice to see you again." She leaned a curvy hip against Michael's desk. "Do you work here too?"

"No, Jenessa's a reporter for the Hidden Valley Herald," Michael said. He could feel a layer of sweat forming on his brow. He pulled at his collar to get some air. Jenessa was holding a pink box from The Sweet Spot too, and he suspected it was for him. He followed her gaze to the top of his desk, then caught the change of expression in her eyes.

"Did you bribe Ruby to get back here too?" Provenza asked.

"No, she just buzzed me through and told me to join the party." Jenessa pitched a quick glance at Josie, before shifting her attention back to the silver-haired detective.

George grunted. "I'm going to have to have a talk about protocol with that woman."

"I'm sorry if I'm interrupting something here," Jenessa said, keeping her eyes on Provenza. "I just need a few minutes of your time, George. I have a few questions for you about the Stone case."

"Sure, let's step into the conference room," Provenza replied, gesturing with an outstretched hand toward the door. "What's in the box?" he asked as they walked down the hallway.

"I'll be there in a minute!" Michael called after them, wanting to get away from his ex-wife. "Geez, is it getting hot in here?" He wiped his hand across his forehead.

"So, Jenessa is a reporter," Josie said, adjusting the hem of her snug t-shirt over her tight-fitting jeans. "I met her a couple of times at the coffee shop, but she never said what she did."

"Yep, she's a reporter." He sat back down, choosing not to respond to her comment about having previously met his girlfriend. "She covers the big stories in town. We used to be on the school newspaper together in high school."

"Did you date back then?"

"No, we were just friends." Michael shuffled a few papers around on his desk. "Thanks for stopping by, but I really have a lot of work to do."

"Are you two dating now?"

His gaze met hers. "What makes you ask that?"

"You told me you were dating someone. The way you reacted to her seeing us together tells me she's more than just a reporter looking for a story. Simply having her and me in the same room is making you break out in a sweat."

"Well, okay, yes, we're dating."

"Is it serious?"

"Not yet," he paused, hesitant to say too much, "but it could be, someday." How much should he tell her?

Josie moved closer to his chair and rested her backside against his desk. "Being away from you and Jake has given me a lot of time to think."

Her perfume was intoxicating and his heart rate felt like it was picking up speed.

"I miss you both so much. I miss us being a family."

"Since when?" He asked, fighting his unwelcome reaction to her nearness.

"Now, I realize I may have lost my window of opportunity to make things right again—since you've started dating someone else. But before it gets serious with her, I want you to know that I would love the chance to make it up to you." She traced a finger down the buttons of his shirt, toward his waist. Her flirty touch caused him to push back a little. "And the chance to have our family back together." She inched closer. "I'm ready to be a mother again, and a wife—your wife."

His eyes were riveted to her sensual lips as she spoke, but he couldn't believe what she was saying. He raised his gaze to meet her eyes, which held his until he broke away and bolted out of his chair. "Too much has passed between us to go back and start over again. We can't just take up where we left off. You broke my heart and you abandoned your own child."

"But, Michael—" She pushed away from the desk and stood before him, so close that her breasts were brushing against his chest.

His gaze came defiantly back to hers and he took a small step back. "You chose a career in Hollywood over your family, Josie. I can't forgive that, or act like it never happened."

"You don't have to decide right now. Take some time to think it over, babe. Maybe you'll change your mind—maybe we can be a family again."

"Don't count on it."

"Why not?" Her enticing lips formed a perfect pout. "Because of that woman?"

"No, because of you. How do I know you won't take off? Break our hearts all over again?"

"Are you telling me you know beyond a shadow of a doubt that Jenessa won't ever break your heart?"

He had to admit that no one could know with a hundred percent certainty, but there was no way he would admit that out loud to Josie. "I think it's time for you to leave. I have work to do."

"Just think about what I said, Michael." She moved to the door and lingered there, seductively leaning against the doorframe. "Jake and I will be waiting for you at home. See you for dinner?"

He crossed his arms, feeling the need to protect himself from her magnetic draw. "I'll have to see how my day goes."

"I'm making your favorite, fried chicken and mashed potatoes. Our son misses you when you're not home," she said, giving him another little pout.

"That's Jake's favorite, not mine. Besides, I have a murder case to solve." He wasn't falling for her ploy to tug at his heartstrings. "Normally when I can't be home for dinner he's at his grandparents' house and he's fine eating without me."

"That's not what he told me." She peeled away from the doorway and disappeared down the hall, leaving him to wonder if she might be telling the truth.

Their chemistry was undeniable, but he couldn't let her coax him back into her web. Dating Jenessa aside, Josie couldn't be trusted, no matter what she said. He'd have to be more guarded around her than he had previously thought.

He straightened his collar and ran a nervous hand through his hair. Now he'd have to face Jenessa. She would certainly have questions, and not just about the case. He pulled in a heavy breath and exhaled a sigh as he marched out of his office to find her.

CHAPTER 12

"WHAT CAN YOU TELL ME about the progress you've made so far on the Daphne Stone murder case, Detective?" Jenessa asked, seated across the table from George Provenza. She'd been sure to use his title in an effort to get more information out of him.

"Nothing that we want to see in print yet."

"Can't you give me something? Charles is breathing down my neck for another story. I need something my readers can sink their teeth into."

Provenza eyed her, his lips drawn tight, as if he was weighing what he should tell her. Finally he spoke. "We're working our way down the suspect list."

"Which I figured."

"You'll be glad to know your aunt no longer seems like a viable suspect to us, but we're not ruling her out completely."

That wasn't what Jenessa wanted to hear, but she couldn't belabor it. "So who's next on your list?"

"We haven't brought him in for questioning yet, so

I really can't release that information."

"Drew Stone?" After what her aunt had said, he was likely the next suspect.

A light of recognition flashed in the old detective's pale eyes. "Who told you that?"

"No one had to tell me, George. It just made sense to me, since he had been stepping out on his wife."

A slight frown wrinkled his brows. "You already knew that?"

"Don't forget, my aunt was a close friend of the victim."

"What do you need to be interviewing me for then, Miss Jones? Seems like you're already getting your information from another source."

She gave him a little smile and clasped her fingers together on the table. "I just needed to confirm the husband was next on the suspect list, which you just did," she said with some satisfaction.

He cleared his throat with a huff. "I didn't say he was next."

"You didn't have to."

The door opened and Michael stepped into the room. "What did I miss?" He slipped into a seat next to George.

"We were just discussing how you're going to be investigating Drew Stone next," Jenessa replied.

Michael's head snapped toward George, with eyes wide. "You told her that?"

Provenza shrugged sheepishly. "Not in so many words."

"This probably doesn't need repeating, but if you guys feed me information, I'll feed you back. It's a win for both sides."

"What have you got to offer?" Michael inquired.

"Maybe I can get more details from my aunt."

"Like what?" Provenza was quick to ask.

"Aunt Renee said that Daphne wanted to leave her marriage, but her husband wouldn't let her out, that he was holding something over her head," Jenessa said. "So when you're questioning Drew Stone, that's something you fellas need to press him about."

"Hmm, that could be useful," Provenza replied.

Jenessa leaned an elbow on the table and volleyed back. "So what have you got for me?"

"That's not how—" Michael started to argue, but he was cut off mid-sentence.

"Agreed," Provenza said, "as long as you don't print anything until we give you the go-ahead on it." He settled back in his chair. "If you jump the gun, your young man here could lose his job."

"What about you?" Michael glared at Provenza.

"Heck, I'm going to be retiring soon. Besides, the captain is fully aware that I know where all the bodies are buried."

Bodies are buried? Could there be a seedy underbelly to this quaint little town that most residents were totally unaware of? Jenessa filed that tidbit away for future reference.

Michael let out a nervous laugh and rose to standing. Did he think George was only joking? "If that's all, we need to get back to investigating the cheating spouse."

"Speaking of spouses," Jenessa said, "what's with Josie bringing you coffee and goodies?"

Michael's Adam's apple bobbed as he swallowed hard. "She was just trying to be nice."

"Is she still staying at your house?" Jenessa asked.

Provenza's head whipped toward Michael so fast he could have wrenched his neck. "She's staying at your house? Oh, Michael, Michael, Michael." He shook his head slowly as he rose and pushed the chair back in. "I thought you were smarter than that," he muttered as he walked out.

"You had to bring that up? In front of him?" Michael asked, his annoyance obvious.

"You didn't answer the question, Michael. Is she still staying at your house?"

His irritation appeared to dissipate as his gaze fell to the floor. "She is."

Jenessa stood and collected her things. "Then we're done here."

As she walked past him, toward the door, he caught her arm to stop her. "Please don't be like that. Josie will be gone soon. Don't let her mess up what we have."

She met his gaze, trying to read his eyes, their warm brown simmering with intense feelings. "What exactly do we have, Michael?"

He ran his hands nervously up and down her arms. "Well, I, I, I..." he stammered, clearly at a loss for words.

"Just say it."

His arms slid around her and he pulled her close. "I think I'm falling in love with you, Jenessa."

His lips came tantalizingly close to hers and she could feel the heat of his breath.

"Did you hear me?" he asked softly, searching her

106

eyes, anxious for an answer.

She blinked and gave a quick nod, but could not reply. Her throat tightened and her heart rate soared at hearing him say those three little words for the first time.

"I love you," he repeated, whispering the words against her lips before he kissed her.

~*~

After Jenessa left, Michael returned to his office where he found Provenza on the phone.

"Put them in the interrogation room," he said, then hung up. He raised his eyes to Michael. "Drew Stone and his attorney are here."

"That didn't take long." They had only called the man an hour ago to ask him to come in to answer a few questions. "Guess he's anxious to get this over with."

Provenza grabbed the file and got up from his desk. "I thought we'd have time to talk to Buck Baird first."

Michael followed Provenza out and down the hall. "Bringing his attorney along says something about him."

Provenza chuckled. "Yeah, that he's no dummy." He paused at the door to the interrogation room.

"I meant it was more like he had something to hide."

"That's what I meant too." George pushed the door open and they went in. He introduced himself and Michael to the attorney.

"James Winslow, attorney-at-law," the lawyer said.

"I thought I knew all the lawyers in town," Provenza remarked. "You must be new."

"I am," Mr. Winslow responded. "But not new to

trial law. Now let's get down to business."

"All right, then." George settled in a chair and placed the file on the table, lacing his hands over it, but Michael chose to stand. "Tell us again where you were between seven am and noon on the day your wife was murdered."

"Like I told you before, I was teaching an early class, then I went home sick. Is that what you called me down here for?"

"No, there's more." George opened the file. "Are you having an extra-marital affair, Mr. Stone?"

A frown bloomed on the man's brow and he turned to his attorney.

"Don't answer that," Mr. Winslow instructed his client.

"It's a simple question," Michael stepped in. "Yes or no. Either you were or you weren't. Which is it?"

Drew sat stone-faced, eyeing the detectives.

"Do you have any other questions?" the attorney asked.

"We haven't finished with this one," Michael shot back. "Mr. Stone told us when we visited him last that his marriage was fine, but we have reason to believe otherwise. Something about a blond mistress?"

Anger flashed through Drew's eyes—or was it surprise? Either way, the jig was up. "It's not what you think," he mumbled.

Provenza raised his hand and cupped his ear as he inclined his head. "What's that?"

"My client is not answering that question," the attorney said. "Move on, if you have anything else. Otherwise, we're leaving."

Provenza picked up the file and leafed through a few pages. "We've found in our investigation that your wife recently changed the beneficiary in her Will." He looked up, focusing on the suspect. "Were you aware of that, Mr. Stone?"

Again, the same flash of anger or surprise—or maybe both—momentarily lit up his eyes.

"Don't say anything," the lawyer warned, throwing an arm out in front of Drew, as if to hold him back.

Drew did not answer, but his expression screamed that he had not known.

"I think we're done here," Mr. Winslow said, lifting his briefcase from the floor.

"Not so fast," Provenza said. "I have one more question."

Winslow set his briefcase down again, with a low groan. "What else?"

"In going over Mr. Stone's phone records, we noticed several phone calls late at night. We thought maybe they were to his mistress, but in checking we found they were to an ex-con who works in the maintenance department at Whitfield College, the same place your client works. The same place Daphne Stone was murdered."

Drew's eyes rounded at what Provenza had said, but soon the expression was replaced by a quizzical frown. He turned toward his attorney, leaning over and whispering something into his ear. Mr. Winslow nodded at him to answer.

"I know for a fact that I have never made a phone call to any maintenance man at the college late at night. They must have been wrong numbers or something."

"Well, no," Michael said, tugging a chair out and sitting down. "Each call was at least five minutes long. That tells us they were not wrong numbers or hang ups or anything like that. They were definitely conversations."

"The maintenance worker's name is Buck Baird," Provenza added. "What did you discuss with him?"

"Honestly, I have no idea what you're talking about," Drew said. "Did you also happen to see, when you were checking out my phone calls, that I phoned my wife repeatedly the day she died?"

Provenza nodded. "I had seen that, but what of it?"

"Drew." Winslow put a cautionary hand on his client's arm.

"No, he needs to hear this," Drew responded, shaking his lawyer's hand off and leaning forward as he faced the detectives. "Think about it—why would I call my wife if I knew she was already dead?"

"To cover your tracks," Michael said.

"Have you even listened to the voicemails on Daphne's phone?" Drew questioned.

Provenza gave Michael a quick glance before answering. "Not yet."

"You'll find I left several voicemails. Her doctor's office called the house and said it was urgent she call them back. They wouldn't tell me what it was about."

"We'll have to check with the doctor and make sure you're telling the truth," Provenza said. "Just because you left her messages, like Detective Baxter said, you could have been setting it up to cover your butt."

"I'm telling you the truth," Drew moaned. "I loved my wife."

Winslow tugged on Drew's arm again, as if he hoped to quiet him before he said too much. "If that's all." The attorney stood, briefcase in hand. Drew stood too.

Michael whispered a reminder to George.

"Oh, I almost forgot," Provenza said, "there was one more thing."

The attorney scowled. "You said the question before was the last."

Provenza breathed a laugh. "I must've been having a 'senior moment.' Have a seat, please." He gestured toward the chairs. "I promise this is the last question."

"For now," Michael added, crossing his arms as he leaned back in his seat.

Mr. Winslow and his client sat down again. "What is it, Detective?" the attorney huffed.

"According to someone who knew your wife," Provenza began, "Dr. Stone knew about your affair and wanted a divorce from you."

"That's a lie," Drew spat.

"Now, wait." Provenza raised a hand. "There's more. Your wife told a friend that you wouldn't give her a divorce and that you forbade her to file against you. Seems there's something you were holding over her head."

"That's preposterous!" Drew snapped.

"A secret you knew about her, maybe?" Provenza went on. "What was it, Mr. Stone?"

Winslow jumped to his feet. "My client is not answering that question. Sounds to me like you should have brought your rod and reel, Detective."

"Oh yeah?" Provenza's brow furrowed. "Why's

that?"

"Because you're obviously on a fishing expedition. If you had any real evidence, you'd be arresting him. Let's go, Drew."

Both men marched out.

"What do you think he was holding over her?" Michael stood and went for the door.

Provenza shrugged, walking out first. "Maybe she was having an affair with this Buck Baird character."

CHAPTER 13

"BUCK BAIRD?" MICHAEL QUESTIONED as they walked down the hallway. "You think an academic like Dr. Stone was having an affair with an ex-con maintenance man?"

They stepped into their office.

"Well, I didn't mean she was having a relationship with him." Provenza took a seat at his desk. "But if her marriage was on the rocks, maybe this guy somehow came into her life at an opportune time. If she was depressed over her husband's infidelity, maybe this guy made her feel desirable and he was able to get her into bed—you know, the sexy bad boy hooking up with the straight-laced professor—I've seen it happen before."

"In movies, maybe," Michael replied with a chuckle as he sat.

"Not just in movies." Provenza didn't laugh. "When you've been around the block as many times as I have, you see a lot of things, Baxter. Trust me, it happens."

"Then why don't we get over to the college and

have a conversation with Mr. Baird?"

~*~

"But, Aunt Renee," Jenessa argued, "it's not as simple as that."

Aunt Renee took a seat at her breakfast bar, a tall glass of iced tea sitting in front of her. "It couldn't be any more simple, dear girl. Josie Baxter is back in Hidden Valley to insert herself, once more, into Michael's life, and probably his bed."

"Her screen name is Josie Renner," Jenessa corrected, standing at the counter, making sandwiches for the two of them.

"Whatever her name is, that girl is trouble."

"Michael swears she's just here for Jake's birthday."

"Didn't he also say she had no money for a hotel?"

"Yes."

"So, either she's an out-of-work actress or she's lying so he'll let her stay at his house."

Jenessa laid the sandwiches on a couple of plates. "Maybe she figures she can spend more time with Jake if she's staying at their house." Assuming Josie's motherly feelings were back from hiatus.

"What else does Michael have to say about all this?" Aunt Renee asked.

"He said he loves me."

Aunt Renee's eyes grew wide. "He did? When?"

"This morning, after Josie left his office."

"What did you say?"

"I didn't say anything." Jenessa handed her aunt

one of the plates.

"Why not?"

"Because I didn't have a chance, he kissed me as soon as he said it."

"Do you love him?"

"I think so."

"You think so? What kind of answer is that?"

"I hadn't expected him to say it yet. Sure, things are moving along well, but I didn't think we were at that point so soon." Jenessa took a sip of ice water. "I need to be absolutely certain I want to commit to him before I tell him I love him. You remember what happened the last time I told a guy I loved him, don't you?"

"You mean Logan?" Aunt Renee took a small bite of her sandwich.

"Exactly. Disaster. And now with Josie back in the picture, staying at Michael's house, playing the doting mother to their son, well, I'm just not sure I'm ready to say it back."

"Be honest with me, Jenessa. Are you in love with Michael?"

"I am, but—"

"Then you need to fight for him," Aunt Renee advised. "Don't let her win because you're too afraid to fight for what you want. Forget about Logan. You were just a kid when you told him you loved him—you made a mistake."

"A whopper."

"Don't let that cloud your judgment now. If you love Michael, fight for him, because men like that don't come along every day."

That was true. Michael was sweet and strong. An

ex-army ranger turned policeman turned detective, not to mention a loving father. But he had a weakness for beautiful damsels in distress.

Aunt Renee's phone rang on the breakfast bar. "Hello," she answered brightly.

Her aunt listened briefly, then her expression darkened. "Oh, hello, Drew." Her voice was cool and even. Her lips pressed into a tight straight line, as if she was trying to keep them from saying something she'd regret.

What could he possibly want with her?

"All right, I'll be over in a little while," Aunt Renee said before hanging up.

"You will? But why?" Jenessa asked, incredulous Drew Stone had the nerve to call her at all.

"He asked if I'd come over and pick out something for Daphne to be buried in. He said he couldn't bear going through her things right now."

"But they haven't released her body to the funeral home—as far as I know. They're still working the case."

"He knows that. He said he wanted to be ready when they did. Making the arrangements with the funeral home somehow was giving him closure, but he had no idea what she would want to be buried in."

"Do you think it's just a ploy to make himself appear innocent of her murder, like he really did love her?" Jenessa asked.

"I couldn't tell you. I know they were happy together for a long time."

"What changed?"

"Daphne became suspicious, depressed, angry. They would argue all the time, Daphne told me."

"When he began cheating on her?"

"It's hard to say. It's like, what came first, the chicken or the egg?" Aunt Renee asked. "So I don't know, dear, which was first—the affair or the change in her personality. My guess is the affair, but it just as easily could have been her suspicions and anger that drove him into another woman's arms."

"Is that what you think I might do with Michael? Drive him into Josie's arms?"

~*~

Aunt Renee asked Jenessa to go with her to the Stone house, to which she happily agreed, knowing her aunt would need support going through her dead friend's personal things.

As they stood on Drew Stone's porch and rang the doorbell, Aunt Renee appeared nervous while she waited for him to answer the door. Jenessa took her aunt's hand and gave it a little squeeze.

"I'm here for you," Jenessa whispered.

Aunt Renee nodded and took a deep breath.

The door opened and Drew greeted them with a somber expression, holding a little Yorkie in one arm. "Please, come in." He stepped back to let them by. "I so appreciate your coming, Renee."

"This is my niece, Jenessa," she introduced. "I don't recall if you've ever met."

"No," he extended his hand with a little smile, "I don't think so."

"Yes, the day someone took a shot at your wife." Jenessa shook his hand, seeing just a faint redness in the

117

whites of his hazel eyes, a slight expression of a grieving husband. Was he putting on a brave face for Aunt Renee? They had been romantically involved at one time, after all.

"That's right," he said with a bit of a nod.

"What a cute dog," Jenessa said. "What's her name?"

"Buttons. She was Daphne's dog."

"I'm so sorry for your loss, Mr. Stone."

He set the little dog down and she scampered off. "Well, we best get to it."

Drew climbed the stairs and the two women followed him. They walked through double doors into a large, well-decorated master bedroom. "The closet is there," he said, gesturing toward a short hallway. "I'll leave you to make a selection. Just drape the outfit across this chaise." He turned and left them alone.

Jenessa followed her aunt down the short hallway that opened to a generous master closet, decked out with multiple cedar drawers, rows of clothes, and racks of shoes. In the center was a wide tufted bench covered in ivory leather.

"Wow, what a closet," Jenessa exclaimed.

Aunt Renee began flipping through Daphne's dresses and suits. "She was always dressed exquisitely. I'm sure she'll want to look fabulous when friends and family see her for the last time."

Who wouldn't?

"Here," Aunt Renee declared, "this one is perfect." She pulled out a silky sheath with small abstract red flowers and a touch of green leaves on a creamy background. "This one always made her glow."

That made sense, with her auburn hair and her deep green eyes.

"Yes, this is the one," Aunt Renee said, like she was confirming it to herself.

"Here are some shoes that'll look stunning with it." Jenessa pulled a pair of red leather pumps with three-inch heels off the rack. As she stuck her fingers into the tops to pick them up, she felt something in the toe of one of the shoes. "What's this?"

Aunt Renee spun toward her, with the dress draped over one arm. "What did you find?"

Jenessa dug out a small prescription pill bottle and held it up to read it. "It says it's Oxycodone."

"Let me see that." Aunt Renee plucked it from her hand and studied the label. "The police said Daphne was on antidepressants, but why painkillers?"

"And why was it stuck in her shoe?" Jenessa asked. "Was she hiding it from her husband?"

Aunt Renee stared at her with a blank expression, her mouth hanging slightly open, as if she was trying to come up with an answer.

"Any ideas?"

Aunt Renee settled on the edge of the ivory bench, staring at the bottle in her hand. "I do remember her saying she was having some awful headaches."

Jenessa took the pills back and stuffed the bottle in her purse. "I'll have Michael check into it."

Her aunt nodded.

"And don't breathe a word about these pills to her husband," Jenessa warned. "I don't trust him."

~*~

119

After dropping Aunt Renee off at her house, Jenessa headed down to the police station, calling Michael on the way. "I've found something I think you and George need to take a look at. I'm on my way to the station."

"Sorry, Provenza and I are at the college. We'll be back soon."

"What's going on at the college?" Was there a new development in the case?

"Hey, there he is!" Michael called out.

"There who is?"

"Sorry, I can't talk now."

The line went dead.

CHAPTER 14

"Buck!" Michael shouted. "Stop!"

A young man in a tan maintenance uniform jogged around the corner of a building at the college. Michael sprinted after him, Detective Provenza trying to keep up. When Michael rounded the corner, Buck was grabbing the handle of a door and yanking it open. But Michael, with his long gait, reached him before he went inside and disappeared.

Michael seized him by the collar of his shirt and spun him around, pushing his back against the brick exterior. "Buck Baird?"

The man nodded.

"Why'd you run?" Michael asked, still holding him by his shirt.

"I didn't know who you were."

"Are you in some kind of trouble?" Provenza asked.

"I don't know, am I?" Buck answered with a bit of sarcasm.

"Depends." Provenza shot a look of irritation at

Michael, then pulled out his shield and flashed it at the man. "We're police detectives. I'm Provenza, this is Baxter."

"What's this about?"

"Dr. Daphne Stone's murder." Michael said.

"What? You think I had something to do with that?"

"Possibly," Michael replied. "Did you?"

"Kill Dr. Stone? Hell no!" Buck's expression changed to indignation.

"We have some questions for you," Provenza said.

"What do you want to know?"

Provenza signaled with his thumb toward his car. "Let's take a ride down to the station and discuss it."

~*~

Jenessa stopped by The Sweet Spot to kill some time before Michael got back to the station. She swung the door open and caught Ramey's eye when the little bells chimed. Ramey was waiting on a customer, but flashed her friend a welcoming smile.

As the customer stepped away, Jenessa moved up to the counter. "The usual."

Ramey leaned over and whispered, "Look over there." She motioned with her expressive blue eyes in the direction of a couple sitting at a table.

Jenessa turned her head slowly, not wanting to be conspicuous with her curious stare. Seated at a table by the window, laughing and talking, were Josie and Logan. Her head snapped forward.

"What do you think of that?" Ramey asked in a low

voice.

Well…when he was asking her to dinner for the umpteenth time, Jenessa had suggested to Logan that he check out the new dark-haired beauty in town—but that was before she knew the sexy brunette was Michael's ex-wife. Visions of the future exploded in her mind. She saw herself and Michael fighting Josie and Logan in the courts for the right to raise Jake, which caused a terrifying chill to snake down her back. She shook her head, dislodging the horrifying image.

"Jenessa?" Ramey asked.

The room suddenly became suffocating, her brain screaming *Run, before they see you.* "Sorry, Ramey, but I have to go." She bolted out the door, hopefully unnoticed, and climbed into her car.

She could see Logan and Josie through the glass, laughing and conversing, not taking their eyes off each other in that flirty way. Her heart pounded at the possibility that those two could become a couple and what it could mean. Those troubling thoughts sent blood painfully pulsing to her head. She closed her eyes and massaged her temples.

Just breathe. You can handle it. Just breathe.

A sharp rap at the car window almost brought her out of her skin. It was Ramey. Jenessa rolled the window down.

"Are you okay?" Ramey looked worried.

Jenessa's cheeks warmed with embarrassment. "Sorry I ran out on you like that."

"No need to apologize. I get it." Ramey handed a coffee through the open window. "Maybe this will make you feel better."

"Thanks, but I think it's going to take a lot more than a cup of coffee." She offered Ramey a wan smile. "I'd better get going before they see me."

"Too late."

Jenessa looked toward them. Logan waved and smiled before turning his attention back to Josie. "Oh geez." She started her engine. "I'm out of here."

~*~

"Have a seat," Detective Provenza ordered Buck Baird as they ushered him into the interrogation room at the station.

Buck dragged a chair out and sat. Provenza took a seat across from him, setting the growing file on the table. With arms crossed, Michael stood in the corner, observing.

"You have the right to remain silent," Provenza began and continued to read the man his rights.

"Am I under arrest?" Buck asked.

"Let's just say you're a suspect, so we have to Mirandize you."

"A suspect?" Buck squirmed a little in the chair. His nervous gaze flew to Michael in the corner, then back to Detective Provenza. "What's this about?"

"I'll ask the questions," Provenza replied, opening the file and laying it flat. "What is your connection to Professor Drew Stone?"

"I don't have any."

"Now, that's no way to start this thing off," Provenza said.

"What do you mean?"

"By lying to us." Michael stepped toward the table and leaned down on both hands. "It only makes you seem guilty."

"So let's try that again," Provenza said. "What is your connection to the murder victim's husband?"

"Uh, well, we work at the same place."

"You've got to give us more than that," Michael said forcefully.

"I don't know what you want me to say." Buck crossed his arms and fidgeted in his chair. "I didn't have anything to do with killing Dr. Stone. I liked her, she was nice to me."

Provenza lifted a few pages from the file. "This says that you spent time in prison for assault. You nearly beat a man to death."

"What's that got to do with Dr. Stone? I heard someone poisoned her."

"Well," Provenza set the papers down and raised his gaze to the man, "phone records indicate the good doctor's husband made several calls to you, late at night, prior to her death. Can you tell us what that was about?"

"Never happened," Buck replied emphatically.

Provenza chuckled. "You're saying the phone company got it wrong?"

Buck shrugged and looked away.

"Were you sleeping with Daphne Stone?" Michael asked.

His gaze snapped back to Michael. "No, it wasn't like that." Buck seemed to relax, casually hanging an arm over the back of his chair as he looked across the table at Provenza.

Provenza folded his hands on the file and leaned

forward. "Then tell us what it was like."

Buck suddenly looked away. Was he thinking about how to answer the question? Or was he considering just how much of the truth to tell?

"Well?" Michael asked after Buck took a long pause.

Buck's gaze returned to Provenza. "I want a lawyer and a deal, then we can talk. I will tell you this, though, I did not kill Dr. Stone, but I think I know who did."

"If you didn't kill her, then why do you want a deal?" Provenza asked. "Why don't you simply tell us what you know?"

"Let's just say I may have bent a few laws."

Provenza met Michael's gaze for a moment, then his attention moved back to the suspect. "Well, young man, we don't generally arrest people for bending the law, but we do for breaking it. Are you really trying to say you may have broken a few?"

Buck tilted his chair back, knitting his fingers behind his head. "You get me a lawyer and see what you can do for me, then I'll tell you what I know."

~*~

"Is Detective Provenza or Baxter in, Ruby?" Jenessa asked when she reached the police station.

"I'll check. Last I saw of them they were dragging some guy into the interrogation room."

Jenessa's interest piqued. *Who could it be?*

Ruby phoned the detectives' office and let them know Jenessa was there to see them. She hung up and looked at her over her glasses. "Detective Baxter said to send you back."

"Thanks, Ruby." Excitement danced down Jenessa's arms as she made her way back to their office. "Knock, knock."

Michael was on the phone, but he looked up and smiled at her, then covered the receiver with his hand. "Give me just a minute," he said before returning to his call.

"Hello, George," she greeted the elder detective, keeping her voice low. "Any big breaks in the case?" Anxious to know who they hauled in, she took the seat beside his desk. "Anything I can print?"

"We're working on something, but it's too early to say."

"A little bird told me you brought someone in here for questioning. Sounds promising."

"A little bird with a big mouth." Provenza frowned and gave his head a shake. "I really can't talk about it yet."

"That was the assistant DA," Michael said after hanging up the phone. "He's on his way over here to—" He stopped short, his gaze darting to Jenessa, apparently seeing her eyes light up with interest. "Uh, well, let's just say he's on his way over later this afternoon."

"What's this about?" she asked, looking from one man to the other. "Does it have anything to do with that suspect you have in interrogation?"

Provenza's phone began to ring. "Saved by the bell," he quipped before answering it. "Detective Provenza," he said turning away.

He listened for a bit. "Uh-huh. Okay," he said. "Sure, we'll be right down."

"Who was that?" Michael asked.

"Dr. Yamamoto."

"The ME?" Jenessa inquired.

Provenza nodded. "Some tests have come back and there's something he wants to tell us." He stood and grabbed his jacket. "We'll be back before the lawyer for you-know-who shows up."

"Can I come?" Jenessa pleaded.

"Not a good idea," Michael said.

Jenessa grimaced. "What happened to you scratch my back and I'll scratch yours?"

Provenza raised a brow. "You have something to trade?"

"As a matter of fact I do," she crossed her arms and replied with a bit of smug satisfaction.

CHAPTER 15

"WHAT DO YOU HAVE FOR US, Miss Jones?" Detective Provenza asked.

"Depends. Are you going to let me go to the ME's office with you?"

"Jenessa," Michael said, "you can't be withholding evidence from us. If you know something, you have to tell us."

If she didn't stand her ground and dangle a carrot or two, these guys wouldn't give her anything for her stories, so she had to play the game. "Tit for tat, Michael."

He scowled at her response.

"Okay, okay," Provenza groaned impatiently. "You can go with us. Now, tell us what you've got."

She dug around in her purse and pulled the little bottle of prescription pills out. "Oxycodone," she said, setting it, with a snap of the bottle, on the corner of the desk.

Provenza picked it up and read the label. "Daphne

Stone's prescription." His gaze sailed to Jenessa. "Where did you get this?"

"At her house."

"But we searched the whole house," Michael said. "How did you find it?"

She explained how Drew Stone had phoned her aunt earlier in the day, asking her to come and pick an outfit for Daphne to wear at the funeral, once her body was released to the funeral home. "I happened to be with my aunt when he called, so she asked me go to with her. We were going through Daphne's enormous closet, trying to choose the right outfit, and that's when I found it, in the toe of a pair of red leather pumps. I felt something when I picked up the shoes—it was that bottle of pills."

Provenza scratched his head. "I wonder what it means."

"Aunt Renee said Daphne had been having terrible headaches lately, and some serious mood swings. Maybe there was something wrong with her, something more than simply depression."

"Whatever it was might have nothing to do with her murder," Provenza said.

"On the other hand…" Michael raised his eyebrows to his partner. "Who's the doctor on the bottle?"

Provenza lifted it up. "Says Dr. Eugene Tierney, Walnut Grove."

"Maybe we should go and pay Dr. Tierney a visit," Jenessa suggested. "Walnut Grove's not that far."

"Whoa," Michael breathed a laugh, "we agreed you could go to the ME's office with us, but don't get it into that pretty little head of yours that you're going to be following us on every lead."

She stood and smiled sweetly at him, liking the compliment he just paid her. She ran her fingers through her long tresses, brushing them back over her shoulders with a naughty grin. "Well, as long as you put it that way."

"All right, all right," Michael acquiesced. He rose too and grabbed his jacket off the coat rack. "Let's get over to Yamamoto's office and see what he has for us."

"As long as she stays quiet as a church mouse," Provenza muttered, glaring at her. "Got it?"

Jenessa winked at him and went for the door. "I call shot gun."

~*~

"What do you have for us, Doc?" Detective Provenza asked as the three of them strolled into the cool antiseptic morgue.

"Hello, Miss Jones," the ME said, seeming a little surprised to see her there.

"Hello," she answered, but kept her response short, apparently not wanting to stand out, for she had been warned by Provenza she could come if she remained silent.

"Doc?" Provenza said, bringing the man's attention back to him. "What do you have?"

"Oh, yes, I got the secondary test results back today and they showed some interesting things. Not only did Dr. Stone have Phenelzine in her system, I found she had traces of Oxycodone as well, although that's not what killed her. It was definitely the Phenelzine and vinegar."

"Oxy, huh?" Michael fingered the pill bottle in his pocket.

"Any idea why she would have been taking Oxy?" Provenza asked.

"Not yet, but she also had some suspicious anomalies in her blood work. I'll have to keep studying the test and finish the autopsy, but I wanted to let you know that there may be more to this than we originally thought."

"We're anxious to know what you find, Doc," Provenza said. "Anything else?"

"Yes, as a matter of fact." The doctor moved to his desk and retrieved a file. "The blond hairs we found in Dr. Stone's office also match hairs we found at the Stone's home."

"Neither Daphne nor Drew have blond hair," Jenessa said.

Michael and George both cut disapproving looks her way and she backed up a step.

"Continue, please," Provenza said.

"The lady's right, neither are blonds, but the test results show the hairs are synthetic," Dr. Yamamoto said, "meaning they were from a wig."

"So we're not necessarily looking for a blond mistress," Michael surmised.

Provenza rubbed his jaw. "Since you found those hairs at Dr. Stone's office and at her home, I wonder if she ever wore a blond wig."

"I can ask my aunt if she knows," Jenessa offered.

George frowned at her.

"There's more." The doctor flipped through the file. "I found a set of fingerprints on the bottle of cranberry juice that I haven't been able to identify yet. They match ones we took from Dr. Stone's desk, so I'm guessing they belong to her assistant."

"They should be easy enough to get," Michael said. "It would make sense her prints would be all over Dr. Stone's office."

"Anything else?" Provenza asked.

"That's all for now."

"We'll get out of your hair then." Provenza turned to leave and the others followed. "Let us know as soon as you have anything more, Doc," he pitched over his shoulder.

~*~

When they returned to the station, Michael walked Jenessa to her car.

"Want to get something to eat?" she asked.

"No, I'm having a quick bite with Jake tonight, before I head back to work."

"And Josie?"

"Well…" He paused, drawing out the word as if he were searching for a way to answer her question, his gaze drifting a bit before returning to Jenessa. "She did mention she was making dinner for us, and that Jake really wanted me there. I don't want to disappoint him."

Jenessa leaned her hips against her car and folded her arms. "Kids always seem to have the dream that their parents will get back together."

Michael rested his arm on the top of the vehicle and leaned close, his face within inches of hers. "I don't think Jake dreams about that."

"All kids do, Michael."

"How do you know that?" His gaze moved from her eyes to her lips.

Her heartbeat picked up the pace, sensing he wanted to kiss her. "It's common knowledge." She watched as he moved a little closer.

"Oh, is it?" He closed the gap between their lips and kissed her tenderly. "Maybe we can have dinner this weekend."

"What about your houseguest?"

"Josie?" His lips curled into a mischievous smile. "She's on her own. Besides, she'll probably be doing something with Jake while she can."

"Are you sure she's going back to Los Angeles after Jake's birthday?"

Michael pulled back. "Why wouldn't she?"

Jenessa wondered about Josie and what looked like her new relationship with Logan. Had there been sparks flying between them, or was Jenessa making more out of it than there really was? After all, it was Jenessa who had suggested he ask her out.

It was possible they were just having a friendly conversation—no more, no less—because when Jenessa had seen the ex-wife in Michael's office earlier with a box of bakery treats for him, not to mention the overt kiss on the cheek, Josie seemed like her sights were set on Michael. Was she truly only in Hidden Valley for Jake's birthday, to spend some time with her son—or something else?

"Maybe she's broke and has nothing to go back to," Jenessa said. "You told me she didn't have the money for a hotel room, so it could be that her career has hit a snag or something." Was the woman out of money and out of luck? Was Josie hoping Michael would take her back because she had no place else to go? Like she could just step back into her little ready-made family like nothing had happened?

Michael's eyes grew pensive. "She did mention she hadn't been hired for a part in quite a while, but I never thought she wouldn't go back and keep working at it."

"What if she decides to stay? Where does that leave us, Michael?"

Michael had told Jenessa that he loved her, though she hadn't yet found the words to say it back. But there it was—he had said it. So why would he declare his love for her if he still had feelings for his ex-wife?

Jenessa's chest tensed as another side to the story popped into her mind. Not to be overlooked was the fact that Josie was the one that left Michael. She was the one who had broken his heart—not the other way around. It was very possible that he still had feelings for her, deeply buried, feelings that made him long for what they once had. If Michael could put his family back together, would he?

"If she decides to stay, that might make things difficult for a time," he admitted, "but don't worry, we could work it out."

Her heart sank. *What does that mean?*

CHAPTER 16

MICHAEL PUSHED AWAY FROM THE CAR, and from Jenessa. The look on her face told him that she didn't like his answer. *It might make things difficult for a time? But we could work it out?*

What was he supposed to say?

He looked at his watch. "I need to check in on Jake and then get back to work. We'll talk more about this later." He had too many things on his mind to discuss his ex-wife right now.

"Yeah, later." Her voice was flat, emotionless, like the expression on her face. Her gaze fell to the sidewalk, then drifted down the block, like she was avoiding making eye contact with him. Was there something in her eyes she didn't want him to see? "You'd better get going."

He needed to go, but he wanted to stay, wanted to make this right. She was definitely thinking way more than she was saying.

"Are you going to be questioning that suspect

again?" she asked. "You know, the one you wouldn't tell me about?"

"The suspect?" His head jerked toward the police station. By now, Buck Baird's lawyer should have arrived. His gaze returned to her. "Yes, that's why I've got to get back in there. We're hoping he can tell us something that'll break this case wide open."

"Then maybe I'd better drop by later to see if you have a statement for me." Her lips curved into a smile that somehow failed to make it all the way up to her eyes.

He hated to leave her this way. He brushed a few strands of her long dark hair away from one side of her face, weaving his fingers through her tresses as his hand cradled the back of her head. He leaned down and kissed her deeply, hoping to convey his love for her, his desire to be with her and only her.

She let him kiss her, even responded, but then she pulled back. "You'd better go."

Michael went inside, still tasting the sweetness of Jenessa's lips. He checked on Buck Baird. His attorney hadn't shown up yet, but Provenza said the woman was on her way.

"I also called that doctor over in Walnut Grove. His receptionist said he's on vacation this week. Be back on Friday."

Michael nodded. "We'll have to take a drive over there as soon as he gets back."

"That's assuming we haven't solved this case by

then." Provenza grinned.

"Mind if I run home for a quick bite with Jake? I promised I'd have dinner with him tonight."

"Go on ahead. I'll call you when the lawyer shows up."

"Thanks, George."

As Michael stepped out of their office, he heard Provenza call out, "Say hello to that pretty little ex-wife for me."

Michael didn't need that. He silently groaned and hurried out.

~*~

As soon as Michael stepped through his front door, Jake came running. "Daddy, Daddy!"

Michael whisked him up in his arms and whirled him around. "Hey, big guy. Did you have a good day?"

Jake nodded with a big grin. "Mommy's friend took us for ice cream."

"Mommy's friend?" Michael looked past Jake to Josie, who was standing in the doorway to the kitchen, with a wooden spoon in her hand.

"Dinner's ready," she said, turning to go back in.

"What friend?" Michael set Jake down and marched to the kitchen. "Who's Jake talking about?"

"Oh, I met someone today at that cute little coffee shop. He said he went to high school with you."

"Does this someone have a name?"

"Of course, silly." She stirred the spaghetti sauce on the stove. "Logan."

Logan? The thought aggravated him. He wasn't

sure why, but it did. "You just traipsed off with someone you hardly know and let him buy our son ice cream?"

Josie glared at him, her eyes darkening. "You make it sound like I let him take us out of the state or something." She shook her head and went back to stirring the sauce. "The glasses are on the table. Can you pour some drinks please?"

"Sorry." Irritated, he did as she asked and gathered their son into a kitchen chair.

Josie brought a large bowl to the table, full of spaghetti and meaty marinara. "You didn't have any vegetables or I would have made a salad, but we do have rolls."

"The pasta's fine," he ground out as he watched her scoop some spaghetti into their little boy's pasta bowl. "I can't stay long, I've got to get back to work."

"Oh, come on. Jake and I were looking forward to seeing you tonight. Weren't we, Jakey?"

Jake nodded, digging a forkful of saucy spaghetti out of his bowl and sticking it in his mouth, creating a messy red outline around his lips. "Mmm."

"Use this, Jake." Michael handed him a paper napkin to wipe his face. "I've got a murder case I'm working on and I need to get back."

"Here I made us a nice dinner," she said, gesturing toward the spaghetti bowl, "thinking you were actually going to spend time with your family."

He inclined his head toward her. Keeping his voice down, he spoke. "You haven't been part of this family for a long time."

"I'm here now," she replied softly, faint tears beginning to glisten in her eyes.

Her tearful reaction made him straighten in his seat. Were they real tears? "You wanted to spend time with your son, now here's your chance. Make the most of it."

Was she seriously trying to make an attempt to be part of the family? Or was she simply playing him? After all, she was an actress.

Michael turned his attention to his son. "Is that good, Jake?"

The boy nodded with a smile but didn't stop eating to answer him.

Chilly silence hung between Michael and Josie. He filled his bowl and quickly downed his spaghetti, not even looking her way. He sensed she was trying to pull him back in, as she had at his office when she'd unexpectedly shown up earlier.

And what was the deal with Logan? He couldn't put his finger on it, but there was something about Logan taking them for ice cream that grated on him. Maybe it was simply the fact that it was Logan.

"Thanks for dinner," he said in her general direction. "Jake, Daddy has to go back to work for a while. You be a good boy for your mother, okay?"

"Okay, Daddy."

Michael kissed the boy on the head and walked out the door.

~*~

"Hey, I was just about to call you," Detective Provenza said as Michael entered their office. "Baird's attorney is in with him now." He paused and eyed Michael with interest. "Everything okay?"

"I don't want to talk about it." Feeling squeezed between Jenessa and Josie was uncomfortable and he'd have to find a way to resolve it, especially if Jenessa's fears about Josie staying turned out to be right.

"Suit yourself," Provenza said. "Just offering a friendly ear while we're just standing around waiting."

"Thanks, but I need to concentrate on this case."

Before long, the suspect's attorney let them know they were ready to talk. Michael grabbed the file, and he and Provenza took their places across the table.

"Listen, fellas," the lawyer said, "if you had more than just a phone record showing a few calls between my client and the victim's husband, you would have arrested him. I have advised him not to talk to you. So unless you have something more and you're going to arrest him, I'm taking my client home."

"That's bull!" Michael shot up, sending his chair crashing back against the wall. He slapped both hands on the table and glared at Buck Baird. "You had to have done something more than make a few phone calls."

"Settle down, Detective," the woman warned.

"Have a seat, Baxter," Provenza said.

Michael dragged the chair back to the table and sat down. "Your client clearly knows something about Dr. Stone's murder because he offered to make a deal in exchange for the information."

"That was before he had the benefit of legal counsel," she said, "and your theatrics won't help. If you find something else, something you can actually charge him with, then we'll talk." She rose and turned to her client. "Let's go."

Buck shrugged apologetically and followed her out.

"Now what do we do?" Michael growled and he got to his feet. "We were this close," he said, pinching his thumb and forefinger almost together. "That guy knows something—I'm sure of it." He shoved the chair against the table with a huff.

"What's eating you, Baxter?" Provenza stood, picking up the file. "It isn't like you to lose your temper like that."

"Sorry, I just have other things on my mind."

"Yeah, I got that, but you need to get your head on straight and help me solve this case."

Michael nodded sheepishly. "You're right."

"There's nothing more we can do tonight. Go on home and see your kid."

Michael half-expected a glib remark from Provenza about seeing his ex-wife too, but none came. "See you in the morning."

~*~

"Come set the table," Aunt Renee called from the kitchen to Jenessa, who was seated in the great room, talking to her sister. "Ramey says dinner's almost ready."

"Be right there," she called back, then finished what she was saying to Sara. "He claims she'll be gone as soon as Jake's birthday party is over…well, by the next day at least."

"If Michael were my man, I'd keep a close eye on that woman. Have you seen her?"

"Jenessa!" Aunt Renee called again.

"Coming."

As soon as Jenessa had the table set, Ramey presented a platter of sliced pot roast surrounded by roasted potatoes, carrots, and onions. "Voilà," she said with a flourish, a glow of pride lighting up her whole face. She set the platter down in the middle of the table and smiled.

"Looks delicious, dear," Aunt Renee said, and everyone agreed as they took their seats.

"Oh," Ramey gasped, her head snapping toward the oven. "I almost forgot the rolls."

Jenessa jumped up. "I'll get them. You've done enough." She dashed to the kitchen.

"What's Michael up to tonight?" Sara inquired as soon as Jenessa returned to the table. "Have you seen him much with this murder case he's working on?"

"Sara," Ramey scolded, gesturing with her eyes toward Aunt Renee, as if reminding her the victim was their aunt's friend.

"Sorry," Sara said glumly. "That was insensitive of me."

"It's okay." Aunt Renee affectionately patted Sara's hand. "Yes, I'm sad, of course, but life goes on. I just hope they can solve her murder and catch whoever did this horrible thing to my friend."

"A drug interaction, wasn't it?" Ramey asked, tucking a strand of red curls behind one ear.

Jenessa nodded. "That's what the ME said and—"

"Didn't your first husband die of a drug interaction?" Sara asked her aunt.

"Oh, that reminds me, Jenessa," Aunt Renee said, changing the subject, "did you tell Michael about the bottle of pills?"

Did her aunt not hear Sara's question, or did she change the subject on purpose?

CHAPTER 17

JENESSA GLANCED ACROSS THE DINNER table at Sara, who looked confused as to why her aunt seemed to ignore her question. Had Aunt Renee's first husband, in fact, died of a drug interaction? If so, she would have known the particulars of how that could happen.

No, it would be crazy to think she had anything to do with his death…or Daphne's. She claimed she didn't know Daphne was taking antidepressants—was it true? An icy chill shimmied across her shoulders at the possibility her aunt was involved and she shuddered.

"Jenessa, did you hear me?" Aunt Renee questioned.

"Sorry, yes, I did tell him, and Detective Provenza too, but I don't know what it means yet. Maybe we shouldn't talk—"

"What pills?" Ramey asked, wide-eyed.

"Let's change the subject," Jenessa suggested before taking a bite of pot roast.

"It's kind of creepy knowing there's a murderer

walking our streets." Sara ignored what Jenessa just said and looked right at her. "Who do they suspect?"

"Really, Sara," Jenessa said, "let's change the subject."

"I'm sure Luke can find out for me," Sara muttered as she stabbed a piece of beef.

"Luke's a patrolman," Jenessa reminded her, "not a detective. Besides, even if he—"

"I have a new subject," Ramey shouted over the sisters' bickering. "Jake's birthday party. I'm making a big cake and a whole slew of cupcakes with Teenage Mutant Ninja Turtles on them. You're going, aren't you, Jenessa?"

"Of course," she said, not looking forward to seeing the gorgeous Josie there. Would everyone be fawning over the beautiful actress?

"Charlie's really looking forward to it," Ramey continued.

"Isn't Charlie quite a bit older than Jake?" Aunt Renee asked.

"Yes," Ramey replied, "but Jake's been like a little brother to him."

Jenessa's ears perked up. "So Charlie is an only child?"

Ramey nodded. "Calista had a hard time getting pregnant, Charles told me, so they stopped at one."

A hard time getting pregnant? Maybe they adopted?

Ramey moved on to a new topic. "What do you think is going on between Logan and Michael's ex-wife?"

"Josie? With Logan?" Sara directed her question at

Jenessa, her eyes growing big. Sara had pined for Logan, unproductively, until Luke Baxter came along. "Tell me, what is going on?"

This was not the conversation Jenessa wanted to have. "Don't ask me," she said, looking down at her plate as she took a few quick bites.

"Do you think she'll invite him to Jake's birthday party?" Ramey asked.

She wouldn't, would she?

Jenessa shrugged her answer, concentrating on eating her dinner.

"They do make a striking couple," Ramey added.

"They're a couple?" Sara gasped. "Jenessa?"

"You girls leave Jenessa alone. You're making her uncomfortable," Aunt Renee reproved. "Look at her shoveling that pot roast into her mouth like she hasn't eaten in days, just so she won't have to answer you."

At her aunt's absurd comment, the pot roast stuck in Jenessa's throat and she almost choked. Her eyes watered and she took a few long swallows of water to clear it. This was going to be a long evening.

~*~

The next morning, Michael snuck out of his house early, before Jake or Josie were up. The less drama the better. After the argument he'd had with her the night before, it was best he let her get Jake off to school herself.

"You're in early," Provenza remarked as the senior detective strolled into the office, causing Michael to look up from his computer. "You look like hell."

"Didn't sleep much last night," Michael muttered. "Got a lot on my mind."

"I hope you're talking about the case." Provenza shrugged his jacket off and hung it over the back of his chair. "We've got to find something that's going to make Buck Baird tell us what he knows."

"Yeah, that's on my mind too, but I was talking about Jenessa and my ex-wife."

"Oh, I see," Provenza grumbled. "Well, as much as I'd like to hear about it, we need to focus on this case. So if you can manage to push your personal life to the side for a few hours, the citizens of this town, who pay your salary, would appreciate it…if you know what I mean."

"I'm trying."

George's phone rang on his desk. "Detective Provenza."

His eyebrows raised as his gaze moved to Michael, while he listened to the caller. "Thanks, Doc."

"What did he say?" Michael asked.

"Remember how someone took a shot at Dr. Stone a short while back?"

"Yeah…"

"One of the CSIs dug the bullet out of her car and sent it to the county crime lab. They've been a bit backed up, and I guess it was low priority since the bullet hadn't hurt or killed anyone, so they just got around to trying to pull any usable prints off it."

Michael perked up. "And?"

"Seems they pulled a pretty good partial thumb print off the bullet."

"Whose?"

"Buck Baird's."

~*~

Jenessa was up early, working at her laptop in her home office, trying to piece together a story from what she knew so far of Dr. Stone's murder and the suspects surrounding it. There wasn't much of anything new she had permission to report, but Charles McAllister had already called her that morning asking for an update on her story.

She had previously written two short articles on Daphne Stone, having stretched them out with what little facts she had, but now her editor was hounding her for something new. She had done the obituaries yesterday, had a society wedding, and a renewal of wedding vows ceremony to write about this coming weekend, but maybe she could come up with some other interesting story to cover.

Grey Alexander. Logan had given her a *heads-up* about him a week or so ago, but with Daphne Stone's murder, she had put it on the back burner and forgotten all about it. She didn't want to have to go to Logan for an update, but she needed a new story to write.

She phoned him and invited him to have coffee with her, not telling him the reason. He happily agreed to meet her at The Sweet Spot at ten. Knowing what he liked, she was waiting at a table with drinks already sitting on it, hoping to keep their discussion strictly about his father and not leave a lot of room for the personal stuff.

"Logan," she called to him when he entered the

coffee shop, waving her hand to get his attention.

He smiled, his sky-blue eyes lighting up, and he moved toward her. "I was a little surprised you called and invited me for coffee." He took a seat across from her.

"We hadn't talked for a while and I wondered if you'd heard anything more about your father's early release."

"What, no small talk first? No polite foreplay before getting down to business?"

Was she that transparent? "Sorry. How have you been, Logan?"

"I'm doing well. I took your advice and tracked down that woman you told me about. You were right, she's a beauty."

Josie. "Happy to hear it," she said, lying through her teeth.

"Someone told me she's an actress," Logan went on, "although I don't think I've seen any of her work."

"Me either." At least not on the screen.

"Did you know she was Michael's ex-wife?"

"I didn't when I recommended her." Heat crept up her neck to her cheeks. "I do now."

He grinned at her, like he was pleased with her discomfort.

Enough about Josie.

"Let's get to the point, Logan. You told me last week your father had reason to believe he would be getting out of jail early. What is the latest on that front?"

He seemed a bit annoyed. "Are you writing a story about it?"

"Possibly." Was there some reason she shouldn't?

"I only told you because I thought *you* should know."

"But it's news that the whole town would be very interested in, Logan."

"I guess that's true enough."

"So, tell me, what have you heard?"

He took a sip of coffee, his eyes going to the cup before he set it back down. "Thanks for the coffee by the way. I'm touched you remembered how I like it."

She gestured for him to continue.

"Anyway, Dad phoned me last night, said he has reason to think his lawyers are close to a deal. He could be home in as little as a week."

A week? Her chest tightened at the news and her hands balled into fists. *So soon?*

Logan's warm palm enveloped her clenched fist as it rested on the table. "Relax." He'd noticed her tense up at his statement. "Nothing is for certain."

The jangling above the door drew Jenessa's attention toward it. *Shoot.* It was Michael. He took one look at her with Logan's hand on hers. His lips pressed into a harsh, straight line and his eyes narrowed with anger.

Jenessa's hand recoiled. Her heart pounded as the misunderstood situation seemed to unfold in slow motion. Michael's eyes shimmered for a moment, then he turned and rushed back outside.

She dashed after him, but his gait was long and he was already halfway down the block. She called his name, but he didn't stop, didn't acknowledge her, just kept walking and rounded the corner back to the police station.

That was the last thing she needed. Had she just helped to drive him back to Josie?

Deflated, she dragged herself back to The Sweet Spot, knowing Logan would still be waiting for her. Not even the colorful autumn artwork painted on the shop's windows brought a smile to her face. Of course, seeing Logan's barely disguised grin beyond those windows didn't help.

"Sorry about that," she said, taking her seat again, trying to act like it was no big deal. "It was only—"

"I saw," Logan said before she could finish making up some excuse. "He'll get over it." He paused, giving her time to calm down. "Now, where were we? You wanted to know more about my father's situation?"

She appreciated his not belaboring the scene with Michael or trying to use it as an opportunity to ask her out again. "Yes, that's right. You had said last week that his lawyers may have found a loophole to get him out for time served, but you never said what the loophole was. Do you know?"

Logan shook his head. "Dad wouldn't tell me, said he was afraid it might jinx it."

Jenessa grinned at the thought. The almighty, powerful Grey Alexander, king of his own universe, who got whatever he wanted, never took no for an answer, and never seemed afraid of anything or anyone. "Funny, I never took your dad for the superstitious type."

"I think going to jail changed him." Logan's eyes softened as he put his hand on hers again. "You changed him."

"Me?" She pulled her hand back. "How did I change him?"

"He always thought he was invincible, but you found a way to take him down."

"And now he'll be after my head when he gets out." It didn't seem so funny anymore.

He leaned an arm on the table, drawing closer to her. "I would never let that happen, Jenessa. I'm no longer that eighteen-year-old boy who let you down when you got pregnant." He straightened in his chair. "Dad put me in charge of his businesses while he was gone, and I've done a good job—exceptional, even. I think the board members have appreciated the way I'm running things too. When he does get out, whenever that is, I intend to go to battle with him to keep my position in the company."

This was a new side of Logan she hadn't seen before—stronger, more self-assured. But what about his apparent relationship with Josie? If Jenessa continued to spurn Logan's advances, she'd be sending *him* straight into Josie's arms. After what just happened with Michael, then Josie would be the one having to choose between Michael and Logan—if she decided to stick around.

"I like this new Logan." She gave him a smile. "You've grown up."

"So you'll—"

"Not so fast," she jumped in. "Just take the compliment and leave it at that."

He stood and swigged back the last of his coffee. "I'll take what I can get." He paused, smiling, as if he was waiting for her witty reply, but Jenessa was silent, afraid to give him further encouragement. "I've got an important meeting to get to, so I'm out of here. Let's do this again, soon."

She nodded. "Soon."

The second Logan was out the door, Ramey slid into his empty seat, her deep blue eyes as wide as the saucer under Jenessa's cup. "So, what's up with you and Logan?" she asked, twirling a strand of her curly red hair around her finger. "You two looked awfully chummy."

"I was interviewing him for a possible article about his father."

"Grey? Why?"

"I can't say just yet. It's a developing story idea," Jenessa explained. "Did you happen to see Michael when he came in?"

"No, I was in the back for a bit. Did he catch you with Logan?"

"Catch me? Like we were doing something wrong?"

"Well, were you?"

"No, but he did see Logan with his hand over mine."

"Oh my."

"It was just a friendly gesture, Ramey."

"Bet Michael didn't like that."

"No. He stomped out of here. I went after him, but he wouldn't stop and talk to me."

"Sounds like seeing you with Logan made him mad."

"Or hurt him," Jenessa added. "I've got to go talk to him. Explain what was really happening."

Chatter drew their attention as several new customers waltzed through the door. "I'd better get back to work," Ramey said. "Keep me in the loop." She hurried back to her place behind the counter.

Jenessa took a long drink from her cup. She hadn't gotten enough from Logan to write a story, but she would keep her notes to begin building one.

As she finished her coffee, she glanced at the people in line. She recognized one of them. It was Daphne Stone's assistant, Ashley. Had the crime lab figured out if the unknown fingerprints on Daphne's juice bottle belonged to her?

After the young woman picked up her coffee and moved toward the door to leave, Jenessa rushed to catch her. "Aren't you Ashley?"

The young woman stopped, looking a bit surprised. "I am."

"You worked for Dr. Stone, didn't you?"

"Yes," she answered with a note of suspicion.

"We met at her office, the day you discovered her…well, you know, at her desk."

A hint of recognition lit up Ashley's eyes. "You're the reporter, right?"

"That's right. Mind if we sit and chat for a while?"

"I'd love to, but I'm kind of in a rush right now." Her eyes looked suddenly nervous. "Maybe some other time."

"It won't take but a minute."

"I can't, really. Some other time." Ashley pushed through the door and dashed away.

Jenessa stepped outside and watched as the young woman quickly made her way down the block and climbed in the passenger side of a small, dark sedan. The driver turned his head toward her as she got in. From that distance away, Jenessa couldn't be sure who it was. Might it have been Drew Stone?

CHAPTER 18

JENESSA HURRIED ON FOOT, from The Sweet Spot to the police station, hoping to find Michael and explain what he'd seen. Yes, Logan still tugged at her heartstrings, but it was Michael she wanted—steady, strong, a family man.

Logan had been the love of her life, the high school quarterback, handsome and rich, and good to her—until he got her pregnant. Michael, on the other hand, had been a high school geek, a good friend who worked on the school paper with her. But he had grown up, become an army ranger, then a cop, and now a full-fledged police detective. He had been nothing but sweet to her, and now that she was back in Hidden Valley, she was falling for him—and his little boy.

As she approached the entrance to the police station, Michael and Provenza were coming out, heading for their vehicle. If she didn't stop them now, she didn't know when she would have another opportunity to explain herself.

"Michael!" she called out.

He stopped and looked in her direction. She moved toward him. "Sorry, I don't have time to talk," he said brusquely, opening the passenger-side door.

"Let's go, Baxter," Provenza hollered from inside the car.

"It's about the case," Jenessa said to Michael, huffing from the run. She hoped that would be enough to make them stop. "Did you hear that, George?"

"I heard," he groaned. "But we've got to go. We won't be long."

Michael climbed in the car without a word.

"I'll be right here when you get back," she managed to squeak out before he closed the door.

~*~

"What was that about?" Provenza asked as they drove to the college.

"Haven't a clue," Michael replied, staring out the side window, hoping his partner would let it drop.

"She said it was about the case," Provenza said. "Why don't you call her and see what she has?"

"I'm sure it can wait."

"What makes you so sure?"

"Just a feeling."

"You don't want to call her, do you?" Provenza paused and waited for a response, but Michael gave him none. "What's going on with you two?"

How could he respond? George had told him that morning to push his private life aside while on the job, now he was pressing him about Jenessa.

"The ex-wife again?" Provenza inquired.

"Oh, it's an ex all right," Michael muttered, "but not my ex."

"Oh." Provenza clammed up and drove the rest of the way in silence.

When they reached the college, they went to the administration building and had one of the secretaries page Buck Baird to the office. After a brief wait, he meandered through the double doors where the detectives stood waiting.

"Mornin', Detectives," Buck said with a cocky grin.

"Good morning," Provenza answered. "We need you to come with us for more questioning, down at the station."

"My lawyer said I'm not allowed to talk to you without her present."

Michael took hold of one of Buck's arms. "You can call her from the station."

Buck pulled his arm away, glancing around the reception area. "I don't want to lose my job, guys. I'm happy to go with you, but don't make it look like you're arresting me, please."

Michael looked to George, who nodded his approval. "All right, but don't even think about running."

"Hey, Jenny," Buck said to the secretary behind the counter, "I'm taking a break. It's almost lunchtime, so I'll be back about one."

"Got it," she replied with an uncertain look on her face.

"Let's go, boys," Buck said lightly.

~*~

As Provenza and Michael entered the police station with their suspect, Jenessa stood from one of the chairs in the waiting area. "Can you give me just a minute?" she said, hurrying toward them.

"We're a little busy," Michael said gruffly.

Not to be deterred from the job she had to do, she held firm. "I just need a minute, Michael."

"I'll put our suspect in the interrogation room, Baxter. You stay and find out what she's got." Provenza took hold of Buck's arm and led him down the hall.

"You said you had something regarding the case?" Michael's usually warm greeting felt frigid.

"I do," Jenessa replied. "Is there someplace we can talk?"

"Here is fine."

She glanced over at the reception area where Ruby sat smiling at her. "Somewhere out of earshot." Jenessa pitched her head slightly in Ruby's direction.

He followed her lead. "Outside then." He held the door open and Jenessa stepped out into the crisp sunshine. "What is it?"

"A couple of things. First, I saw Ashley earlier at The Sweet Spot."

"Ashley?"

"Daphne Stone's assistant."

He nodded in recognition. "And?"

"I tried to talk to her, but she made some lame excuse and ran off. I saw her get into a car and the driver looked kind of like Drew Stone."

Michael's eyebrows raised. "You think she's the

one he's having an affair with?"

"Could be. She is blond."

"But the ME said the blond hairs that were found were synthetic."

"It is possible she's wearing a wig, maybe a really good one."

"I'll have to recheck Mr. Stone's phone records, see if there were calls between them."

"I wonder if Daphne thought her assistant was the one Drew was sleeping with," Jenessa said.

"If it's true—and we don't know that it is—it would give Ashley a good motive to want to get rid of her competition. We'll have to chat with her."

"You want to go now?" Jenessa asked, wanting to get some answers from the young woman. "I'm free."

"I meant Provenza and me." His words were short and curt. "What was the second thing?"

"What you saw between Logan and me, well, I think you misunderstood."

"You were holding hands over the table. What's to misunderstand?"

"No, that wasn't it at all," she insisted. "Logan was telling me about his father's fight to get out of prison early, which was making me turn into a tense ball of nerves. My fist was clenched so tight my knuckles were turning white and he simply put his hand over mine for a second and told me to relax. That's what you saw, Michael, swear to God."

"You know I love you, but it seems Logan is always around. If things don't work out between us, well, I'm a big boy and I'll get over it. But my son is falling hard for you, Jenessa." He took her by the arms.

He looked like he wanted to kiss her, smooth things over, but something was stopping him. "If things go south with us, he'll be devastated."

"I love that little guy. I'd never do anything to hurt him." Her gaze was locked on his. Her heart was thumping.

"Not on purpose maybe, but you're letting Logan get between us," he moaned.

She could hear the pain in his voice, but it was hurting her too. She pulled back from him. "And you're letting Josie get between us."

"At least she'll be gone soon. Hopefully."

"Hopefully?" Jenessa gasped, her muscles tensing. "You don't sound so sure."

"She told me the other night that she doesn't have any work right now and she's thinking of moving back here, to see more of Jake."

"And you too?" *I knew it*. Couldn't Michael see how Josie was trying to weasel her way back into his life?

"I love you, Jenessa. You have to know that."

She nodded, trying to work up a smile. She was angered by Josie's ploys and irritated by Michael's blindness.

"We'll talk more later," he said. "I've got to get back inside."

Her personal feelings aside, she needed to get more information on the murder investigation before he left. "Who was that man George was putting in the interrogation room?"

"I can't—"

"Hey, no fair. I just gave you some info on Ashley

and Drew. Surely you can tell me who your latest suspect is."

His gaze lowered to the sidewalk for a moment, as he considered her request, then bounced back up to her eyes. "Okay, but it's got to be off the record. If you put this in print, Provenza will have my head, and probably my badge."

"Okay, off the record."

"It's Buck Baird, a maintenance worker at the college. That's all I can tell you right now." He paused. "I mean it, I'd better not see that in print until Provenza gives you the go ahead." He started to turn to leave.

"Hey, wait!" she called, moving toward him. She took hold of his dark blue necktie and gently pulled his face down, close to hers. "I love you too, Michael Baxter."

He closed the gap and kissed her ever so briefly, mindful of nosey town folk in the vicinity. "Finally," he said with a big grin, and he was gone.

~*~

After a brief wait, Buck Baird's attorney showed up and was escorted into the interrogation room to meet with her client. Provenza and Michael stood in the observation room, with the speaker off, waiting for the opportunity to go in and question the man.

Eventually the lawyer came to the two-way glass and rapped on it, motioning for them to come in. Provenza and Michael took their seats across the table from Buck and his lawyer.

"I told you the last time we were in here," the

attorney began, "that you'd better have something you could arrest my client for before he said anything to you. If this is a ploy to—"

"As a matter of fact, ma'am," Provenza interrupted, folding his hands on the table and leaning forward, "we have a nice fat ol' thumb print of his on the bullet that was fired at Dr. Daphne Stone the week before she was murdered."

Baird's cocky expression changed. His eyes rounded and his jaw went slack.

"Can you explain that?" Michael asked.

"It's not what you think," Buck spit out.

"Oh, do tell." Provenza leaned back in his chair, crossing his arms.

"What kind of deal are you offering for information?" the attorney asked.

"Depends on what you have to tell us, young man," Provenza said, not looking at the lawyer. "The better the information, the better the deal. As we have it right now, we can charge you with attempted murder."

"I never tried to kill her, I wouldn't. I liked the doc. She was my therapist."

"Yet you shot at her," Michael said with a frown.

"It wasn't like that. It was her idea."

CHAPTER 19

MICHAEL LAUNCHED OUT OF HIS CHAIR, nearly lunging at Buck Baird. "What do you mean, it was her idea?"

Buck jumped back, eyes wide, his gaze rising to Michael's six-foot-four frame. "Uh…uh, that's right. It was her idea."

"Now this is all hypothetical," the attorney jumped in, "that is, until we have a deal."

"Settle down, Baxter," Provenza said. "Take a seat."

Michael slowly sat down again. "You'd better explain yourself, Baird—hypothetically."

"Go ahead, Mr. Baird," the lawyer urged.

"Let's say…what if Mr. Stone, the professor, had paged me to come to his office and he had a maintenance issue. And what if, when I got there, he told me he knew about my prison record and asked if I was interested in doing a side job for him."

"Go on," Provenza said with a nod.

"And let's say I really needed the extra money, hypothetically, so I might have asked him what he wanted me to do—like handyman work around the house or something."

"What did he want you to do?" Michael asked.

"Uh, well, let's just say he might have wanted me to kill his wife."

"Now we're getting somewhere," Provenza muttered. "What did you say?" `

"Well, if he had asked me to do that, I might have asked him why he didn't just divorce her. Then he could have said something about their prenup, and that he wouldn't get anything if they divorced."

"What did he offer you?" Michael asked.

Buck looked at his attorney, his eyes asking permission to speak. She leaned over and whispered something into his ear.

He nodded. "Okay, so if that all had happened, he might have said he'd pay me five thousand dollars after the job was done. Oh, and he would probably have threatened me. Said if I told anyone, he'd drum up some story and make sure I'd go back to prison for a long time. He's an English professor, you know, so he knows how to spin a good story."

"Did you agree?" Provenza questioned with an unyielding stare.

"Remember, Detectives," the attorney interrupted, "this is all hypothetical."

"Oh, of course." Provenza's mouth twisted with annoyance.

"Well, I knew the doc, she was a nice lady. I'd helped her fix a flat tire in the parking lot, and we got to talking a little. She knew I'd been in prison and she offered me a few free therapy sessions if I ever wanted to talk."

"You're not answering the question," Michael growled.

"I'm gettin' to it."

"It's no secret that I really needed the money—my mom's sick and she's in a nursing home—so I might have told him I'd do it, that is, if he had asked me. I wouldn't have wanted to, but I would have figured the mister would get somebody to take the job, so why not me."

"So that's when you shot at her?" Michael asked.

"Did I say I shot at her?" Buck asked sarcastically.

"Let's cut the hypothetical crap and get to the point," Provenza growled. "Just tell us the truth."

The attorney slapped her hand on the table. "As long as you understand we're still only talking hypothetically. My client is not admitting to anything here until we have a deal."

"Oh, don't get your bloomers in a bunch," Provenza snapped. "We have his thumb print on the bullet, so we know he shot at Dr. Stone. Loaded the gun at least." He turned his focus on the suspect. "Just tell us what happened. Is that when you shot at her?"

"No," Buck said, settling back in his chair. "I told the husband I needed a few days to set it up. I didn't really want to do it, even though I needed the money. So I figured out a way I wouldn't have to kill her, but I hoped I could still get some money out of the deal. I went to the missus and told her that her husband had hired me to take her out for five thousand dollars. She offered to match that if I could help her set him up for trying to murder her."

"Now it's getting interesting," Provenza said.

"I agreed, and she called me a few times, late at night, after her husband was asleep, she'd said, to talk about what we should do."

Was that why there were phone calls from Drew Stone's cell phone to Buck Baird? Had Daphne called him from her husband's phone? That'd be a good way to tie him to Buck should she wind up dead.

"So why'd you try to shoot her in the college parking lot?" Provenza asked.

"It was part of the plan, the set up," Buck replied with an impish grin. "She was at least ten feet away from the car when I fired. Then she phoned nine-one-one and reported being shot at. It was part of her plan to make it look like her husband was trying to kill her."

"We'll need this all in writing," Provenza said.

"And don't forget to include the times and dates of Dr. Stone's phone calls to you," Michael added with a firm voice.

"You know," Buck said thoughtfully, "she always recorded our sessions with one of those little doohickeys."

"Micro-recorders?" Michael guessed.

"Yeah, one of those things. She probably has our planning session on tape too."

"That would help corroborate my client's story," the lawyer suggested. "Wouldn't it?"

Provenza nodded. "Assuming we find it."

"So, is that enough information to get my client a deal?" the attorney asked.

"I'll have to run it by the District Attorney," Provenza closed the file, making a slapping sound as he did so. "Assuming Mr. Baird here is telling the truth."

"Find the doohickey," Buck told them.

"But that still doesn't tell us who really killed her, who put the vinegar in Dr. Stone's cranberry juice," Michael said.

"Sounds like Drew Stone to me," Buck said, pursing his lips.

~*~

Jenessa left the police station and headed to the college, hoping to track down the illusive Ashley Brandon. She tried her office first, the one next to Dr. Stone's office that still wore yellow crime scene tape across the entrance. The door was closed, but when Jenessa tried the knob she found it was not locked.

She knocked lightly. "Hello," she called out as she pushed the door open. No response.

The room was about ten feet by twelve with a generous window overlooking the parking lot. A desk abutted one wall, a row of bookcases and file cabinets on another.

Not knowing how much time she had, Jenessa quickly scanned the desktop, then rifled through papers and folders, looking for any sign of something suspicious. She opened the lap drawer and rummaged through the various items, looking for hidden love notes, a loose key, anything that might tie the young woman to Drew Stone.

Below a box of staples was a small, weathered

photo, partially sticking out of a white envelope. Jenessa pulled it out and held it up to inspect it more closely. It was a picture of a dark-haired woman, maybe in her thirties, with a child whose hair was long and light brown, a little girl about seven, if she had to guess. She flipped the photo over, finding a name scribbled on the back—Madalyn Makovsky.

Did it mean anything? Probably not. She slipped it back into the envelope, making sure it would appear undisturbed.

Jenessa continued her search through the assistant's drawers, looking for anything connecting Ashley to Drew Stone…and possibly to Daphne Stone's murder. Could it have been a love triangle gone wrong? The handsome mature man throwing his middle-aged wife, albeit attractive, over for a sweet young blonde—emphasis on *young*.

She pulled the lap drawer out farther. There in the far right corner, at the back, was a small black phone. It looked inexpensive. A disposable one, perhaps.

The door had been left slightly ajar, and the faint sound of female voices wafted in. They seemed to be growing louder as the women moved down the hall toward the office. Was one of the voices Ashley's?

How was Jenessa going to get out? There was only one exit from this office. She couldn't have Ashley find her snooping through her desk.

"I'll talk to you later, Maggie," a female voice said to someone in the hall. Jenessa recognized the voice was Ashley's. "Back to work." The young woman stepped through the door and began to close it. "Oh!" She jumped.

Jenessa was leaning against the empty wall behind the door, her arms crossed casually across her chest. "Sorry, did I scare you? I thought you said one o'clock."

"We had an appointment?" Ashley's brows knit in suspicion. "I don't remember setting a time." She stepped behind her desk, appearing to check the items on top of it. Was she trying to see if anything was missing?

Jenessa pushed away from the wall and stood across the desk from her. "Sorry, I must have heard you wrong. When you dashed out of The Sweet Spot, I could have sworn you said we'd meet later, at one o'clock."

Ashley pushed a strand of hair from her blond bob behind her ear. "No, you must have misunderstood."

"My bad." Jenessa shrugged and gave Ashley her best apologetic smile. "I found the door unlocked, so I thought you'd be right back and I should wait. I hope you don't mind."

Ashley's demeanor appeared to lighten. "No, it's no problem." She even spoke with a little smile.

"As long as I'm here…"

"Sure." Ashley settled into her chair. "What was it you wanted to talk to me about?"

Jenessa studied the young woman's hair as she spoke, doing her best to be inconspicuous, trying to determine if it was a wig or her own hair. "Well, you probably know I'm covering the story of your boss's murder."

"I assumed as much, with you being a reporter and all."

"I thought, with your working so closely with Dr. Stone every day that you could give me some insight into her life and her relationship with her husband, the professor." Jenessa looked closer at Ashley's hair, but it was hard to tell.

Ashley ran a hand lightly over her head, as if she sensed Jenessa looking. "Insight? Like what?"

Maybe Jenessa hadn't been as inconspicuous as she'd hoped. She compelled her eyes to meet Ashley's. "Like did he ever bring her coffee in the morning? Did he have a habit of dropping by her office to take her to lunch? Did they seem happy? Did you ever see them argue? Did he ever make her cry? Stuff like that."

"So basically you're trying to dig up dirt on her? Write one of those kinds of stories that ends up on the cover of The National Inquirer?"

"No, not dirt, just trying to understand her and her life, figure out what might have led to her death. You want to help find out who killed her, don't you?"

"Well, of course I do. She was a great lady."

"Then help me understand her."

Ashley paused and eyed Jenessa for a moment before proceeding. "Well, the professor didn't drop by very often, but Dr. Stone didn't seem to mind at all. She had very busy days with her teaching and department meetings, not to mention she was seeing a few private clients on the side."

"How long have you worked for her?"

"About nine months. I started at the beginning of the last spring term."

"Mid-year? What happened to her previous assistant?"

"I'm not sure. Why?"

"No reason, just curious." *Very curious.* "Let's get back to Dr. Stone. So, she never mentioned her husband, places he took her, vacations they spent together, anything like that?"

Ashley shook her head. Her hair certainly moved like it was real. "She didn't discuss her personal life with me. I think she liked to keep her private life private."

Never discussed her private life? Was it time to drop the bomb? Time to watch the sparks fly?

"Ms. Brandon—"

"Call me Ashley, please."

"Ashley," Jenessa corrected, "I've heard rumors that you and Drew Stone have been having an affair for the past few months."

"What?" Ashley screeched. "Where did you hear that? I mean, Professor Stone is kind of hot for an old guy, but eww, no. Besides, he's a married man, I would never—" Her face began to turn red. Was it anger or embarrassment?

"So you're saying it's not true?"

"Absolutely not true! Who would say such a hurtful thing?" Tears flooded to her eyes.

The girl was about to blow a gasket. Now was probably not a good time to ask her if Drew was the one who had picked her up from The Sweet Spot.

~*~

Michael and Detective Provenza had gone to Drew Stone's house to bring him in for further questioning. Before he was in the back of the police cruiser, Drew was already on his cell phone to his attorney.

Now, Michael and Provenza sat across the interrogation table from Drew and Mr. Winslow, a thick, contentious atmosphere hung in the air. There were important questions to be asked, but would the attorney allow his client to answer any of them?

"What have you dragged Mr. Stone down here again for?" Mr. Winslow questioned. "And this had better be good."

"Oh, it is." Provenza flipped through the file and stopped mid-way into it. "Last time you were in here for questioning, we asked you if you knew a maintenance man at the college by the name of Buck Baird. You claimed you did not."

"That's right," Drew replied.

Provenza chuckled sarcastically. "Well, I have a copy of a sworn statement right here, from Mr. Baird, stating that you contacted him and hired him to murder your wife. What do you have to say about that?"

"So basically it's a case of he said-he said?" the attorney questioned.

"We've got several late-night phone calls from your client's cell phone to this ex-con," Michael said. "What else were they discussing? Who was going to win the World Series? How many light bulbs the professor needed changed in his office?"

Although Michael knew the calls were most likely from Daphne, Drew didn't know that. If he thought they really had something on him, maybe he would be more forthcoming with answers.

"That doesn't prove anything," Winslow maintained.

"I have a sworn statement from the man on the other end of that phone conversation," Provenza stated. "He says your client offered him five thousand dollars to kill his wife and your client's financial records show him withdrawing that exact amount around that same time."

Sweat began to form on Drew Stone's forehead.

Mr. Winslow leaned over to his client and whispered something in his ear.

Drew answered him with a loud whisper. "But I changed my mind."

CHAPTER 20

"YOU CHANGED YOUR MIND, MR. STONE?" Michael jumped in. "So you admit you approached him for the express purpose of hiring the hit?"

"No," Drew said adamantly.

"My client admits to nothing." Mr. Winslow turned to Drew. "Stop talking and let me handle this."

"But he just said—" Michael gasped.

"You have no way of knowing what I said to him that elicited that response," the attorney responded. "He was merely responding to what I said, not referring to your ludicrous accusation."

"Like hell," Provenza growled.

"How do you know this Baird fellow is telling the truth, Detectives?" Winslow asked. "Didn't you say he was an ex-con?"

"Yes, but that doesn't mean it didn't happen," Provenza replied.

Winslow rested an elbow on the table. "What exactly are you promising Mr. Baird in exchange for this so-called testimony?"

Provenza's gaze met Michael's, but he said nothing.

Winslow sat back. "Yeah, that's what I thought."

"According to your financials, you withdrew five thousand dollars from the bank around that time. What was all that money for?" Provenza asked.

"It was to buy an anniversary gift for my wife. You can ask the jeweler. I picked out a beautiful diamond necklace for her."

"What's the name of the jewelry store?" Michael asked.

"Dupree Jewelers over on Fourth Street in Walnut Grove."

"Can you produce this diamond necklace?" Provenza asked. "Because she wasn't wearing it when she died."

"And the receipt," Michael added.

"Uh, well, yeah. I'll have to look around the house to see what she did with it. It's probably in her jewelry box."

"Whoa," Winslow exclaimed. "You'll need a court order before my client hands those things over."

Detective Provenza flipped the file shut. "I'd think your client would want to clear his name before his reputation is totally destroyed."

Winslow shot his client a quick look, then turned his attention back to Provenza. "I'll see what we can do."

"No. Wait," Drew said. "I think she was wearing it the day she died."

Provenza opened the file and perused a page. "It wasn't among her personal effects."

"I could have sworn she had it on when she left the house."

"You'll have to do better than that," Michael said.

~*~

After Drew Stone and his lawyer left, Provenza suggested to Michael they walk over to The Sweet Spot for a cup of coffee. "Maybe they'll have a good maple bar to go with it."

"You sound like a typical cop," Michael kidded.

"What can I say? I've been a cop for thirty-five years and I love doughnuts." Provenza chuckled.

As they approached the front of the shop, with the picture windows still decked out in painted pumpkins and green and gold leaves, Detective Provenza took a phone call. "It's the crime lab," he told Michael after answering it. "I've got you on speaker phone."

"You're not going to believe this, George," the CSI said.

"What's up?"

"As a matter of procedure, you know we run the fingerprints of the deceased to confirm identity. We've been a bit backed up, you probably heard, so I didn't run them right away on Dr. Stone. After all, we knew who she was, so I thought my time was better spent on more important things."

"What's happened?" Provenza asked impatiently. "Why are you calling?"

"When I got around to running them, they came back with a different name. So I ran them again to make sure."

"Are you saying our victim is not Daphne Stone?"

"Her prints came back as Suzanne Tremont. She's wanted by the FBI."

In that moment, Jenessa came out of the coffee shop. "Who is wanted by the FBI?"

Provenza frowned at her nosey intrusion, then returned to his call. "Thanks for letting me know." He clicked the phone off. "Hello, Miss Jones."

"Hello, George. Michael." She gave Michael a wink. "Who is wanted by the FBI?"

"You weren't supposed to hear that," Provenza said.

"Then you shouldn't have had it on speaker." She flashed a grin. "Does it have anything to do with this case?"

"Can you do something with this woman, Baxter?" Provenza complained.

Michael raised his hands in surrender as he moved a few feet away, within reach of the door to the coffee shop. "I think you can handle her, Boss." He had his own battles with her, he didn't want to add to them. Besides, this way he maintained deniability.

"Listen, I've got some information to share," Jenessa said, "if you want to hear it, *Detective*. But you've got to give me something in exchange. That's how it works."

"What do you have?" Provenza seemed interested, his growl melting into a friendlier tone.

"You first," she said.

"That's *not* how it works," he came back, "you know that."

She pitched Michael a grin, then turned back to

George. "All right, you win. Happy?"

"Thrilled," George replied, the word sizzling with wry sarcasm.

"Ashley Brandon, Daphne's assistant, she has a burner phone in her desk. Why would she need a phone that can't be traced?"

Provenza grimaced. "How do you know she has a phone like that in her desk?"

"You don't want to know, George. Trust me." She shook her head at him. "There's something else."

His expression perked up.

"I saw her getting into a car today by The Sweet Spot. I didn't get a real good look at the driver, but it could have been Drew Stone. Ashley Brandon might be the other woman." Jenessa looked over at Michael.

She had already told him about having seen Ashley, but he had forgotten to mention it to George.

"Did Michael tell you that?"

"No, not yet," Provenza replied. "We've had a busy afternoon."

"I've done my part, George, so now it's your turn." Jenessa eyed him expectantly. "Who is wanted by the FBI?"

He leaned close to Jenessa and lowered his voice to almost a whisper. "This goes no further than right here. This is absolutely not for publication until we solve this case."

She nodded her agreement.

He looked around, making sure no one else was within earshot, except for Michael. "Apparently Dr. Daphne Stone wasn't who we thought she was. Her real name is actually Suzanne Tremont."

Jenessa pulled back. "Daphne Stone is Suzanne Tremont?"

"Shhh. Keep that under your hat," Provenza warned.

"Any idea why she would take on another identity?"

"Not yet," Provenza replied, "but you can be sure we'll find out."

"If I can be of any help, George—"

"I think we can take it from here," he replied. "Now, if you don't mind, we'd like to get our coffee and get back to work." He blew past her and went inside.

Michael hung back. "Are we okay?"

Jenessa moved closer to him, her jade-green eyes floating up to his. "I hope so, but we haven't spent much time together lately. If you don't have any plans later, I'll be home if you want to stop by."

"I can't make any promises, with this case and all, but I'd like to."

"I miss spending time with little Jake too."

"He's crazy about you," Michael said, taking her hand in his.

"I'm sure he's not missing me one bit, not with his mother here." She glanced to her feet for a moment, as if she wanted to hide the telling expression in her eyes. "Don't get me wrong," she said, lifting her head, but her eyes drifted down the street, rather than to Michael. "I think it's great she wants to spend time with him, but how's he going to feel when she leaves again?" Her gaze finally returned to him. "She is leaving again, isn't she?"

How could he answer that? He wasn't about to tell her that Josie had made overtures, that she had hopes of

184

putting her family back together. The thought of Jake having both his mom and his dad together again seemed right, just as Michael had always had both of his own parents to raise him.

Yes, he had told Jenessa he loved her—and he meant it—but if he was being completely honest with himself, he would have to admit that some small part of him was still in love with Josie, even after what she'd done.

"You know," Michael lifted her hand to his lips and kissed the back of it before letting it go, "Josie told me this morning she has plans tomorrow evening. How about you and Jake and I do something?"

Her face lit up. "I'd like that."

"Then let's plan on it. We'll talk more." Michael turned to push the coffee shop's door open. "I'd better get inside or George'll be grumbling about heading back to the station and I'll be SOL."

"Then skedaddle." She giggled and put a hand to the side of her face, with thumb and pinky extended. "Call me," she said as she walked away.

~*~

"Did you know that vinegar would interact with Daphne's anti-depression medication?" Jenessa asked her aunt, as she sat behind her father's big oak desk in the study, talking on the phone.

"Of course I know you can't mix those two. That's how my first husband died, remember?"

Jenessa did remember. That's what prompted the question, the comment someone made at dinner, saying as much. The observation had made Jenessa wonder, if only for a fleeting moment, if her aunt could have been involved somehow.

"But remember, Jenessa, I didn't know she was on that medication until after she died."

Jenessa wanted to believe her.

And then there was the money. Jenessa hadn't known her aunt was having money troubles until the police brought up the fact that Daphne Stone had changed her Will and left Aunt Renee the bulk of her estate.

As much as Jenessa didn't want to think it, let alone believe it, she recognized that sometimes people desperate for money will do things they ordinarily wouldn't do under normal circumstances. She had written stories about just those kinds of people— embezzlers, thieves, sometimes murderers—when she was on staff at a major newspaper in Sacramento.

"Why do you ask, dear?"

"Just curious." There was no way Jenessa would tell her aunt what she was thinking. "What about Daphne? She must have known to stay away from vinegar, right? Her doctor would have warned her."

"I'm sure any respectable physician would. What are you getting at?"

"Did she ever ask you about Uncle Henry's death?"

"Well," the phone line went silent for a few moments, "she did ask me if it was a painless death, which I thought was odd."

"When was that?" Jenessa asked.

"A few days before she died, the day we were having coffee together, before she ran off to her doctor's appointment."

"Do you think it's at all possible that she might have killed herself?" Jenessa asked.

CHAPTER 21

AS RELUCTANT AS JENESSA WAS to discuss the idea of Daphne having committed suicide, particularly over the phone, the fact that it was a glaring possibility compelled her to bring it up. With care, she eased into the difficult conversation with Aunt Renee.

"They say when someone commits suicide it's generally because they're in so much pain they just want to make it stop, even emotional pain."

"There's no doubt she was in emotional pain, but suicide? Daphne?" Aunt Renee questioned. "She was a strong woman. I would never have thought her the kind to...you know."

"Think about it," Jenessa gently urged, "you said she wanted to divorce Drew, but he wouldn't let her out of the marriage, that he was holding something over her head, right?"

"Yes," Aunt Renee replied slowly, her skepticism evident in her voice.

"We know she had been taking medication for her

depression, so clearly she was depressed, and then we found that bottle of Oxycodone she was hiding. Do you think she might have been addicted to pain killers?" Jenessa made a note to pay a visit to the doctor on the pill bottle.

"Oh, dear girl, I wouldn't have thought so, but—"

"There were obviously secrets in the Stone house, secrets that not even you, as her good friend, knew about. Maybe they were enough to drive her over the edge."

"When you put it all together like that, it does sound possible," Aunt Renee conceded. "Maybe that's why she changed her Will right before she died."

"Because she knew her death was imminent," Jenessa finished her aunt's thought, "and she didn't want her husband to get anything. It's definitely something the police should consider."

And then there was the question of Daphne's true identity. Had Aunt Renee known that Daphne was really Suzanne Tremont? Did Drew know?

Perhaps there was a scandalous reason for her new identity and that was exactly what Drew had been holding over her head. Jenessa wanted to ask Aunt Renee about it directly, wanted to know if Daphne had ever let her in on her deep dark secret, but she held back. She had promised Detective Provenza she would keep her mouth shut about it, so she did.

However, maybe there was another way to ask her. "Don't you think it's odd, Aunt Renee, that Daphne never told you what her husband was blackmailing her with?"

"No, I wouldn't say it was odd. I didn't want to

press her on it because the poor woman was frazzled enough."

"Frazzled? You mean the mood swings?"

"That's right—the mood swings, the marital problems, the depression—and I figured she'd tell me when she was ready."

"So you have no idea what it could possibly be?"

"None," Aunt Renee replied flatly, then her voice took on a suspicious tenor. "Why do you keep asking me? Do you think I'm holding something back, that I know more than I'm saying?"

"Of course not." Jenessa ended her line of questioning before her aunt became too suspicious and started asking questions of her own. "I'm just trying to be thorough."

"As long as that's all it is," Aunt Renee said, not sounding like she completely believed her. "Let's change the subject."

"What did you have in mind?" Jenessa asked.

"I was wondering how things are going with you and that handsome boyfriend of yours. You two seemed to have hit a snag with his ex-wife back in town."

"We're fine." There was more to it than that, but Jenessa wasn't going to go into the details of their private conversations and struggles. On the surface things did appear to be fine, but deep down something wasn't sitting right with her as far as Josie was concerned, and Logan's repeated presence in her life wasn't helping things with Michael either. Though she would rather cry on her aunt's shoulder about the emotional battles she was fighting, instead of keeping things bottled up as she tended to do, for now she'd keep them to herself and wait to see how they played out.

"Fine, huh? Sounds like there's something *you're* not telling *me*."

~*~

Michael went home after an exhausting day. When he stepped through the front door, he found Josie and Jake sitting on the living room floor playing Chutes and Ladders. Josie was laughing, and Jake let out a squeal of delight as he moved his player across the game board, sliding it up the ladder to the end.

"I win! I win!" Jake exclaimed, shooting his little hands in the air.

Josie reached over and tickled him under his arms and he rolled onto his back on the floor, giggling with delight as his mother continued to tickle him. Then she threw her arms around him and gave him a big hug as he pretended to try to wriggle out of her hold.

Michael stood watching, not wanting to interrupt their fun. This was the way Jake should have always had it—a mother spending the afternoon laughing and playing with him.

"I love you, Jakey," Josie said, planting a shower of kisses on his chubby cheeks. Their little boy laughed uncontrollably, both of them apparently unaware of Michael's presence.

Michael sniffed the air. Something smelled good. "What's for dinner?"

Josie snapped her head toward Michael and flashed him a big smile, her eyes twinkling like violet lights as she let go of the boy and sat back on her heels.

Jake scrambled to his feet and came running. "Daddy!"

Michael scooped him up and held him, savoring the huge grin on his son's face. He was generally a happy, well-adjusted kid, but since Josie had shown up, Jake was simply effervescent.

"Mommy made macaroni and cheese," Jake said, his eyes wide as he licked his lips.

Josie got up off the floor and joined them. "Pulled pork, too. I know how much you like that, Michael."

Everything seemed perfect as he held his son. What more could a man ask for? A beautiful woman, a happy child, and his favorite food for dinner in his cozy home. Wasn't this the way his life was supposed to be?

Josie had already told him she wanted to put their little family back together again, but did she mean it? Would she stay this time? Be happy with the small-town life? Or would the glittering lights of Hollywood draw her away again?

"Penny for your thoughts," Josie said, a smile teasing at the corners of her mouth.

How could he answer? He set Jake down and his gaze lingered on her face. Gawd, she was beautiful. "Just happy to be home."

Josie didn't press it, and Michael was relieved she hadn't. She turned and started for the kitchen. "Dinner's almost ready."

The tight jeans she wore hugged her body and the curve of her swaying hips caught Michael's eye as she walked away. "I'd better go wash up." He hurried to the hall bathroom and ran the cold water, splashing some on his face and running his wet hands through his hair.

"Is your head dirty, Daddy?" Jake asked, standing in the doorway, as he watched his father drying it with a towel.

"Yeah, a little, big guy. Here, let's get your hands washed."

They left the bathroom and gathered around the table to eat the dinner Josie had prepared. Conversation was easy, the way it should have been—if they had stayed married and kept their family together. Maybe there would have even been another child or two by now.

Josie had come for Jake's other birthdays, but this time it felt different. Usually, she stayed at a hotel and was in and out of town in a matter of a day or two, always seeming anxious to get back to the big city, back to an acting gig. This time she would be here for at least a week or more. What changed?

Had she suddenly recognized that her life was shallow and empty, and finally wanted something real? Did she realize she'd had a good thing and let it slip away? Had she woken up one day and longed for the love she and Michael once shared? Longed to hold her son and have a meaningful relationship with him?

Jake wolfed down his mac and cheese and asked to be excused to go and watch his favorite TV show.

"One hour of television," Michael said firmly as Jake slid off his chair, "and then it's time to get ready for bed."

"Julia Roberts doesn't let her kids watch television," Josie said when Jake was out of earshot. "Neither do Kate Hudson or Ben Affleck."

Was that what this was about? The big names in

Hollywood were having kids and she wanted to fit in? Would she be asking to take Jake back to Hollywood with her to hobnob with celebrities and their children?

"How do you know that?" Michael asked, a little perturbed by the thought.

"Oh, I read it somewhere," she said with a dismissive flip of her hand. "We should really limit how much TV our son watches and encourage him to do more creative things. Do you think we should have him start with piano lessons?"

"He's only five."

"He'll be six in a week. Did you forget about the birthday party?"

"No, I haven't forgotten. I've just had a few other things on my mind." Michael paused, feeling a prick of guilt because maybe he had, just a little bit. After all, he had other things to think about—urgent, important things. Besides, the party would be at his parents' house and they always handled everything for him. "Speaking of the party, once it's over, you'll be gone, won't you?"

"That depends," she replied, the raise of her perfectly-shaped eyebrows suggesting it was up to him.

"On what?" he asked anyway.

"On whether I'm wanted here, of course."

"What about your career, your life in Southern California? Isn't that why you left us in the first place?" His throat suddenly thickened at the mention of it.

Her thickly-lashed eyes lowered to her plate and she nodded. "But things have changed." Her gaze raised to meet his. "The movie and TV roles haven't been coming in like they used to, which has given me a lot of time to sit and think about my life, and Jake…and you."

"But Jake and I have moved on, Josie. Well, at least I have. Jake will always love his mother."

Josie got up slowly and came around behind Michael's chair. She draped her arms loosely around his neck and bent down, her mouth touching his ear. "Won't you always love his mother too? At least a little bit?"

CHAPTER 22

JOSIE'S VOICE WAS LOW AND SULTRY and her breath was warm on Michael's ear. "Will you always love me?" A rush of prickly heat spread down his neck.

If he was being honest with himself, he'd have to admit that some part of him would probably always love her. He had taken a vow of commitment before God and his family to love her forever—but that was before she ran off and left them. In his family, they married for life—but not so with he and Josie—they destroyed the family's proud heritage of lifelong marriages.

Yet here she was, attempting to make amends, asking for another chance. Should he believe her and do all he could to restore their marriage? Was he honor-bound to try?

He put a hand lightly on one of her arms laced about his neck. He didn't know why, but it just felt natural. Still, he was wary of Josie and her real motives. It was probably safest not to lower his guard around her, not to let her in again, for she would probably end up breaking his heart into a million pieces once more.

"I told you, I'm involved with someone else," was all he could think to say.

"You didn't answer my question."

Michael kept his mouth shut.

"Is it that Jenessa Jones woman?" Josie asked sharply, as if she didn't already know.

"You know it is."

Josie straightened and pulled her arms off him. "But it can't be that serious. You've only been dating a few months, right?"

"What difference does that make?"

Before he knew it, she stepped around and backed herself into his lap, wrapping an arm around his neck. "Does she kiss you like this?" Without waiting for a reply, Josie pressed her moist, full lips against his, forcing them apart with her tongue.

Her kiss was heady, and his body vibrated with desire. Memories of when they'd made love—made Jake—flooded his mind and his body began to react. His arms encircled her and he pulled her closer, his lips eagerly responding.

What the heck am I doing?

He pulled back and pushed her off his lap and onto her feet.

She breathed a deep throaty laugh, as if she knew she had gotten to him.

"That's not funny." Michael wiped his mouth with the back of his hand.

"It wasn't meant to be funny. And you seemed to be holding your own there, mister." Her lips curved into a seductively playful smile. "We had a good thing once,

Michael, and we can again. We can be a family—if you let us."

She was putting the onus on him? He got up and walked away, heading down the hall to his bedroom.

"It's because of Jenessa, isn't it?" Josie called after him.

He did not reply, just kept walking. Jenessa's image popped into his mind—her long, dark tresses, her engaging smile, her jade-green eyes that sparkled when she laughed. He had just declared his love for her a few days ago and she had returned his sentiment. What was he doing feeling this way about Josie? It had to be physical chemistry and not love—didn't it?

Michael had to get away from her, with thoughts running through his head, testosterone coursing through this body. How could he answer her, feeling pulled in two different directions? This voluptuous, sexy ex-wife of his was going to ruin everything he had with Jenessa, but only if he let her.

He went into his bedroom and shut the door, leaning his back against it. He thought of Jake. Didn't his son deserve to be raised in a home with both of his parents? Wasn't it his duty to try to put his family back together, given the chance?

But what if he chose Josie, for Jake's sake—and a little for his own—and she ended up leaving them again? Would he and Jake survive?

He couldn't count on Jenessa to be there to catch them, to pick up the broken pieces left in Josie's wake. What woman with any self-respect would stick around?

Worse than that, his choosing Josie over her might even drive Jenessa back into Logan's arms. Could he live with that? Seeing Jenessa and Logan together? In this small town, there would be no way for him to avoid it.

A sharp pain stabbed at his temple, settling behind his eyes. He massaged his fingers into each side of his head, trying to make it stop. It was the piercing ache of being pulled in two different directions at once. What was he going to do?

~*~

"Here we are," Jenessa declared, setting a couple of plates on her dining table. Each dish held a pile of noodles and a few indistinguishable lumps, covered in a white sauce.

Ramey looked down at it, wrinkling her nose, and poking at the lumps under the sauce. "What is it?"

"Fettuccini Alfredo with chicken."

"Oh." Ramey slid her napkin onto her lap, picked up her fork, and paused, her gaze stuck on the mystery food.

"Try it," Jenessa encouraged as she took a seat. "It won't bite you."

Ramey lifted her eyes to Jenessa, an obviously forced smile spreading on her face. "Okay. Here goes." She twirled some pasta on her fork and pierced a chunk of chicken. She hesitantly looked at Jenessa again, the fork hovering between the plate and her lips.

"Go on," Jenessa urged.

Ramey opened her mouth and took a bite.

"Well…how is it?"

Ramey chewed and nodded slightly, her gaze

meeting Jenessa's. "Not bad." She reached for the salt and pepper shakers and sprinkled them both liberally on the food. "Could use some seasoning, and the chicken pieces should be bigger, and preferably grilled and not boiled."

"Besides that?" Jenessa asked, smiling hopefully.

"The sauce could use more Parmesan cheese and a little butter added to it, but beyond that, I think it's good."

"Really?" Jenessa asked excitedly.

"Sure," Ramey replied. "Next time, though, cook the fettuccini a few minutes less, but other than that, I think you did a pretty good job."

"Thanks, Ramey." Jenessa jumped from her chair and gave Ramey's shoulders a quick squeeze.

"Why the sudden interest in cooking?"

"I'm going to make this for Michael and Jake tomorrow night." Jenessa sat back down and scooped a forkful. "I hope they like it."

"Is Josie a good cook?" Ramey took another bite.

"Why would you ask that?"

"Well, she's been staying at Michael's. Is she cooking for him and Jake?"

"I don't know. I hadn't really thought about it," she lied.

"Haven't you guys discussed her staying there?"

"Yes, but only why she's there and not in a hotel—and when and if she's leaving."

"If?" Ramey gasped, throwing a hand over her mouth to keep the food from shooting out. "When did that become a question?"

"Michael keeps saying she's leaving after the party,

but I get the vibe from him that she wants to stick around awhile longer."

"Doesn't she have to get back for work?" Ramey asked.

"It didn't sound like it. Maybe her acting roles have dried up."

"I saw her on that TV series on cable, you know the one about the FBI chasing white-collar criminals. I thought she was pretty good."

"I never watched it, but that reminds me, she had a small part in that big movie, that one about the superheroes trying to save the planet," Jenessa added. "I never saw that either."

"Oh, she was good in that too, but I haven't seen her in anything since." As Ramey took a sip of white wine, her eyes got big, as though a surprising thought popped into her mind. "You don't think she wants Michael back, do you?"

"I don't know what to think." Jenessa refilled Ramey's glass. "One minute I think she's after Michael, and the next I see her looking awfully chummy with Logan."

"Logan?" Ramey's eyes lifted toward the ceiling, as if she was considering the possibility. "Hmmm."

"What?" Jenessa questioned the I-suddenly-figured-everything-out look in Ramey's eyes.

Ramey took another long sip of her wine, drawing out the suspense of her answer. "Think about it, Jen. If Josie hooked up with Logan...that would solve your problem."

"How so?" Jenessa asked.

"You'd get Logan to stop trying to woo you back,

and Michael would be free of his ex-wife. And you want both those things, don't you?"

CHAPTER 23

WITH RAMEY'S CHIN PROPPED ON THE back of her hand, she gazed at Jenessa with expectancy in her eyes.

Logan to stop wooing her? Michael free of his ex-wife? That was what she wanted, wasn't it? Why was she hesitating to reply?

Something changed in Ramey's eyes, her eyebrows wrinkled in dismay. "You like Logan pursuing you, don't you?"

"I didn't say that," Jenessa was quick to refute. Maybe too quick.

Ramey sat up and dropped her hand to the table, her gaze not leaving Jenessa's. "Then what are you saying?"

"With Josie here, things have gotten…complicated."

"I don't understand. Michael is crazy about you,

and you're crazy about him. What's so complicated about that?"

"I'm not convinced Josie is going to leave after Jake's party."

"Why wouldn't she?"

"I can't really say. Just a feeling." Jenessa picked up the dinner plates and took them to the sink. "Maybe I'm just being silly."

"You can't think Michael would take her back after how she abandoned him and little Jake. What's it been— almost three years?"

Jenessa turned the faucet on and rinsed the plates. "What if he did? What if he still has feelings for her?" Her chest began to tense with emotion. She willed herself not to cry. "After all, she's the one who left him, not the other way around."

"So then what? Logan is a backup in case things don't work out with Michael?" Ramey brought the glasses to the sink.

"I don't know." Jenessa gave a slight shrug, her eyes lowered to the dishes in the sink.

"Sounds to me like you're looking for trouble where there may not be any. What is it Aunt Renee says? You're putting the cart before the horse." Ramey draped an arm loosely around Jenessa's shoulders. "Why don't you wait until after the party to start getting all upset about Josie staying? When you know if she is or not."

"You want some dessert?" Jenessa asked, turning away from the sink, hoping to change the subject. "You didn't eat much of your dinner."

"What do you have?"

"Rocky Road ice cream."

Ramey nodded as her eyes lit up. "Sounds good."

"Have a seat and I'll scoop us some." Jenessa pulled the carton from the freezer. "So how are things going between you and my boss?"

"Oh, Jen, Charles is the most wonderful man. He amazes me at how thoughtful and patient he is." Ramey was almost glowing as she spoke about him. "Especially with Charlie."

Charlie. Jenessa's mind drifted to the photo of Charles and his son, the one in his office, and to her thoughts that maybe that's what her own baby might have grown up to look like—sandy-blond hair, green eyes. Her little boy would be the same age as Charlie too. A tingle of excitement danced across her chest at the remote possibility that he could be that baby. With all that had been going on, she hadn't had time to dwell on those thoughts.

"Jenessa? Did you hear me?"

Ramey's question brought her mind back to the present, and she began scooping ice cream into the dessert bowls. "Sorry, what?"

"I said I think I'm falling in love with him."

Jenessa dug another scoop of ice cream out of the carton. "Who?"

"Charles, of course. Who do you think?" Ramey asked with a frown. "You haven't heard a word I've said."

Jenessa handed Ramey a dish of ice cream. "Do you know if Charlie was adopted?"

"Adopted?" Ramey took the bowl. "What makes you ask that?"

"Just curious." Dare she tell her? Jenessa spooned

more ice cream into her own bowl. "Was he?"

Ramey paused and thought for a moment, taking a seat at the table. "I couldn't say. It seems that when Charles and his late wife moved here, they already had him. He was just a tiny baby then. Maybe Aunt Renee knows. Why are you so curious about that?"

Perhaps she should tell her? But Ramey might think Jenessa was crazy if she shared what she'd been thinking.

"What's going on in that head?" Ramey said, wagging her spoon at Jenessa.

Here goes.

"Grey Alexander placed my baby for adoption, and I was wondering if there was a slim chance Charlie could be him."

"Oh, Jenessa, you've got to let it go." Ramey put her hand on Jenessa's forearm. "He's someone else's son now, wherever he is." She put a spoonful of ice cream into her mouth. "Besides, wouldn't it have been the adoption agency that placed him, not Logan's father."

"That's what they'd like me to think, but I can't imagine the great and powerful Grey Alexander letting just anyone raise his grandson." Besides, he had hired Charles to work at the newspaper he owned. What better way to keep tabs on them?

"Have you tried tracking him through the adoption agency?" Ramey asked.

"Yes, but they're out of business."

"There are places that try to match adoptees and birth mothers if they both want to be found."

"My son would be too young to use one of those sites."

"Too bad your mom and dad both passed away before you could ask them. They might have known." Ramey took the last bite of her ice cream.

"I don't think they would have told me, even if they did know."

"Have you asked Aunt Renee?"

"Not yet, but I have asked Ian McCaffrey."

"The attorney?"

Jenessa nodded, spooning her ice cream.

"What did he say?"

"That it was a closed adoption and he couldn't divulge any of the details."

"And you're not going to leave it at that?"

"Of course not, but I'm not sure what my next step is. Ian said he'd see if there was a way for me to find out, but I think he just said that to get me out of his office. I doubt he'll do anything about it."

"Then I'd ask Aunt Renee," Ramey suggested. "See if she can be of any help. Your mom and Charles's late wife were close friends. Maybe Aunt Renee knows something."

If Jenessa's mother knew who had adopted the baby, she might have purposely made friends with the wife to keep an eye on her grandbaby. It was an ever-so-slim chance, but still an angle worth exploring.

"Would that be weird for you, Ramey? If Charlie turned out to be my son?" Knowing sweet Ramey, she would never say unless asked.

Ramey took a moment to think before she replied. "A little, if Charles and I end up getting married. But let's not get the cart before the horse, again." She grinned. "Charlie is probably not the baby boy you hope he is."

~*~

Early the next morning Jenessa slapped at the alarm clock buzzing on her nightstand. She dragged herself out of bed and down to the kitchen to make coffee to help her get an early start on her day.

Her editor was on her about another story, updating the citizens of Hidden Valley on the Daphne Stone murder investigation. She wasn't getting much information from Detective Provenza, or Michael for that matter, at least any she was allowed to print. She was determined to take matters into her own hands, gather information on her own, so she wouldn't need their permission.

How was she going to find out what Daphne Stone was suffering from? Besides depression, she must have been in pain from something, otherwise why take the Oxycodone?

She looked up the doctor in Walnut Grove and gave his office a call. She was able to snag an appointment for later that day, making up some ongoing malady. She'd have to come up with a pretty good story to wrangle any information out of the doctor, but it could be done.

After a quick breakfast, she sat before her laptop, pulled her notebook out of her bag, and positioned it beside her computer. Suzanne Tremont was scrawled across the top of the page.

"So, Daphne Stone," Jenessa said to herself as she opened a Google browser, "let's see who you really were." She typed *Suzanne Tremont* into the search bar and a page of links appeared on the screen.

Jenessa methodically clicked on each link and read the stories associated with the name. From what she could gather in these articles, about fifteen years ago Suzanne Tremont had been a participant in a bombing at an animal testing lab belonging to a large cosmetics company. She'd been involved with an animal rights group, when she and another member, who had never been identified, had allegedly set a bomb to go off, late one evening, in the office portion of the facility. They had hoped to destroy computers and years of research from the company's testing, believing it might put the company out of business—or at least convince them to stop testing their products on poor defenseless animals.

The news articles claimed the pair hadn't planned on a cleaning lady being in the offices that late at night, or anyone else for that matter. The woman was tragically killed by the blast.

No wonder she changed her name and disappeared.

But who was her partner in crime?

~*~

"Jenessa Jones," a nurse called out into the waiting room.

Jenessa set her magazine down and stood to follow the nurse down the hall to an examination room.

"Up on the table and I'll take your vitals before you disrobe for your exam," the nurse said.

After taking her temperature and blood pressure reading, she handed Jenessa a disposable gown and asked her to get undressed. "The doctor will be with you in about ten minutes," the nurse said as she slipped out the door.

Jenessa put the folded gown on the table, then sat and waited for Dr. Tierney. What she had to discuss with him didn't involve him probing her naked body, but she had better come up with a compelling way to finagle information out of this small-town doctor.

CHAPTER 24

AFTER FIFTEEN MINUTES OF WAITING, Dr. Tierney stepped into the exam room. He looked down at the chart. "Jenessa Jones?"

"Yes, that's me."

His thick, graying eyebrows lowered in a slight frown. "You haven't changed for the exam."

"I don't really need an exam, Doc. I just wanted to talk to you," she said, perched on the edge of the examination table, "and this seemed to be a good way to speak in private."

His eyes filled with suspicion. "About what?"

"Aunt Daphne—Daphne Stone. It's so terrible…what happened to her."

His brows lifted. "I can't discuss a patient—"

Jenessa jumped in and cut him off before he could go through the normal spiel about doctor-patient confidentiality. "I think you'll want to hear this, Doc. Aunt Daphne told me that Uncle Drew didn't think you did all you could for her—under the circumstances, that is."

"Of course I did," he shot back defensively.

"Aunt Daphne spoke so highly of you. She knew you were just trying to help her." Jenessa wiped at an imaginary tear near the corner of her eye. "So tragic…anyway, I thought I should come to warn you. Uncle Drew is talking about suing you."

"Suing me?" the doctor gasped, color draining from his face. "There was nothing more I could do for her."

"Nothing?" Another fake tear. "I mean, I thought these things could be treated, you know, beyond pain medication…" She lifted an unconvinced eyebrow, hoping to draw more information out of him in his defensive state.

"The cancer had spread so quickly. There was nothing anyone could do but try to alleviate her suffering."

Cancer?

"That isn't what Uncle Drew is saying. He's consulting a specialist, and an attorney—"

"Wait a minute, young lady." His lips grew tight with anger. "I referred her to the best oncologist that specializes in brain cancer. If your uncle wants to sue anyone, it should be him."

"That's what I tried to tell him, Dr. Tierney, but you know Uncle Drew—"

"No," the doctor snipped, "I don't know your uncle."

Jenessa was glad of that. "Well, he sure seems to

know you. He says you were the one giving my aunt the Oxycodone, so…"

The doctor paused and his expression softened as he replied to her, perhaps the Oxycodone statement hit him in the right spot. "Like I said, she was too far gone by the time she came to me. The only thing I could do was help her manage the pain."

Would the doctor spill more details if she made it sound like she knew a lot about Daphne's health? "Are you saying she should have come sooner? When she first started getting those bad headaches and mood swings? That she shouldn't have waited until…"

"Exactly—she shouldn't have waited until the small growth was protruding from the inner part of her eye. She waited too long. I knew before I sent her to Dr. Sakani that it was probably too late, but I prayed there was something he could do for her." Dr. Tierney's expression turned fearful. "Listen, I'm just a small-town doctor, a malpractice suit would destroy me. We don't have to go to court over this. Please tell your uncle I did everything I could. He needs to talk to Dr. Sakani before he starts any legal proceedings."

"Don't worry, Doc," Jenessa slid off the table and patted him on the arm, "I'll do all I can to make sure he understands what happened."

He nodded. "I appreciate that." The doctor pulled the door open to let Jenessa leave first.

She headed down the hall, toward the reception area. As she approached the end of the hall, she heard Detective Provenza's voice. She peeked around the corner of the wall and saw Provenza and Michael talking to the receptionist, their backs almost facing her.

Jenessa slipped around the corner and made it to the door without being seen by them.

"Miss Jones," the receptionist called out just as Jenessa put her hand on the doorknob.

Provenza and Michael spun around.

She was caught.

"You'll need to pay for your visit before you leave," the receptionist continued. "Let me get your chart from the doctor." She left her desk and disappeared around the corner.

"What are you doing here?" Michael asked.

"What? I can't have a doctor's appointment?" Jenessa pulled three twenty dollar bills out of her wallet and dropped them on the desk. "You want to know about my female issues?"

"Oh, no, no," Provenza stuttered, "that's all right."

Michael shook his head in agreement with the senior detective's discomfort.

"I'll talk to you guys back in Hidden Valley." She hightailed it out of the doctor's office before the receptionist came back and the guys could ask her any more questions.

~*~

"Female issues make you a little queasy, Detective?" Michael jabbed.

The receptionist's return saved Provenza from having to respond.

"Where did the young woman go?" she asked.

"She said she had to get back to work," Michael covered for her, "but she left you sixty bucks there on

216

your desk."

The woman clipped the bills to Jenessa's chart. "So, what can I do for you detectives?"

Michael leaned an arm on the raised counter. "We'd like to speak with Dr. Tierney."

"He's got appointments all morning. If you'll have a seat, I'll let him know when he's finished with—"

Provenza cleared his throat in the middle of her sentence. "This is official police business, ma'am. We need to speak to him now."

Glaring at the elder detective, she rose from her seat. "He won't like being interrupted when he's with a patient, but I'll tell him you're here." She disappeared, again, around the corner.

Michael's gaze moved to the main door, visualizing Jenessa scurrying out of there. Had she really been there for a doctor's appointment? In Dr. Tierney's office? The same doctor she knew he and Provenza wanted to interview?

The receptionist stuck her head around the corner and motioned for the detectives to follow her. She showed them to the doctor's private office and opened the door.

"Come in, gentlemen," Dr. Tierney said, seated behind his impressive oak desk. "Have a seat."

They did as the doctor requested and sat across the desk from him.

"I'm Detective Provenza, this is Detective Baxter. We don't want to waste your time, Doc, so we'll get right to it. We're here about Dr. Daphne Stone. We understand she was a patient of yours."

His face seemed to register shock at the mention of

the name. Or maybe Michael was reading things into it.

"Yes, she was," he replied, "but doctor-patient confidentiality prevents me from divulging any of her personal information or health records."

Michael shifted in his seat and pitched forward. "This is a murder investigation, Dr. Tierney."

"Murder? I thought she died from—" His eyes lowered and he paused, appearing to be thinking over what he should say.

"From what?" Michael asked.

The doctor raised his eyes and continued. "I thought the news reported she died from a health-related issue."

"It was first reported that she had a heart attack," Michael said.

Dr. Tierney's eyebrows shot up. "A heart attack?"

"You sound surprised, Doc," Provenza remarked. "What health issue did you think she died of?"

"I really can't say."

"Your patient is dead, Dr. Tierney," Michael said. "Murdered."

"You said that, but how? Why?"

"We were hoping you could tell us why she was coming to see you. Maybe it could help us put the puzzle pieces together."

"I told you I can't—"

"If you know something that could help us find her killer, I'd think you would want to do that," Provenza barked.

"All I can tell you is that she was very, very ill."

"What did she have?" Michael asked.

"I can't say, but I doubt she had long to live—a few weeks maybe."

Michael turned and met Provenza's gaze, the elder man's eyes looking pensive. "Is that why she was taking Oxycodone?"

The doctor's eyes rounded and he shot up out of his chair as if something spooked him. "I'm sorry. There's nothing more I can add."

"Did her husband know about her condition?" Provenza asked as he stood, eyeing the man.

The doctor nodded slightly. "I have reason to believe he did, yes."

Michael got up too, his hands on the edge of the doctor's desk as he leaned toward him. "Reason to believe? So, Dr. Stone never actually said she told him?"

"Not in so many words."

"What reason do you have to believe he knew?" Provenza questioned.

"I've said too much already. I'll have to ask you to leave."

~*~

"What do you make of that doctor?" Provenza asked as they left Dr. Tierney's office and headed to their car.

"Hard to say," Michael replied. "Like most doctors, he refused to break doctor-patient confidentiality. I get that, but when the patient is dead, does that still apply?"

"No, it doesn't, but from my experience, the doctor is often hesitant to divulge private information. If the relatives don't want a family member's info shared, he'll most likely fight it."

"You think Drew Stone told the doctor not to

disclose what his wife was dying from?" Michael asked as they climbed in their vehicle.

"Who knows," Provenza shrugged. "With the contentious relationship those two seemed to have, we can't even be sure the husband knew about her illness. The doc was probably just trying to cover his behind." The elder detective raked his fingers through his short crop of gray hair. "Let's head over to that jewelry store where Mr. Stone claimed he bought the anniversary gift for his wife."

"An anniversary gift," Michael huffed, "for the wife he wanted to have killed. What's wrong with this picture?"

CHAPTER 25

A LIGHT AUTUMN RAIN had begun to fall as Detective Provenza pulled the car to the curb in front of the jewelry store. The two men sprinted into the shop, a melodic tone chiming as they entered.

The young man behind the glass cases, dressed in a stylish suit and tie, greeted them with a bright smile. "Good afternoon, gentlemen. How can I help you today?"

"I'm Detective Provenza," George introduced. "This is Detective Baxter. We have a couple of questions."

"Shoot."

Michael tugged a photo of Drew Stone out of his breast pocket and showed it to the man. "Have you ever seen this man in your store?"

The salesman took the photo and studied it for a

moment. "He does look familiar." He handed it back to Michael. "Why do you ask?"

"We're not at liberty to say," Provenza replied, "but we need to know if he purchased anything from your store."

"I can see if he's in our system." The young man stepped to the computer on the counter. "What's his name?"

"Drew Stone," Michael said.

"Drew Stone?" the salesman echoed.

"Yeah, why?"

"You're the second one asking about him today."

Provenza leaned an arm on the jewelry case. "Who else was asking about him?"

"A pretty girl, long dark hair, beautiful green eyes." *Jenessa.*

Provenza frowned. Apparently he had the same thought Michael just did. "She didn't happen to tell you her name, did she?"

"No, but she said Drew Stone was her father, that he had a brain tumor that was making him do all sorts of crazy stuff and she needed to find him before he burned through all of the family's money and left them destitute."

"Oh really." Provenza's mouth twisted with obvious irritation. "What else did she say?"

"Well, she asked if he had bought anything here, so I looked up the records and told her what he bought. I felt sorry for her, guys, but I made it very clear to her that all sales are final."

"What did he buy?" Michael asked.

"A diamond necklace."

"A necklace, huh?" Provenza muttered, rubbing his jaw. "How much was it?"

"Around five thousand dollars."

"Anything else you can tell us?" Michael inquired.

"Well, let's see." His eyes briefly rose toward the ceiling. "I recall he paid in cash. All hundreds."

"Cash, you say?" Provenza's gaze slid over to Michael's. "Was he alone?"

"Now that you mention it, he did have a good-looking blonde on his arm." The young man's gaze flickered between the detectives. "She wasn't the girl's mother?"

"Her mother?" Michael asked, assuming the blonde would be young. "How old would you say the lady was?"

"Maybe around forty-five. She was pretty hot for an older woman."

Renee Giraldy?

~*~

The rain had stopped by the time Michael and Provenza returned to their car, leaving a fresh sheen of moisture on everything. The cottony gray clouds hung low and heavy, threatening to drop more showers.

"That girl of yours beat us to the punch," Provenza grumbled from behind the wheel. He looked over his shoulder to check for traffic, then pulled out onto the street.

George sounded irritated, but Michael grinned inside. "Sure looks that way," he said, trying not to sound like he was gloating.

"Female problems," George muttered, almost to himself.

Maybe she'd beat them to two punches. Perhaps she was able to get more information out of the doctor too.

"Why don't I call her and have her meet us at the station when we get back?" Michael suggested, trying not to let the grin show up on his face. "We can compare notes."

"All right," Provenza grumbled.

While Michael dialed, Provenza drove them to Hidden Valley.

"We're on our way back," Michael told Jenessa. "We need to talk."

"About us…or the case?" she asked.

He paused. "About the case." Did she think they needed to talk about them? "Can you meet us at the station?"

"No problem. I'll see you in about thirty minutes."

Michael stuck the phone in his pocket and peered over at Provenza. "She'll be waiting."

~*~

As promised, Jenessa was sitting in the reception area of the police station when Michael and Detective Provenza returned. She popped up out of her seat as soon as they walked in the door. "Hello, boys."

"Miss Jones." Provenza gave her a slight nod.

Michael gestured toward the door with an outstretched arm. "Why don't we go back to the conference room for a chat?"

"Am I in trouble?" she asked. Not that she had done

anything wrong, at least not in her own mind, but sometimes the detectives didn't appreciate her antics.

"Should you be?" Provenza growled.

She glanced at him, then silently went through the doorway.

Once they were seated around the conference table, she posed the question again. "So, really, am I in trouble?" The first time she'd asked, she was half-joking, but now...

Michael put a hand over hers. "No, you're not in trouble. We just want to compare notes."

Provenza cleared his throat. "So, miss reporter, what did you find out from Dr. Tierney?"

Apparently they weren't buying her story of having an actual doctor's appointment with the man. "Well," she considered her words carefully, "I found out that Daphne Stone had a cancerous brain tumor and was going to be dead within weeks."

"How did you get that out of the good doctor?" Provenza asked. "He wouldn't tell us diddly."

Jenessa suppressed a grin. "I can't reveal my secrets, Detective."

"Were you able to get anything else?" Michael folded his arms on the table and leaned toward her.

"He said he had prescribed the Oxycodone to help manage her pain, then he referred her to a cancer specialist, but because of how the cancer had presented itself, he was certain it was already too late to save her."

"Presented itself?" Michael's brow lowered with the question.

"Apparently it was pushing its way out at the inside corner of one of her eyes, a tiny gray bulge."

Provenza grimaced at the description. "I thought I'd seen it all."

"Aunt Renee told me Daphne had been having mood swings the past few months," Jenessa went on, "which I thought could have been a side-effect of the antidepressant, but now it looks like it must have been the brain tumor."

"Yeah, I've heard those things can completely change someone's personality," Michael said. "You think Drew knew about his wife's condition?"

"That, I couldn't say," Jenessa replied.

"Surely he wouldn't have tried to have her killed if he had known," Provenza said. "What would be the point?"

"What?" Jenessa gasped. "He tried to have her killed? When was this?"

Michael looked to Provenza for permission to reply. Provenza gave him a nod, so Michael proceeded to explain what Buck Baird had told them.

"Now, we can't say for certain that Baird is telling us the truth," Michael said, "but he and his lawyer are asking to cut a deal in exchange for his testifying against Drew Stone."

Jenessa's mind began racing with questions. Where should she start? "This changes everything."

"Would you like a glass of water, Miss Jones? You're looking a bit pale and your eyes are doing a weird little dance."

She closed her eyes for a moment and took a deep breath. "No, George. I'm fine." Physically, at least, but mentally, her thoughts were shooting off like rockets. When she opened her eyes, her mouth engaged. "How did Drew connect with Baird? Why would he want Daphne dead? Did he know how sick she was? Did he know Daphne was really Suzanne Tremont and that she was a wanted felon?"

"Whoa," Michael said, "slow down."

Her gaze bounced between the two detectives. "Had Drew been hiding her secret? Was that what he was holding over her head? Maybe he was her unknown accomplice."

"Take a breath," Provenza warned.

"He's definitely hiding something," Jenessa said. "And who was the blonde with him at the jewelry store?"

"The jewelry store, huh." Michael cut in when Jenessa paused and finally took a breath.

"Yes," she replied, her gaze settling on Michael. "The salesman said Drew was with an attractive blonde when he purchased a diamond necklace."

"He told us the same thing," Provenza added. "But how did you know about the jewelry store anyway?"

"Aunt Renee mentioned something about Daphne receiving a gift from there."

"Oh, she did?" Provenza questioned, his gaze connecting with Michael's momentarily.

"Could the blonde have been Ashley, Daphne's assistant?" she questioned.

"No, it couldn't," Michael replied.

"How do you know?"

"Because he said the woman was older, around forty-five," Michael replied. "Maybe it was Renee."

"My aunt?" Jenessa gasped.

"Guess you didn't get *all* the facts from him,

missy," Provenza quipped.

"I just assumed when he said blonde he—"

"You know what they say about assuming?" Provenza began to ask, a snarky edge in his voice.

"Hey, you two," Michael cut in, before the contention escalated, "we'll know for certain soon enough. The sales guy said he'd have the store's security footage sent over as soon as he could speak with the owner."

An older blonde? Could it really have been Aunt Renee?

CHAPTER 26

"DID EITHER OF YOU RESEARCH DAPHNE'S real identity?" Jenessa asked.

"Of course," Provenza replied. "This is not our first rodeo."

"Nor mine." She grinned. "I'm working on a story about her secret past and how she's been able to hide it all these years."

"I'd rather you held off on that," Provenza said.

"It's public information, George." Jenessa dipped her chin and gave him a questioning look. "Anyone can read the information on the internet."

"That's true," Michael said, "but it could have something to do with her murder and you might be tipping the killer's hand, letting him know we're onto him."

"Or her," Jenessa corrected.

"Well, yes, of course," Provenza muttered.

"I've got to write about something, guys. Charles is on me to give him something more to keep the readers buying the paper."

"Give us a few more days," Michael appealed. "Hopefully we can nail down the killer soon and then you're free to run with your story."

"Don't you have some society weddings to cover?" Provenza grumbled. "Some feature stories like someone's dog saving their kid from drowning or something like that?"

Jenessa eyed him with a frown. She had been a relentless investigative reporter on a big newspaper until her job had disappeared due to downsizing. George was right, though, she was now covering weddings, ribbon-cutting ceremonies, garden-club events and the like, when she wasn't sinking her teeth into a juicy murder story like this one.

"I'm sure I can come up with something to appease Charles, but I am still working on this story so it'll be ready to hit the press the second you arrest the murderer."

"That's my girl," Michael said with a smile. "Now get out of here and let us get back to work."

"Walk me out?" she asked, getting up from her seat.

Michael followed her down the hall and escorted her to the front door of the station. "We're still on for tonight, aren't we?"

Excitement rose in her chest at his reminder. "You, me, and Jake?"

"That's right," he replied with a little smile.

"What about Josie?" An unexpected prickle

scurried up the back of her neck as the name slipped past her lips. "Won't she want Jake to herself?"

"Remember, she said she has plans and I could have Jake tonight."

"Sorry," Jenessa replied with a little grimace. "I've had so many other things on my mind lately that I completely forgot."

So, Josie had plans—with whom? Logan?

Stop that!

She willed her focus back to Michael. "Sounds like fun," she replied, grinning at him. "When will you be by for me?"

Michael took a quick glance over his shoulder at the receptionist, who must not have been watching them, for he bent down, slipped a hand around her waist, and kissed her briefly. "We'll see you at six." He tossed her a sexy smile as he turned and walked away.

"Can't wait."

~*~

Jenessa rolled her wrist to check her watch. At four she had an appointment with the head of the Chamber of Commerce regarding the plans for the Oktoberfest celebration. If she was quick, she'd have time to stop by The Sweet Spot and pick up a latté before her meeting.

She drove a few blocks over, swung her sports car into a space in front of the coffee shop, and paused to once more admire the autumn artwork on the large front windows. Fall was her favorite time of the year—cool, crisp, sunny days, the leaves changing colors, the delicious vanilla soy lattés and pumpkin bread.

A chilly rush of wind blew into the shop when Jenessa opened the door, drawing attention to herself as she entered. Josie stood at the cash register, holding Jake's hand, and turned at Jenessa's breezy entrance. A sudden awkwardness filled the atmosphere in the café as their eyes met, then they both looked away.

"Jenessa!" Jake hollered and ran toward her.

Bending down, Jenessa caught him as he flung his arms around her in a big hug. "Hey, Jake." Jenessa glanced up at Ramey, who was watching from behind the counter. "How're you doing, big guy?"

"I just got out of school and Mommy said we could come by for a cookie."

"She did?" Jenessa asked with as much cheer in her voice as she could muster, while trying not to lock gazes again with Josie. "That was nice of her."

Jake nodded his head dramatically. "I picked chocolate peanut butter."

Josie's well-shaped legs appeared next to Jake's little body, covered in black leggings stuffed into high-heeled, short black boots. "It's time to go, Jakey."

Jenessa crouched down in front of the boy, her face not far from his. She wanted to scoop him up into her arms and kiss his chubby little cheeks, but she didn't dare. Instead she ruffled her fingers through his shiny dark hair. "See you later, okay?"

Josie took his hand.

"Okay," he said with a grin as his mother led him away.

Jenessa straightened and watched through the window as Josie and Jake walked hand in hand down the street. Where were they going? She stepped closer to the window, but they turned the corner.

It wasn't that she had any right to know, but if she and Michael were a couple, the natural progression of their relationship would be marriage and she would become Jake's stepmom.

Jake's stepmom? That was the first time she said that to herself.

As his stepmom, she would only have to endure Josie in their lives for one week out of the year—that is, if the woman did leave and return to Southern California after Jake's birthday party.

"Unless you have x-ray vision, my friend, you can't see them through the buildings." Ramey slung an arm around Jenessa's shoulders.

"See who? I was just looking at the weather. There seems to be some dark clouds moving in from the west."

Ramey dropped her arm. "Have it your way." She went back to the cash register. "Did you want to order something?"

"A pumpkin soy latté, please."

The bells on the door jingled again, and Jenessa spun around, half-hoping Jake had run back to her. But no.

In walked her boss, Charles, along with his son, Charlie. Something about seeing Charlie, with her maternal instincts already on fire from having just been with Jake, hit her like a blast from an invisible force field. She took a step back to steady herself and drew in a deep breath before plastering a smile on her face.

"Good afternoon, Charles," she said, but her eyes were on Charlie. He looked so much like Logan. Could she be right about him? Was it possible that he could be the baby she had given up?

"Hello, Jenessa." Charles's gaze flew beyond her to Ramey as he approached. "There's my girl. Couldn't go an afternoon without seeing your beautiful face."

"Geez, Dad," Charlie moaned. "Do you have to go all mushy in front of me?"

"Yeah, Charles," Ramey said with a beaming smile, "you should save your mushy stuff for when we're alone."

Charlie hissed his exasperation.

Ignoring his son, Charles leaned over the counter to give her a quick kiss.

Charlie's face screwed into a scowl. "That's gross."

"So, Charlie," Jenessa did her best to draw his attention away from the happy couple, "are you enjoying your new class? Sixth grade, right?"

"Yeah, sixth," he replied with a nod. "It's okay. Mr. Makovsky isn't so bad."

Makovsky? Why did that name sound familiar?

"That's good to hear." Jenessa checked her watch again. Time was running short. She cleared her throat, hoping to get Ramey's attention. "My latté?" she asked when Ramey looked her way.

"Oh, yes, sorry. Right away." Ramey set about making Jenessa's drink.

Charles turned toward Jenessa, resting an elbow on the counter. "So, how's the story on Dr. Stone's murder coming along? I'll need something soon."

Jenessa stepped close to Charles and lowered her voice. "The police are playing this one close to the vest. They don't want to release any information that could jeopardize their case."

He groaned a breath. "Don't you have anything?"

"I'm working on it," she assured him, giving him a pat on his shoulder. "I'll get it to you as soon as I can, but I wouldn't hold a space in tomorrow's paper, except for my Oktoberfest story, that is."

~*~

Michael phoned the jewelry store and spoke to the young salesman they had interviewed. "When will we see that security video you promised us?"

"I only promised I'd ask the owner about it. Sorry, but he said I can't give it to you without a court order."

"What's he got to hide?"

"He said he has a lot of high-powered clients that wouldn't be too keen on being seen on camera. They're very private people."

"We're only interested in the footage where Drew Stone was purchasing the necklace," Michael replied.

"He's the one in charge and he said no court order, no video."

"Then we'll be getting one," Michael said. "You can count on it." He hoped they could secure a warrant and serve it before the video mysteriously disappeared.

Detective Provenza was listening to Michael's conversation, when his own phone began to ring. "Provenza," he answered.

Michael clicked off his call and turned his attention to his partner.

"Dr. Yamamoto, what do you have for us?" Provenza asked. "Uh-huh." He paused. "Thanks for letting us know." He hung up the phone and his chair squeaked as he leaned back in it.

"What's up with the ME?" Michael asked.

"He finished the autopsy on Daphne Stone and found a large malignant brain tumor."

"Just as Dr. Tierney said."

"But did her husband know?" Provenza wondered. "That's the important question."

"We'd better get on that court order for the security video quick, before it no longer exists."

~*~

In the middle of Jenessa's meeting at the Chamber of Commerce, a thought popped into her head like a light bulb turning on. She suddenly recalled where she'd encountered the name Makovsky—the old photo she found buried in Ashley Brandon's desk.

"Are you all right, Miss Jones?" asked the elderly head of the Chamber.

Embarrassed by the odd expression she must have had on her face, her cheeks blushed warm. "Oh yes, yes, I'm fine. You know when you've been trying to remember something and then it just comes to you out of nowhere?"

The man's bushy gray eyebrows sank into a frown as he nodded suspiciously, as if he was wondering where this conversation was going.

"That's what I had, sir, a sudden revelation about another story I'm writing. Sorry for the interruption, now let's get back to the Oktoberfest."

By the time her half-hour meeting concluded, Jenessa had all the information she needed to write a nice piece about the upcoming town event. She sped back to the paper and began writing the story, but she couldn't get the name Makovsky out of her mind. So, once the Oktoberfest article was put to bed, she set about researching it further.

Jenessa typed the name into the search bar and a number of links popped up on the computer screen. She scanned the various articles, mostly regarding an array of people with the last name Makovsky. But there it was, the fourth link she clicked on—Madalyn Makovsky was the cleaning woman killed in the explosion set by Suzanne Tremont and her unidentified partner.

She sank back in her chair. "Makovsky," she muttered.

"Makovsky?" Charles poked his head into her cubicle. "Are you talking about my son's teacher?"

Was it possible they were related somehow?

CHAPTER 27

"NO, I WAS TALKING ABOUT THE WOMAN killed in the explosion Daphne Stone set at the cosmetics testing lab years ago—when she was Suzanne Tremont."

"I can't wait to read what you have on that story," her editor said. "I'd like to run it as soon as possible."

Detective Provenza had asked her to hold off for the sake of the case, but that wouldn't fly with her editor for long and she knew it. "There's so much more research I need to do. Like I said at the café, I'm getting a little info from the detectives, but they're not very forthcoming. They don't want anyone, or anything, to jeopardize their investigation."

"I wouldn't want your story to undermine their catching Dr. Stone's killer either," Charles said, "but we have to print something before the television news scoops us."

"Detective Provenza assured me they're not talking to the press, except for me of course, and I'll have first bite at the story."

Charles sat on the edge of her desk and faced her. "What do you know so far? Who are the cops looking at?"

Jenessa lowered her voice. "Off the record, they've said they're looking at the husband, an ex-con handyman at the college, and possibly my aunt."

"Renee?" His voice rose in question. "Are you serious?"

"I wish I wasn't." She sat back in her chair and crossed her legs. "They searched her house and hauled her into the station for questioning."

Charles sucked in an audible breath.

"I'm not too worried though. At this point, I believe she's been relegated to the end of the suspects list." Or at least she hoped she had been.

~*~

At six o'clock on the dot Jenessa's doorbell rang. Excitedly, she swung the front door open to greet her two favorite guys, both of which were smiling from ear to ear.

"Hello, Michael," Jenessa greeted sweetly.

He bent over and gave her a quick kiss, then she crouched down to the boy's height. "And hello to you too, young man."

He threw his arms around her neck and planted a sloppy kiss on her cheek. She giggled.

"Like that, Daddy?" With an air of pride, Jake

looked up at his father as he untangled his arms from around Jenessa.

Michael's gaze suddenly drifted to the ceiling.

Jenessa arched a brow at Michael as she rose to her feet. So, it was his idea, not spontaneous—but she liked it anyway.

"Who's hungry?" she asked, her attention on the little boy.

"Me!" Jake firmly replied, shooting his hand in the air like he must have learned in his new kindergarten class.

Michael's gaze returned to her, one side of his mouth upturned. "We were thinking pizza at Salucci's."

"Sounds terrific." She plucked her jacket from the coat tree in her entry, relieved he'd suggested it, since she hadn't had time to prepare the fettuccini as she'd planned. "Lead the way, boys."

Soon, the three arrived at the restaurant. When Michael pulled the heavy wooden door open for the others, spicy and savory scents of pizza and marinara sauce drifted out, riding the lively old-fashioned Italian music like a magic carpet.

The hostess seated them quickly and they ordered a large pizza with pepperoni and olives, Jake's favorite.

Jenessa's gaze drifted around the room as they waited for their order, spotting Logan and Josie in a cozy booth in the corner, talking and laughing. She couldn't deny they made a striking couple, sitting together on the same side of the table.

With the tip of her finger, Josie cleaned a drip of sauce off Logan's lip and stuck it seductively into her mouth. *Slut.* Anger tightened in Jenessa's chest. She wasn't sure why, but she didn't like it one bit.

"What do you see?" Michael asked, apparently noticing that Jenessa's gaze was riveted to something behind him. Her face must have mirrored what she was feeling.

"Mommy!" Jake cried out.

Michael's head nearly spun off his shoulders as it whipped around. Then just as quickly, he straightened in his chair, the look in his eyes dark and serious. Was he jealous too?

Too?

"Is Mommy having pizza with her new friend?" Jake asked, staring up at his dad.

"It looks that way," Michael replied, forcing a small smile. His eyes were still brooding.

"Here we are, folks," the waitress said cheerfully as she set the large pizza in the center of the table. "Enjoy."

As soon as the woman was gone, Michael loaded a slice onto Jake's plate. "Try not to wear it, Son."

He grabbed a slice for himself and took a bite before setting it down on his plate. Jenessa pulled a slice and dropped it onto her dish. They ate their pizza in relative silence. Jenessa could tell by Michael's expression, and the lack of conversation, that Josie having dinner with Logan was bothering him even more than it was bothering her. Could it be what she had feared—that he was still in love with her? What did that say about her feelings for Logan?

Jake miraculously devoured more than his share of the pizza, and it took four paper napkins and a joint effort from Michael and Jenessa to clean the sauce off his hands and face.

"Now, what do you want to do?" Michael asked his son, seeming to work at a cheerful tone.

"Miniature golf," came Jake's reply.

"Jenessa?" Michael waited for her response.

Should she put an end to the torment and say she has an early day tomorrow and they should go on without her? Or should she be a good sport and agree to go, for Jake's sake?

"Sure, sounds like fun." She even managed a bit of a smile. Maybe the night would get better once they were out of visual range from Josie and Logan.

~*~

Jenessa was glad she'd agreed to go miniature golfing with her guys. Once they were on the faux greens, with windmills and castles and such to hit the little white balls through, the mood lightened considerably. Before long they were laughing and cheering each other on, especially for Jake, but she couldn't forget Michael's reaction to Josie and Logan— or her own for that matter.

After the round of mini golf, Michael drove Jenessa home. On the way, Jake fell asleep in the back seat.

"That was entertaining," Jenessa said as they drove through town. "It's been a while since I've played."

"We'll have to do it again, soon, before the weather turns too cold."

She smiled at Michael and nodded. The conversation remained light, as if they were purposefully making no mention of Josie or Logan.

He pulled the car into her driveway and walked her

to the door. "I'd better get Jake home and put him to bed."

From the front door, she gazed at the boy asleep in the car, not much more than the top of his hair showing through the window. "I think he had a fun evening," she said, pulling her focus back to Michael.

"So did I." He rested his forearm on the doorjamb, then leaned in and kissed her, softly at first, then his arms came around her and he pulled her into a deeper kiss.

His passion sent a thrill shooting through her body all the way down to her toes. As blood pulsed through her, she wanted him to stay, but she understood why he couldn't. Little Jake needed to go home and go to bed.

Would Josie be there too, waiting for Michael? Would he be leaving Jenessa to go home to her? Would he be able to resist his draw to her?

The thought made Jenessa suddenly feel sick, like she was the other woman, even though they were no longer married. But Josie was staying at his house, making his meals, sleeping under his roof. Jenessa couldn't shake the memory of the look he wore on his face when seeing Josie sitting close to Logan at the restaurant.

A vision of Michael and Josie together caused Jenessa to pull away abruptly. "I had a wonderful time, Michael, but you'd better get Jake in his bed."

At first he looked surprised at her abruptness, but after he glanced briefly over his shoulder at the car, he agreed. "You're right, I need to go." He turned back and searched her eyes. "Can I see you tomorrow?" There was a lilt of hopefulness in his voice.

"Sure, call me," she replied with a slight nod, uncertain of where their relationship was heading with Josie front and center in the picture.

Jenessa sensed impending heartbreak in her future if she let herself get her hopes up before things were settled where Josie was concerned. Maybe it was best not to give her whole heart to this man yet, as wonderful as he was. She pulled her heartstrings in. "Let's get this case wrapped up so I can get my story into print."

Michael wrinkled his brow. "I wasn't talking about the case."

"I know." She turned and unlocked her door, not wanting to see his expression. "Goodnight, Michael," she said as she stepped inside.

"Did I do something wrong?" he asked.

"I'm just tired."

"Goodnight then," she heard him say as she closed the door.

~*~

Michael took Jake home and carried him to bed. The house was dark when he arrived. He'd half-expected Josie to be there, but it was only nine o'clock. Logan would probably keep her out until late.

Logan.

The thought of him with Josie made Michael's blood boil. *But why?*

CHAPTER 28

IT WAS A LITTLE AFTER NINE AT NIGHT and Michael paced the living room floor. Was Josie toying with Logan to make Michael jealous? To see if she could stir up the latent embers of love he might still have for her? She had said she wanted to put their family back together—yet here she was on a date with the town's *number one son*.

Had she been successful in her game? Was Michael jealous? Or was he upset at the thought that if Logan and Josie became serious, Logan would become part of Jake's life and there wasn't a freakin' thing he could do about it?

A wave of nausea hit him as he considered the possibility of his ex hooking up with Jenessa's ex and the havoc that it would wreak. He dropped down into his armchair and cradled his head in his hands. Exasperated, he growled under his breath.

Was Josie staying or was she going? He wished he knew.

Was his love for Jenessa strong enough to weather this gathering storm, strong enough to build a future with her? Or should he put his own feelings aside for the sake of his young son and selflessly give Josie another chance? His mom and dad would say no—that much he was sure of—but he wasn't so certain they would be right.

Pulsing blood painfully throbbed in his head. He stalked to the kitchen and downed four ibuprofen with a glass of water.

He returned to his chair in the living room and clicked on the television, flipping between channels, trying to find something to watch to occupy the time until the pain in his skull subsided and Josie came home. He needed to know if there was any merit to his fears.

Not being able to concentrate on any one program, at ten o'clock he turned the TV off and went to bed.

Now, if only he could sleep.

~*~

Jenessa lay in her bed, unable to drift off to slumber, questions swirling in her head. Had she been too hard on Michael? Too brusque in her good-bye? He didn't deserve that, but how could she explain to him her need to pull away?

Since giving up her baby at eighteen, she hadn't let any man into her heart. Back then, she had given her whole heart, and her body, to Logan and it had turned out disastrously.

At first, she had tried to forget about the son she'd had to give away, immersing herself in her studies at college, then throwing herself fully into her work at the Sacramento newspaper. Though it didn't succeed in making her forget, at least it helped to protect her heart. She made sure she let no one else in who could break it...not until Michael.

With Josie back in town, Jenessa felt him slipping away. With his words he had said he loved her, but his actions seemed to scream he was still tied to his ex-wife. Which one could she believe?

And why did it bother her so much to see Josie with Logan? As Ramey had so astutely pointed out, that could be a good thing. But Ramey had also noted that perhaps Jenessa was upset because she liked knowing Logan was still in love with her, waiting in the wings for her if things didn't work out with Michael, even if she didn't want to admit it.

After all, Logan had been her first love. Does one ever really get over that?

She sighed loudly and rolled onto her side. "Why does love have to be so complicated?"

Michael woke early on Saturday morning and, being careful not to wake the rest of the house, got ready to head to the police station to work on the Daphne Stone case. Josie had told him days ago that she had made plans to take Jake to the zoo that day, but what if she hadn't come home last night? He slowly opened the door to his son's room and peeked in, finding both Jake and Josie fast asleep in their beds.

Relieved, he quietly shut the door and snuck out of the house. He had wanted to talk to Josie about Logan, but maybe that wasn't such a good idea. If she was trying to make him jealous, he didn't want to give her the satisfaction of knowing she may have succeeded. It was just as well that she had come home after he went to bed.

Slowly he backed the car out of his driveway and drove to work, unable to get his mind on anything else. If he could just get through this week, hopefully things would get back to normal—that is, if he could keep Josie from driving a wedge between him and Jenessa.

Now that acting jobs in LA appeared to have dried up for her, Josie talked about staying in Hidden Valley to be closer to her son. Perhaps her date with Logan wasn't meant to make Michael jealous after all—maybe she was simply looking for a sugar daddy in case Michael refused to take her back. Logan did have the money to take care of her the way she likely wanted.

"Morning, Baxter," Provenza greeted as Michael strolled into their office. "You look like hell."

"Gee, thanks." Michael grimaced. "I didn't get much sleep."

"More woman troubles?"

"How'd you know?"

"I've had my fill over the years." George got up from his desk and moved to the crime board. "Now let's get working on this case."

"Drew Stone isn't giving anything up and we don't have enough evidence to charge him yet," Michael said.

"Buck Baird and his attorney are still trying to work a deal with the DA."

"We should haul him down here on Monday and have another go at him. Stone, too."

Michael propped his tired head on his upturned hand. "We'll need to have a reason."

"Then we'd better get busy poring over those financials, phone records, and anything else we have until we can come up with a new angle or a new bit of evidence to give us a reason."

Michael eyed the stack of files on Provenza's desk. "I'm going to get a strong cup of coffee first, if you don't mind."

~*~

Jenessa sat at her kitchen table, stirring the bowl of breakfast cereal in front of her, thinking about Daphne Stone and what Dr. Tierney had said about her brain tumor. Why had she waited so long to go see the doctor if she'd suspected a problem? The depression and the mood swings must have made her suspect something. Could she have dismissed the depression as being a result of her husband's infidelity and blamed the mood swings on hormones?

Hadn't Aunt Renee noticed anything out of the ordinary? Perhaps they had even talked about it but chalked it up to Drew's affair and pre-menopause.

Jenessa scooped a spoonful of cereal into her mouth. Aunt Renee had mentioned that Daphne said she had something she wanted to discuss, but her husband had walked in and she changed the subject before she had the chance to tell her. What could it have been?

She took her bowl of soggy cereal to the sink and dumped it. Letting the water run as she rinsed it, she stared out the window as more questions rushed into her mind. What was Drew holding over Daphne that she couldn't divorce him? Did he know she was really Suzanne Tremont? Did he know about her brain tumor? With whom was he having an affair? Who was wearing the blond wig? Where is the diamond necklace he purchased? Who was the attractive middle-aged blonde with him at the jewelry store?

Drew seemed to be the only one who would know the answers to all of these questions. If only she could figure out a way to get him to talk to her.

She went into her home office and sat behind the large desk. Flipping open her laptop, she considered where to start. Something about the new teacher, Mr. Makovsky, nagged at her. It was an unusual name. He was new to the area. Charles had said the man's first name was David, and from a conversation he'd had with him at Charlie's back-to-school night, he thought he lived somewhere on the west side of Crane Park.

She opened an internet browser and began to research any news stories related to the name Makovsky. Nothing of importance popped up except the stories about Madalyn Makovsky being killed in the bombing.

Madalyn Makovsky, the name scrawled on the back of the photo she had found in Ashley Brandon's desk. Was it possible he was related to the woman in the photo? Was she his wife? His cousin? His sister?

And why would Daphne Stone's assistant have kept that snapshot all these years?

A burbling growl erupted from Jenessa's stomach. Maybe a nice cup of hot mocha cappuccino and one of Ramey's decadently gooey cinnamon rolls might help her think.

~*~

Jenessa pulled her jacket closed as she climbed out of her car in front of The Sweet Spot. A chilly wind had kicked up, and dried fallen leaves rustled around her feet as they blew down the sidewalk. Before she reached the door to the coffee shop, her phone began to ring. Taking a quick look, she saw it was Michael calling.

She hesitated for a moment, then hit *ignore*. She wasn't ready to apologize yet for her cool good-bye the night before. Maybe once she had her coffee and roll she'd do a better job of being contrite.

~*~

After poring over what seemed like reams of paperwork, Michael took a break and phoned Jenessa. He just wanted to hear her voice, see if she was free for lunch. He didn't like how they'd left things last night.

The call went almost immediately to voicemail. Was she busy? On another line? Avoiding him?

"Hey, Baxter," Provenza said, shaking Michael out of his thoughts. "The video footage just came in from the jeweler. Let's have a look."

Michael rose from his chair and moved to Provenza's desk. He bent down and steadied himself with one hand on the desktop, getting a good view of the computer screen.

Provenza queued it up, then fast-forwarded until he saw Drew Stone come into view. There was, indeed, a blond woman with him, but she hadn't looked up at the camera yet. Who could it be? They both watched and waited as the couple looked at different pieces in the jewelry case. Then the woman looked up, perhaps at the clock on the wall.

"Did you see that?" Provenza gasped.

CHAPTER 29

"SEE WHAT?" MICHAEL ASKED, not quite knowing what Provenza was all excited about as the woman was staring up at the jewelry store's security camera.

"The woman." Provenza pointed at the face frozen on the computer screen and replied with an I-can't-believe-you-don't-see-it tone in his voice.

Michael moved in for a closer look, his brows knitting together in concentration. "Is that...oh my god, it is—Daphne Stone."

Detective Provenza settled back in his chair. "Guess we know who was wearing the blond wig."

"But why?"

~*~

Outside of The Sweet Spot, as Jenessa reached for

the door handle, she was nearly bowled over by a man rushing out of the shop.

"Oh, I'm so sorry," he said, apparently realizing he had almost knocked her down.

"Mr. Stone?" Jenessa asked. "Drew Stone?"

He looked more closely at her, but his eyes didn't seem to register recognition.

"I'm Jenessa Jones, Renee Giraldy's niece."

"That's right. You came to the house with her last week. Sorry, I didn't recognize you."

"Everything okay?" Maybe this was her opportunity to make some headway with the man. "You look upset."

"The darn dog got out again."

"Buttons?"

"You know our dog?" he asked with surprise.

"You had her in your arms when we visited."

"That's right. It's all such a blur these days."

"Aunt Renee told me how Daphne loved that dog."

"She did." He nodded sadly. "I just got a call that someone in town found her and I need to go pick her up before they take her to the pound."

"Someone would do that? Knowing who the owner is?"

"Guess so." Drew quirked one side of his mouth. "He sounded like quite an old grump, but at least he took the time to make the call."

With Drew being in such a hurry, maybe this wasn't the ideal time to talk to him. "I won't keep you." She'd have to keep an eye out for another opportunity.

She watched as he got in his silver Lexus SUV and sped away before she ducked inside the warm coffee shop, incredulous someone could be so cruel as to call animal control on that cute little dog.

"Hey, Jenessa," Ramey called out with a big smile. "What can I get you, missy?"

She couldn't help but smile at Ramey's bubbly personality. "Mocha cappuccino and a cinnamon roll."

"Sorry, but we're out of cinnamon rolls for today. How about a nice bear claw?"

"A bear claw?" It didn't seem to have the same draw. "How about just the coffee?"

"That'll be right up," Ramey said as she stepped to the machine.

Jenessa's gaze floated around the cheery café as she waited. At a small table in the corner sat Ashley Brandon, sipping a drink as she read a paperback book.

Drew Stone had just left The Sweet Spot, and here sat Ashley Brandon. Had they been together when he got the call about Buttons? Was she the mysterious blonde?

"Here we are," Ramey said, drawing Jenessa's attention back to the counter. "That'll be three dollars."

"Hey, did you see that blonde over there sitting with a man?"

Ramey glanced toward the young woman. "Couldn't say. I've been helping one customer after another."

"No problem." Jenessa handed her the cash and picked up her cup. "Thanks a bunch, Ramey. I've got work to get after, but I'll see you soon."

When she turned to leave, Ashley was heading out the door. Maybe Jenessa should follow her and see where it led.

Giving her a little head start, Jenessa tailed Ashley on foot as she strolled down Main Street for a few blocks, then made a left turn right before Crane Park. She hung back a little more, even stepped behind a tall bush to avoid being seen. She peeked around the bush, and when the coast was clear she continued down the street, seeing Ashley step onto a stone walkway leading up to a small single-level bungalow.

Jenessa darted behind another bush, peering just over it, hoping to see who answered the door, or if Ashley would simply walk in. In her research she had found Ashley lived in an apartment on Pine Street—this was Elm.

She watched as the young woman knocked, the door opened, and she stepped inside. Irritated she couldn't see who answered the door, Jenessa moved closer, hoping for some clue as to the resident.

There was a dark green sedan parked in the driveway. Jenessa had the feeling she'd seen it before, but where? A thought popped into her mind—the vehicle that had picked Ashley up outside of The Sweet Spot a few days ago.

Jenessa crept closer to the house, keeping an eye on the front door. The last thing she wanted was for Ashley to spot her following her. To shield herself, she stepped into the street and inched closer to the bungalow from the other side of an SUV parked in front of the house.

As she made her way around it, she noticed the Whitfield College staff parking sticker. She took a small step back and scanned over the vehicle. It appeared to be the silver Lexus she saw Drew Stone get into just minutes ago when he claimed he had to go and rescue poor little Buttons from an old grump.

What a liar!

His convincing little act raised her ire. This was probably his love nest and he had likely raced off to get it ready for his tryst with the lovely young blonde. After all, they had just been together at The Sweet Spot, hadn't they?

On the side of the house, a window stood partially open. As Jenessa tiptoed toward it, she heard voices drifting out. Hopefully she could overhear some useful conversation, like Drew and Ashley discussing how they got rid of his wife.

She took a step closer and a twig snapped under her foot. Had anyone heard it? Probably not, for the female side of the conversation continued. If only she could make out what the woman was saying.

Something hard jabbed her in the ribs as a large hand clamped over her mouth.

"Don't make a sound," a man ordered, his deep voice unfamiliar. "This way," he said, pulling her around the outside of the house to the back door.

~*~

Michael tried Jenessa's phone again and, again, it went to voicemail. *Was she mad at him?*

"Baxter!" Detective Provenza hollered from the office doorway. "Let's roll."

The relentless search through all the documents had produced the name and phone number of Daphne Stone's therapist. Provenza had called and the doctor agreed to meet with them if they came right over.

"What's with the long face?" Provenza asked as they walked to the car.

"Jenessa's not taking my calls and I don't know why."

"Women are a fickle bunch," were Provenza's words of wisdom.

"Sorry, Boss, but that doesn't help."

"Is that sexy ex-wife of yours still sleeping at your house?"

"Yes," Michael replied, drawing out the word hesitantly.

"Then there's your answer, son. It's not rocket science." He breathed a laugh. "You want to get your relationship back on track with Jenessa, you get your ex-wife out of your house. Use a boot horn if you have to, but do it—and do it quickly."

"It's a lot more complicated than that." Michael thought of Jake and how much the boy loved having his mother around. He couldn't bring himself to do that to him.

"In my day, no woman worth her salt would put up with her man shacking up with another woman, especially his ex-wife."

"Not just in your day apparently."

"Grow a backbone, Baxter, and give Josie the boot, or you can kiss a happy life with Jenessa good-bye."

~*~

"Thank you for meeting with us, Dr. Forester." Detective Provenza shook the woman's hand.

She gestured toward the chairs across from her desk. "Please, have a seat."

The doctor was short and plump with her chestnut-colored hair cropped into a pixie cut. "I was so sorry to hear about Dr. Stone's death." She settled into her black leather chair and laced her fingers together on the desktop. "But I can't say I was surprised."

"No?" Provenza asked. "Why is that, ma'am?"

"It was just a matter of time, Detective. As you are probably already aware, she was gravely ill with no hope of recovery."

"Yes, we had discovered that," Provenza replied, the expression on his face a little sad, "but she didn't die from an illness—she was murdered, Doc."

"Murdered?" Her brows lifted briefly, then her face relaxed. "Well, still, I can't say I'm surprised. Either way, her life was doomed to end badly."

Michael scooted to the edge of his seat. "Why do you say that?"

"Ordinarily I wouldn't divulge anything, doctor-patient confidentiality and all, but since she was murdered, that does change things."

"What can you tell us about her?" Provenza asked.

"She began coming to see me a few months ago because she believed her husband was cheating on her, which would throw her into bouts of depression. I gave her a prescription to help even out her disposition, but she claimed she was beginning to have mood swings."

"If she was depressed over her husband's alleged affair, why didn't she just leave him?" Michael asked.

"Well, she wanted to divorce him, but he wouldn't let her, which made her all the more unhappy."

"Do you have any idea why he wouldn't *let* her divorce him?" Provenza asked. "I mean, in this state, we do have no-fault divorces. She didn't need his permission to dissolve the marriage."

"No, but…" Her gaze floated out the window as she considered her answer.

"What is it?" Michael pressed.

Her attention slowly traveled back to the detectives. "I'm not used to talking to someone else about my patients, but I guess it wouldn't hurt Daphne now that she's gone."

"What wouldn't hurt her?" Michael urged, growing impatient.

"My telling you that Daphne had killed someone," she said.

"What?" Provenza gasped, his gaze flying briefly to his colleague.

"Killed someone?" Michael met his partner's gaze, as surprised as George was.

"Accidentally, of course," Dr. Forester clarified, "when she was Suzanne Tremont."

"Oh right, Suzanne Tremont," Michael remarked, relaxing back into his chair. "The cleaning woman that was killed in the bombing she was accused of."

"Yeah, we already knew about that." Provenza shifted in his seat. "Are you saying her husband threatened to expose her to the authorities if she left him?"

"No," the doctor shook her head slowly, her gaze dropping to her lap for a moment as she hesitated, "it was more complicated than that."

"Complicated how?" Michael asked.

"He was trying to protect her."

"Protect her?" Provenza's eyebrows arched. "From what?"

"From herself, of course."

"You're not making any sense, Doc," Provenza spit out as he leaned forward, his eyes narrowing with irritation. "Now I know you're the one with all the degrees, but can you just tell us in plain and simple English what was going on with the woman?"

"Daphne Stone, or Suzanne Tremont, whichever you want to call her, was suffering from dissociative identity disorder."

"Dissociative identity disorder?" Michael echoed.

Provenza rubbed a hand over his mouth as he scooted to the edge of his seat. "Are you saying she was nuts? Crazy? Loony tunes?"

The doctor's eyes popped wide, then settled into a frown. "Now, Detective, those names are totally inappropriate." She crossed her arms defensively over her chest, expelling an irritated huff. "Dr. Stone was suffering from a disorder that was beyond her control, and her husband and I were trying to help her manage it."

Michael put a hand on Provenza's shoulder, seeing the elder partner was about to unleash a totally inappropriate witty comeback. "Ma'am—"

"Dr. Forester," she corrected.

"Dr. Forester," Michael gave a slight nod as he said it, "I think you know why we're here. We're trying to figure out who might have killed Dr. Stone or—"

"Or if she took her own life?" she finished his sentence.

"Exactly," Provenza said, jabbing a finger in her direction.

"I believe it is entirely possible that she may have

taken her own life," the doctor went on, "as her alternate personality."

"Can you explain?" Michael asked, struggling to appear patient.

Provenza settled back in his chair. "Just how many different personalities do you figure the woman had?"

"Dr. Stone had two distinctly different personalities. One was Daphne Stone, as she was known at the college and around Hidden Valley, but at times her alternate personality, Suzi, would take over."

"Suzi?" Provenza muttered to himself.

"I assume she took that name because her real name was Suzanne. She might have been called Suzi to her friends and family back then."

The jewelry store's video footage had shown Daphne as a blonde, as Michael recalled. "Did she ever wear a wig—a blond one maybe?"

"Why yes, how did you know?"

Michael cleared his throat. "I really can't say, but I have reason to suspect she might have."

The doctor seemed to relax a bit, unfolding her arms. "When Suzi came out, she would wear a blond wig. Suzanne had been a natural blonde, but Daphne dyed her hair red when she went into hiding after the bombing. Suzi's personality was much more outgoing than Daphne's too. Maybe it was because Daphne had to hide her true identity and became the stuffy and rigid college professor."

"So you're saying her husband was aware of all this?" Provenza questioned.

From the jewelry story video, it was apparent to Michael that Drew Stone was not only aware of Suzi, but comfortable with her.

"I don't know if I would say *all* of it, but the man was aware of her identity disorder and clearly loved his wife. If he had let her divorce him, and go out on her own, there's no telling what could have happened to her. Like I said, Detectives, he was trying to protect her."

"You said you knew she was very ill. Did you know it was a terminal brain tumor?" Michael asked.

"Yes, Suzi was first to tell me during one of our sessions, although I can't say that's what triggered the dual personalities."

"And they knew about each other?" Michael asked. "The two personalities?"

"No." The doctor gave her head a slow shake. "Daphne was not aware of Suzi, but Suzi knew all about Daphne—perhaps because Suzi was more who the woman really was, the personality Daphne'd had to bury deep so she wouldn't be discovered and arrested."

"Why wouldn't you have tried to tell Daphne about her other half?" Michael probed.

"You have to understand, Detective, her psyche was fragile. I casually asked her one day if she knew anyone named Suzi, but she said she didn't, so I moved away from that tack in our therapy. Mr. Stone and I agreed it was best to deal with Daphne on her own, not burden her with another problem. We didn't know about the tumor until later, and by that time it was so advanced that nothing could be done, so, what would have been the point to bring it up then?"

Michael and Provenza exchanged glances. She should have been told, Michael thought, but he couldn't read his partner's mind. "Even when Daphne suspected her husband of having an affair?"

"What are you implying?" she asked.

"It's our understanding that Daphne began seeing you because of depression over her husband having an affair," Michael replied, "because she had found blond hairs on his clothing. Sounds like it was just her other personality spending time with her husband. You had to have known that."

"I considered it, but I had no way of knowing if there were other blondes in Mr. Stone's life."

Yet he did have other blondes in his life—Ashley Brandon and Renee Giraldy. Had Daphne suspected either of them?

"I think we're done here." Provenza put his hands on his knees and pushed up out of the chair. "I never would have guessed Daphne was her own husband's mistress. It would have been nice if she had figured that out before the end came."

Michael stood, mulling over what he had learned from Dr. Forester.

"Funny," the doctor rose too, "Suzi and Daphne had such differing ideas on how to deal with their final days."

"Oh?" Provenza's eyes lit up, causing his brows to lift. "Differing how?"

CHAPTER 30

JENESSA'S HEART POUNDED IN HER CHEST. Where was he taking her? She struggled for breath against the man's large hand pressed over her face.

If this guy wasn't Drew Stone, who was he?

The man bumped the back door open with his hip and pulled her inside, pain from a hard object still throbbing in her side. Was it a gun?

He hustled her through the kitchen, setting something down hard on a counter. The gun? Whatever it was, the pain was fading from her ribs, but she was unable to turn to look, as he forced her into the living room. "Who do we have here?" he asked sarcastically. "Oh wait, I know this one...the nosey reporter."

But how did he know? Who was this man? Was he talking to himself?

Jenessa glanced around the room with her limited

range of motion. Her focus settled on a man in the corner of the room, tied with thin white rope to a wooden kitchen chair, his eyes closed and his head sloping to one side. Drew Stone? Was he unconscious—or dead? Was this about him?

Apparently Drew hadn't come here on his own after all—and this was obviously no love nest. Her captor must have been the old grump and the call about Buttons a ruse—but why?

Jenessa tried to speak, to find out what was going on, but her words were muffled beneath the stranger's flesh. What had she gotten herself into?

She had followed Ashley to this address, but where was she? Had she scooted out while the man was dragging her to the back door?

What was he planning to do with her and Drew? Leave them bound and gagged in the house so he could make a clean getaway?

Or worse? Would he take them somewhere else? To the lake maybe? Kill them and dump their bodies where no one would ever find them?

"You should have kept your big nose out of the murder investigation," he growled, "but no, you media types have to keep digging and sticking your big nose where it doesn't belong."

Jenessa struggled to break free.

"I can tell this one's going to be a problem," the man uttered as he fought to hold her.

Who was he talking to? No one answered. What was he going to do with her? With Drew?

Whatever he was planning, Jenessa wasn't going to make it easy for him. She began to buck and kick against

THE STONE HOUSE SECRET

the man, whose large hand clamped tighter over her face, his other hand squeezing harder on her upper arm. "Settle down!" he shouted in her ear.

She couldn't breathe, his hand was so big it covered both her mouth and her nose. Whether or not he meant to suffocate her, the result would be the same. Fear and adrenalin compelled her to struggle harder, trying to whip her body out of his clutches, but he only tightened his hold on her. If she didn't get air soon, she'd lose consciousness and then he'd be able to do whatever he wanted with her.

She kicked back at him, trying to jam her heel into his groin, but he was too tall for her to accomplish that. The highest her kick would go was his inner thigh, but she did connect with it. He groaned and spun her around, momentarily releasing his clamp over her mouth. She was able to pull in a quick gasp of air before his fist smashed into the side of her face and everything went black.

~*~

Michael and Provenza left the therapists's office and headed back to the station.

"I thought I'd seen everything," Detective Provenza muttered as he drove. "A split personality? Didn't see that one coming."

"So maybe Dr. Stone did kill herself after all," Michael said.

"Could be, you heard the doc. Suzi told her she wanted to end it before the suffering started." Provenza pulled the car into the station's parking lot.

"Yes, but Daphne didn't. She wanted as many days as she had left," Michael countered. "Remember? She said she had to make amends for what she'd done."

"But how was she going to do that?" Provenza asked, turning into a parking space.

"According to Dr. Forester, Daphne wasn't clear on that point, just that she didn't want to go to her grave until she had tried to make up for what she'd done."

"I'd like to button up this case." Provenza shut off the motor. "So, if Daphne Stone killed herself—"

"But what about the husband?" Michael interrupted, opening the car door. "If he really did try to hire Buck Baird to shoot her, maybe he went ahead and put her out of her misery with the vinegar."

"Let's get Mr. Stone back down here and grill him again with the new information we have." Provenza climbed out of the car and moved toward the station.

Michael stepped out and stopped by the car. "I want to try calling Jenessa again. I'll be inside in a minute."

Provenza waved a hand in the air as he kept walking.

Michael dialed Jenessa's number. It rang four times, then went to voicemail. "Jenessa, babe, please call me back. We need to talk." He paused. What else should he say? "I love you."

~*~

When Jenessa regained consciousness, she found herself bound to a chair by rope, just like she had found Drew Stone, only they were no longer in the living room. The room was almost pitch-dark, making it hard

270

to distinguish where she was being kept—a darkened bedroom or maybe a basement?

She pitched and pulled against the ropes, but they did not give.

"Hey, you're awake," a groggy male voice spoke from behind her.

"Drew?" She tried to crane her head around, realizing they had been tied together, their chairs back to back.

"How did you know?"

"I saw you in the living room after some big brute dragged me into the house. He caught me eavesdropping at the window."

"That brute would have been David Makovsky." He let out a low groan.

The teacher?

Jenessa swept the obscure room with her gaze, looking for anything she could use to cut the ropes, but she could see nothing in the darkness. "We've got to figure a way out of here."

"If only I had protected Daphne like I should have, we wouldn't be stuck here." Drew's voice was high and thin, his throat tight with emotion.

"What do you mean, if you had protected her?" she asked. Jenessa had wanted an opportunity to have an in-depth conversation with Drew Stone about his wife and her mysterious life, but this wasn't what she'd had in mind.

"Daphne was sick, very sick…" His voice trailed off momentarily.

"I know."

"You do? But how?"

"I talked to her doctor, but I don't know everything."

"You should, then you'd understand." He groaned again. "My head is killing me."

"Did he knock you out too?"

"Must have."

Not knowing when she'd have another opportunity to interview Drew, she pressed for more information as she struggled with her bindings. "Tell me about your wife."

"She had a brain tumor that was too far gone...once she finally went to the doctor." He expelled a quiet sob. "I should have made her go sooner. I should have known something was wrong...with the headaches...the mood swings."

"You couldn't have known it was something so serious." Could he? Aunt Renee was Daphne's closest friend and she didn't know. Was that what Daphne had wanted to tell her aunt?

"No one but me and her psychiatrist knew this, but—" He paused, seeming to struggle to focus. Was he contemplating whether or not to tell his wife's deepest, darkest secrets?

"Go on, Mr. Stone," she urged, "I'm a good listener."

~*~

Drew and Jenessa sat bound, back to back, in the dark room. He pulled in a ragged breath. "My wife suffered from a split personality," he explained, his voice slow and weak.

She sucked in a sharp breath at his revelation, glad he couldn't see the expression of astonishment that surely was on her face, though it was doubtful he missed hearing her gasp. "Sorry, but that wasn't at all what I was expecting."

"It is rather shocking, even for me." He paused as if he was trying to work up the strength to continue. "Daphne accused me of having an affair," he let out a shaky moan, then drew in an audible breath. "All because she'd found blond hairs on my clothes, but they were only strands from Suzi's wig."

"Who is Suzi?" Jenessa asked. Was it the mistress? She worked to pitch her shoulders from one side to the other as she fought to loosen the ropes.

"Daphne's other personality," he huffed.

Suzi, as in Suzanne Tremont.

Drew paused again and pulled in a loud, uneven breath, sounding like he was working to stay alert to continue. Did he have a concussion?

She couldn't let him fall asleep. "Tell me about her."

With measured phrasing, he slowly explained how Daphne had believed the brain tumor was a curse, some sort of payback for having caused the death of an innocent cleaning lady, Madalyn Makovsky. Somehow, she'd wanted to make it up to the woman's family before she died, but Suzi hadn't agreed. Suzi wanted to end their shared life before the horrible pain and suffering from the cancer began to ravage them. She'd begged Drew to end the torture that was certain to come in the next few weeks.

With a quivering sadness in his voice, he admitted

that he had reluctantly given in to Suzi's pleading, but only because he loved his wife and wanted to spare her from a tortuous death. So, at Suzi's insistence, he'd contacted Buck Baird, who he knew had served time for a violent offense, and offered to hire him to shoot his unsuspecting wife, painlessly putting her out of her misery before she knew what hit her. But second thoughts plagued him and he couldn't go through with it. He claimed he made contact with Buck again and called off the hit.

The abrasive ropes were tight on Jenessa's small wrists, rasping as she fought against them, but she wasn't going to give up trying to get free. She could only assume Drew was working to get the ropes off too, feeling occasional movement behind her as he told his story.

"When you called him off, he must have known you wouldn't pay him. So why did he go ahead and take a shot at her anyway?"

Drew replied that he didn't know, perhaps the man had hoped to collect the money anyway, maybe he planned to threaten to go to the cops and spill his guts if Drew didn't pay him to keep quiet.

"It was the vinegar in Daphne's cranberry juice that killed her though," Jenessa remarked. "Do you think Suzi could have snuck it in, since you backed out of the original plan?" That would mean suicide of sorts.

"Yeah, I'd thought she might have, because even though Daphne didn't want to end her life early, Suzi was adamant she wanted it over, to be put out of their misery."

"You said you'd *thought* she might have?" Jenessa

asked, trying to tug her hands out of the rope. "But it sounds like something changed your mind."

He seemed to gain a little strength, his words coming more clearly. "This morning I stopped by Daphne's office to pick up some valuable first editions she had in her bookcase, not expecting anyone to be around on a Saturday, but Ashley was in her office and the door was slightly ajar. I didn't think she was aware, but I overheard her talking on the phone. I couldn't make out who she was talking to, but I heard her say she thought getting revenge for her mother's death would have given her more satisfaction."

Ashley's mother? Was she Madalyn Makovsky's daughter? If so, it would make sense why the young woman was part of this, but they'd need confirmation. "Then what did you do?"

"I knocked on the door and went in," he said, "explaining I'd stopped by for the books. I tried to sound casual and friendly, but she must have suspected I overheard."

"What makes you think that?"

"Well, why else would her father have lured me here? I'm sure he's the one who called about our dog getting out. Buttons is probably still at home."

"How do you know he's her father?"

"I can't say for certain he's Ashley's father, that's purely assumption, but I am sure he's Madalyn Makovsky's husband."

Was Brandon Ashley's married name? Or a fake one? Or maybe her mother had remarried, taking the name Makovsky later in life?

"You know that how?" Jenessa asked.

"From the pictures."

She stopped struggling for a moment. "What pictures?"

"My wife kept a scrapbook of the newspaper articles about the bombing and the woman who was killed, and lately I'd find her poring over it more than ever. There's a graveside photo of the grieving husband and her daughter that my wife would stop and stare at."

"But that was fifteen years ago."

"Yeah, the daughter grew up and I'm sure she's changed quite a bit. I can only assume Ashley is that little girl, but the husband looks pretty much the same. I'm only guessing here, but I think that after I left the college this morning she must have phoned David Makovsky. That's probably when they hatched the plan to kidnap me to keep me from going to the police, at least long enough for them to make a clean get-away."

"But you both were at The Sweet Spot when I got there," Jenessa said. "I thought maybe you two—"

"Purely coincidental."

"And you don't believe they plan to kill you?" Jenessa felt a little give in the ropes around her chafed wrists.

"No...well, I didn't until you brought it up."

So, Jenessa's listening at the window must have screwed up the plan. Makovsky had to keep her from exposing him as well. "I hope you're right, Mr. Stone."

"About what?"

"That he's not planning to kill us, like he probably killed your wife."

~*~

276

Unable to reach Jenessa by phone, Michael returned to work.

"Any luck?" Detective Provenza arched an eyebrow at him.

"Just voicemail. Where could she be?"

Provenza clicked his tongue. "I meant about getting Drew Stone down here for further questioning."

"Oh." Michael shook his head at the mistake. "Luke is on patrol this shift. Let me give him a call, and he and his partner can go by the Stone house to pick up the professor."

"Just as well," Provenza said. "That'll give us time to sort through this new information and put together an aggressive line of questioning."

Michael radioed Luke and lined out his instructions. "Bring him down here to the station for further questioning."

"Yes, sir," Luke responded with a hint of familiar sarcasm between the cousins.

Michael and Provenza reviewed the story Dr. Forester had spun for them. If she was to be believed, Daphne's husband might have poisoned her in a mercy killing. Sure, the professor had ordered someone to shoot his wife, Buck Baird had confessed to that, and then Drew claimed to get cold feet and call it off, but the drug interaction would certainly have been a cleaner, more humane way to go, one that maybe he hoped would not be detected. If the ME hadn't been on his game, they would have ruled her death a simple heart attack.

Michael was anxious to hear what Drew Stone had to say about this new information, especially in light of the jewelry store's video.

"You know he'll want his attorney here with him," Provenza said, "so we'll be twiddling our thumbs 'til the suit shows up."

Michael jumped at the opportunity to find Jenessa and get her to talk to him. "Since we're looking at over an hour before Stone and his lawyer are ready, I'm going to run an errand," he said, pulling his jacket off the back of his chair and tugging it on. "I'll be back before long."

"Where are you off to?" Provenza questioned as Michael slipped out the door. "Like I didn't already know."

"I heard that," Michael called back to him.

~*~

"What was that?" Jenessa gasped, trying to keep her voice low in the dark room, still fighting the ropes around her wrists. "Sounds like someone's in the house above us." Were they in the basement?

"The cops, you think?" Drew asked.

Several heavy thuds rumbled across the ceiling like someone of size was stalking around upstairs. Was Michael there looking for them?

Dare she scream out to get his attention? She gave a hard yank against the ropes and one hand came free. The room was too dim to make out exactly how they were tied, but she hastily ran her hand over the knots to discern how she could get free.

"We've got to get out of here, Professor. Keep working your ropes."

Drew groaned as he pulled. "They won't budge and

my hands are numb."

"Shhh, someone's coming," she whispered. With another strong yank, she was able to pull her other hand free. Expelling all the air she could from her chest, she slid her body low and out from under the ropes that had held her petite torso to the chair.

The sound of footfalls intensified through the ceiling. *Please let it be Michael.*

She scanned the dark room as well as she could, but all she found were a few cardboard boxes and she was out of time to rummage through their contents.

A door flew open, shining a faint light down a rickety staircase. A single bulb popped on overhead and she froze in the stark light. Her heart dropped to her stomach like a rock. It was not Michael.

The large man lunged at her, his angry face coming frighteningly into view. He grabbed her by the arms and dragged her out of the room. She began to scream and buck wildly. He put his big hand over her mouth, his other arm clamped around her waist as he dragged her up the steps.

She had seen this man for only a moment, upstairs, before his fist had connected with her head and she fell unconscious. The man had to be David Makovsky.

What was he going to do with her now? And what of Drew Stone?

~*~

Before Michael reached his car, he tried Jenessa's number again. Still no luck. This time it went immediately to voicemail. Had she turned it off?

He climbed into his car and phoned the newspaper. The receptionist informed him she hadn't seen Jenessa all afternoon. So he headed for her house, hoping she was there, just avoiding his calls. He had to know why.

When he arrived, her steely blue sports car was not sitting in the driveway as he half-expected. Maybe it was in the garage.

He went to the front door and knocked—no answer. He waited a minute and knocked again, harder, but still no answer. After hurrying around the corner of the house, he peeked into the window on the side of the garage—empty.

Where was she?

Michael phoned the newspaper again. "Hey, Michael Baxter here."

"Sorry," the elderly receptionist replied, "there's no Michael Baxter here."

"No, Alice, I am Michael Baxter."

"Why didn't you say so?"

He groaned. "Is Charles McAllister around?"

"He said he was running over to The Sweet Spot for an afternoon pick-me-up, and I don't think he meant coffee."

"Uh, okay, thanks." *That was weird.* "I'll find him." He swung his car around and headed to The Sweet Spot.

As he drove, Luke radioed and explained that Drew Stone was not at his house, asking if there was another location for them to check out.

"Try the college," Michael replied. "Maybe he went to his office for some reason."

"Roger that."

Michael phoned Provenza's cell. "Hey, George,

Stone is not at home. I sent Luke to Whitfield to see if he was there. Do you have any idea where he might be on a sunny Saturday afternoon?"

"Hold on a minute and I'll give him a jingle and see." Michael could hear Provenza punching in numbers on the desk phone, assuming he had gotten Drew's number from the inside flap of the case file where they'd posted it. "Damn!" Provenza slammed the receiver down hard in the background.

"No answer?" Michael asked.

"Only that stupid voicemail," he growled. "Now what?"

"Take it easy, Boss," Michael urged. "He'll turn up."

Provenza huffed. "So much for our great plan."

"We'll keep trying to find him and I'll be back to the station soon." Michael clicked his phone off and headed to the coffee shop.

Parked in front of The Sweet Spot was Jenessa's car. Michael's heart lifted—finally he had found her. Hopefully he could get her alone and they could hash out whatever it was that had caused this rift between them.

He pulled open the painted glass door and stepped inside. Glancing around the shop, he looked for Jenessa. There were a few familiar faces, but no Jenessa. In the restroom, maybe?

"Hello there, Michael," Ramey called from behind the cash register. "What can I get for you?"

He rushed to the counter. "I'm looking for Jenessa."

"Haven't seen her for hours."

"But her car is out front."

Ramey's gaze pitched beyond him, out the large

storefront windows to the street where the car in question sat. "Hmm, I hadn't noticed. She was in here a couple of hours ago, but she left."

"Without her car?" Something didn't feel right.

"Maybe she had an appointment, Michael, somewhere within walking distance."

He calmed a little at her words. That made sense.

Charles joined Michael and Ramey. "You looking for Jenessa?"

"Yes." Michael was hopeful Charles would confirm Ramey's suggestion. "Is she on an assignment?"

CHAPTER 31

"AN ASSIGNMENT?" CHARLES ECHOED.

"Yes, man, is Jenessa on an assignment?" He hadn't meant to say it so loud that all the patrons in The Sweet Spot would take notice, but he had to know.

"Not that I know of," Charles said. "As a matter of fact, I've been trying to call her and all I get is voicemail. She had an appointment with the Grovers—"

"The Grovers?" Ramey questioned.

"Oh, you know, Marge and Ray Grover, who own the feed store on Broad Street. They've been married sixty years and their kids are throwing them a big vow-renewal ceremony at the Community Church next weekend. Jenessa was supposed to meet with them this afternoon, but she never showed up."

"That's not like her," Michael muttered.

"Now I am worried," Ramey added.

Logan, who had been sitting with Josie and Jake at a table in the corner, stepped into the growing circle of concern. "What's happening?"

"Jenessa's missing," Ramey declared.

"Well, we don't know that for sure." Why was he joining in? The last thing Michael wanted was for Logan to play the hero and find her.

"Michael?" Josie and Jake joined the crowd. "What's going on?"

He was slightly taken aback by their sudden presence in the group, surprised he hadn't noticed them sitting in the corner during his initial scan of the place, his focus concentrating on locating Jenessa.

"Jenessa's gone missing," Logan said, "and we need to find her, make sure she's all right."

Josie breathed a laugh. "I heard you guys say she's only been gone a couple of hours. What's the big deal?"

Instantly, Logan and Michael both turned and scowled at her.

"What?" she asked innocently.

"Daddy?" The little boy's voice carried a note of concern.

Michael lifted his son into his arms. "Nothing to worry about, Jake." He turned to Josie and set their son down in front of her. "Take him home and wait for me. We have to talk."

"We came in Logan's car, after we went to the zoo together," Josie explained, like she was rubbing in his face the fact that she and Jake had been out having fun with Logan all day.

Her dig was not lost on him. Logan was becoming too much a part of his son's life and he didn't like it one bit. But he'd have to deal with that later. Right now he had to concentrate on finding Jenessa.

"Here." Logan handed Josie his keys. "Take the boy home. I'll get my car later."

"Why don't you go with them?" Michael urged.

"I'm sticking with you, Baxter," Logan shot back. "I want to help find our girl."

Our girl? Michael's jaw tensed at the words, feeling a similar tightening around his eyes.

Keep your cool, Baxter.

"No, Logan, I can handle it," Michael ground out, a prickly heat climbing up his neck. "Besides, it's probably nothing."

"Yeah right." Logan rolled his eyes, quirking one side of his mouth. "You wouldn't have that seriously worried look in your eyes if it was nothing." Logan's blue eyes turned steely as they narrowed. "I won't just sit by when I can help."

"I said I've got it," Michael said through clenched teeth.

"Why don't both of you idiots just go find her?" Ramey shouted.

All heads in the café snapped in her direction, including Logan's and Michael's, seeing the usually bubbly Ramey wearing a rare, irritated scowl.

In the next moment, Logan's gaze met Michael's, as if to challenge his directive.

Michael's glare did not break until Logan turned away and put a hand on Charles's shoulder. "What else was Jenessa working on?"

"Well, the Daphne Stone murder case, of course."

"Anything specific she might have mentioned?"

Michael asked, not about to let Logan control the situation.

A light sparked in Charles's eyes. "Funny thing, I think she was researching my son's teacher, Mr. Makovsky. David Makovsky."

"Makovsky?" Logan asked, his brows wrinkling at the question.

Michael rubbed his chin. "Why does that name sound so familiar?"

"She said it was the same last name as a woman who had died in a bombing about fifteen years ago," Charles explained. "But I didn't know what she was talking about."

Suzanne Tremont's case.

"I should go pay a visit to this Makovsky guy," Michael said, turning to Charles. "You said he's Charlie's teacher. Do you know where he lives?"

"Somewhere near Crane Park."

"Where exactly?" Logan demanded.

"I don't know the address, but I can show you. I had to drop off some paperwork last week. He wanted to apply to be a Boy Scout troop leader for some of the boys in his class. He seemed like a real nice fellow."

"Oh, Charles," Ramey uttered with a shake of her head, "you're too trusting. If that was true, why would Jenessa be doing research on him?"

"She never said," Charles replied with a shrug. "Guess I should have asked."

She wouldn't say—at least until she knew enough. She must have thought he was somehow connected to the woman who died in the bombing. Had this whole case actually been about Suzanne Tremont's death—not

Daphne Stone's?

Michael took Charles by the arm and walked him to the door. "Show us where this Makovsky guy lives."

As the three men headed toward Crane Park, Michael checked in with Detective Provenza.

"Are you still on that *errand*?" Provenza inquired.

Errand? Oh right, trying to talk to Jenessa.

"I was," Michael replied, "but I was speaking with Charles McAllister—"

"The newspaper fella?"

"That's right. He said something that made me wonder if we're looking at the Daphne Stone murder case all wrong. It might have been about Suzanne Tremont instead."

"You think the killer was after her as Suzanne Tremont?" Provenza asked.

"It's looking that way," Michael replied. "But we need to talk to Drew Stone. Any luck locating him?"

"Not yet, so I called in a favor and had a friend of mine at the state police ping the GPS in his phone."

"Did they find him?"

"They said his last location was on Elm Street. It hasn't moved in a while. He must be visiting someone there," Provenza said. "Where are you, Baxter?"

"I'm running down a new lead."

"What kind of new lead?"

"I'm on my way to check out a David Makovsky, who might be involved in Dr. Stone's murder. Jenessa was doing a background check on him, but no one has seen her in a couple of hours. Could you get your friend to ping her phone too?"

"I'm not supposed to, especially if it has to do with your personal matters."

"It's important, George. Besides, I think it has to do with the case."

"I'll try. He owes me another favor—or three." Provenza gave a breathy chuckle as he hung up.

"Turn at the next corner," Charles said as they drove past the park.

Michael looked up at the street sign. It read Elm Street—just what Provenza had said was Drew's last known location. Did Drew know someone else on Elm Street, or was he involved somehow with David Makovsky?

"That's the house," Charles exclaimed, pointing to an old white bungalow.

Michael pulled over to the curb and stopped behind a silver SUV. There was a Whitfield College staff parking sticker on it. Could it be Drew Stone's? Had he and David met somehow? Both wanting to get rid of the same woman, only for different reasons?

Had Jenessa figured it out and done something stupid, something that put her life in danger?

"What's the plan?" Logan asked as he sat in the passenger seat of Michael's unmarked police car.

"You two stay in the car," Michael said. "I'll go knock on the door and see what I can find out."

"That's fine," Charles replied from the back seat.

"I'm coming with you," Logan said. "If something hinky is going on in that house, you'll need backup."

Michael cut him a sideways glare. "Stop trying to play the hero, Logan. You're not a cop." He hadn't wanted Logan to come along at all, but he felt pressed into it. Now he'd have to deal with the overly eager civilian since he had no one else at the moment.

Although Michael should call his partner and wait for backup, he didn't want to look like a fool if it turned out to be nothing. For all they knew, Jenessa could have left her car at The Sweet Spot and walked a couple of blocks to the movie theater to watch the latest flick, accidentally spacing her appointment with the Grovers—it was Saturday after all.

And it was also entirely possible that this David Makovsky was just what he appeared to be—a good teacher who wanted to volunteer his time to be a Boy Scout leader, a nice guy who just happened to have the same last name as the woman who died in the bombing. Certainly there are other people in the country with that name, no?

If he radioed his partner for backup and nothing illegal was going on at this house, Provenza would ride him like a trick pony and never let him forget it, not to mention the captain.

"I'll go and knock on the front door," Logan offered, scanning the property, "see if this Makovsky guy comes to answer it. I can ask him a few friendly questions, like I'm selling life insurance or something, and keep him busy while you go around back and check things out, Baxter."

Maybe he should let Logan help him, at least enough to discover if something was really wrong. It wasn't officially police business yet. What could it hurt to let him talk to the man at the front door? He hoped he wasn't making a big mistake.

"All right, Logan, as long as you don't go inside." Michael gave Logan's casual attire a once over. "Better make that alarm systems you're selling."

CHAPTER 32

MICHAEL AND LOGAN CLIMBED OUT OF the car and gingerly closed the doors. While Logan approached the front of the house, Michael crept down the empty driveway. The sound of Logan's enthusiastic knocking reverberated through the neighborhood. Michael hoped the noise covered his footfalls.

After a few seconds, the loud hammering on the door repeated.

Michael peeked in the windows as he skirted the perimeter of the house. No one appeared to be home.

"Hello?" Logan's voice boomed from the front of the house.

Michael moved to the rear door. He tried the knob—it was unlocked. He opened it and slipped inside. With his hand on his gun, he crept from room to room, wondering what he would say if he found someone sleeping in one of the bedrooms, or worse yet, otherwise occupied in the bathroom.

Each room was vacant, the house eerily silent—until he heard a thumping sound. Where was it coming from? It seemed to be emanating from below his feet. The thumping continued, then a crash.

He frantically searched the house for an entrance to the basement and found a door at the rear of the kitchen. It was locked.

He pounded on the door. "Anyone there?"

In return, a muffled response came, colored with desperation.

Michael kicked the door open and descended the steps into the darkness, feeling around all the way down for a light switch. Finding one, he flicked the light on, a single bare bulb glared from the ceiling.

"Help me," the man cried out weakly, bound to a chair laying on its side on the cement floor.

Michael rushed to his aid. "Mr. Stone?"

"Yeah," he gasped.

Michael looked around. "Are you alone down here?"

"He took her," Drew groaned as Michael worked at the ropes.

"Took who?" Michael asked, fearing what he already knew.

"The girl," Drew huffed, as if his strength was drained.

Michael pulled an army knife from his pocket and began cutting the ropes. "What happened?"

With effort, Drew explained the phone call about his dog and how he entered the house to pick her up. "I stepped into the living room and that's the last thing I remember until I woke up down here, tied to that chair. The girl was tied up too."

"You keep saying *the girl*. What girl?"

"That reporter that's been sniffing around my wife's murder."

"Baxter!" Logan's voice roared down the stairs. "You okay?"

"We'll be right up."

"We? So you've got her?"

~*~

Michael helped Drew Stone up the steep stairs and passed him off to Logan, who was waiting at the top. "Help him to the living room. I've got to radio for help."

"But where's Jenessa?" Logan asked as he steadied the man.

Michael pulled out his radio, about to make the call. He paused, his gaze rose to meet Logan's. "She's not here."

Logan's nostrils flared, the look in his eyes intense as he pulled Drew's arm up and slid his own around the man's waist. "We've got to find her."

"I know that," Michael snapped back.

"So, where do we go from here?"

Michael motioned toward the living room. "To the couch."

Logan pitched Michael an angry scowl, almost dragging Drew to a sofa in the living room. "That's not what I meant and you know it."

"What do you want me to say?" Michael

manipulated the radio. "I have no idea where he could have taken her." He called dispatch for an ambulance and to send a couple of officers, before asking to be patched through to Provenza.

"What's up?" Provenza asked when he came on the line.

"Any luck tracking Jenessa's phone?" Michael held his breath, his nerves pulsating as he waited for a response.

"Funny, it showed her phone at the same location as Drew Stone's last whereabouts."

That's what he was afraid of. "You know that lead I told you about, well it just got a lot more significant."

"What's going on?" Provenza's tone went from interested to deadly serious.

Michael explained the situation as briefly as he could. "The bottom line is it looks like David Makovsky has abducted Jenessa."

"Don't worry, Baxter. I'll have an APB dispatched to all patrolmen and every other law enforcement agency in the state."

"They haven't been gone long, so they should still be in the valley." At least, that's what Michael hoped. With his head injury Drew had no idea how long ago Makovsky had taken her, but he had said it only seemed like a short time ago to him.

"I'm looking up Makovsky's vehicle now on the DMV records." Provenza paused as the sound of clicking keyboard keys drifted through the radio. "Got it. Dark green Mazda, two thousand model. I'll have the description and license number pushed out to everyone, then I'm coming out there."

"Five five six Elm Street," Michael said into the radio.

"Keep your chin up, Baxter. Jenessa is a strong lady—and smart too. Maybe she left us a clue."

~*~

It was dark and stuffy as Jenessa rattled around in the small trunk of David Makovsky's sedan. How was she going to get out, escape from her captor?

Think, Jenessa.

She listened to the road noises. She had pitched from side to side as the car stopped and started, sliding into the wheel well every time it turned, which had been a few times since leaving the house.

The car bounced uncomfortably with an uneven shudder. Were they crossing the railroad tracks?

They made a couple more turns, causing her stomach to lurch from the motion. After what seemed like a few more minutes, the car felt like it was beginning to climb at a slight incline. Was it the on-ramp to the freeway?

Like electrified tendrils spreading across her chest, fear gripped her like none she'd ever known. The farther they got away from Hidden Valley, the less likely she would ever be found. If it was David Makovsky's intention to kill her and hide her body in some remote place, she may never be found. She prayed he wasn't that evil.

Would he need to stop for gas? Was he meeting up with his accomplice? Was it Ashley, perhaps, or someone else? What did he do with Drew?

She blew out a deep breath, trying to relax enough to think clearly. Maybe she was simply a hostage, insurance that he could make a clean get away—then he would set her free. He had no score to settle with her, she had just been in the wrong place at the wrong time.

No matter what his intentions, she couldn't just lay there passively and do nothing—but what could she do? *Think!*

Was there a trunk release? She felt around, but nothing. The car must have been too old.

The taillights?

She'd heard of it in a self-defense class. Maybe it would work.

The left rear taillight was at her feet. With all her might, she began to kick against it, counting on the highway road noise to cover the sound. When Makovsky had shoved her into the trunk, darkness was already beginning to fall. Hopefully, if she could kick out the light, maybe a highway patrolman would notice the car had a taillight out and pull him over. If she could manage that, she'd kick at the trunk like her life depended on it—maybe it did.

After enduring a continuous firing of hard kicks with the heel of her boot, the taillight assembly began coming apart. She continued to strike at it until a hole opened up where the taillight had been.

Would a broken taillight be enough to save her? She couldn't count on it—she needed to do something more.

Though the trunk was small and cramped, she began to twist and turn her body, scooting around until her head was now near the broken opening. As she jammed her hand through the hole, it scraped on the jagged remains of the taillight. The sharp pain would not deter her. She waved her bloody hand around, hoping there were cars behind them that would notice.

Had anyone seen her hand in the evening dusk? Had they called 911? How long might it take a highway patrolman to respond?

She didn't have the luxury of time, or of assuming anyone had seen her small hand bouncing around. How could she make it more obvious? Draw more attention?

A crazy idea came to her. Though the compactness of the trunk hampered her movement, she managed to get her leopard-print bra unhooked. She worked the straps down around her arms and pulled it out from under her dark blouse.

She stuck the bra through the hole, again slicing more gashes into her hand with the shards still protruding around the opening. Blood dripped onto her bra. Fighting through the pain, she held onto it, letting it flap in the breeze. Surely someone would notice something was wrong, that there was a person attached to that bloody hand sticking out of the back of this car.

The minutes seemed to fly by, the car still careening down the highway. The pain no longer mattered and she waved the bra for all she was worth, her wrist continuing to bang against the jagged remains of the taillight.

CHAPTER 33

"TELL ME YOU'VE FOUND JENESSA," Ramey pleaded as she stomped toward Michael, standing in David Makovsky's driveway in the glow of a gathering of headlights.

"What are you doing here?" Michael asked.

"And who let you through?" Provenza questioned, his head jerking around in the direction of a couple of officers standing on the sidewalk talking.

"Obviously you haven't." Ramey grunted, planted her feet, and fisted her hands on her hips, with Charles and Logan at her side. "Charles called me to come pick him up." Her gaze bounced around the property, then slid back to rest on Michael. "I want to know what's being done to find her."

"We don't have time to fill you in." Provenza motioned toward the street. "You people need to get back behind the police cars."

"Ramey, please," Michael said, understanding her concern for Jenessa, "go home. I'll let you know when we find her."

Rather than retreat, Logan stepped closer. "I'm here to help, Baxter, you know that. I can't just sit here and do nothing when Jenessa's out there needing our help. You tell me what to do and I'll do it."

A sarcastic comeback was way too easy, and this was not the time for it.

"There's nothing you can do, except get in our way," Provenza barked.

Thank you, George.

A female voice came over Michael's police radio. A car matching the description was reported as suspicious by a 911 caller on Highway 99, about fifteen miles north of Hidden Valley.

Michael lifted his radio to his mouth. "Provenza and Baxter will be there in ten."

The detectives rushed to their car.

"I'm begging you guys, let me come with you," Logan hollered after them, approaching their car with long strides.

"It's against policy," Michael yelled back, but Logan was stalking toward them anyway.

"I happen to be good friends with the police chief, you know," Logan said as he caught up to Michael climbing into the car. "I'm sure he'll make an exception."

Michael paused and groaned inwardly. He lifted his brow to his senior partner, asking his permission, hoping he'd say no and the onus would be on Provenza.

"All right," his partner growled, "we don't have time to argue. But if you get hurt, that's on you."

"Deal." Logan hopped into the back seat.

The three men raced to the location, Michael at the wheel, with lights on and siren blaring.

"If that man laid a hand on her, I'll k— " Logan started to say from the back seat.

"You'll do what?" Provenza asked, pitching a sardonic look over his shoulder. "You'd better watch what you say around cops, boy, friend of the police chief or not."

Michael peered up into his rearview mirror and caught Logan's eye.

"Can't this thing go any faster?" Logan demanded.

"No one wants to get there any faster than I do," Michael replied, taking a quick glance at the speedometer. "I'm already doing ninety." His heart was hammering with anticipation—he didn't need Logan provoking him too.

~*~

Makovsky's car continued to fly down the highway, Jenessa furiously waving her bloody bra. In the distance she heard something. Was it the wail of sirens? The sound was getting closer, louder. Could it be?

The car began to slow, then the crunching of the tires on gravel crackled from below before the vehicle came to an abrupt stop, sending her rolling toward the back seat. There were voices, men talking, then shouting, but she couldn't make out what was being said.

No matter, this was her chance—maybe her only one.

She yanked her hand inside, but the bra snagged on the broken taillight. Out of pure instinct, she began to kick at the inside of the fenders and pound on the trunk lid above her, screaming for help. At the unmistakable sound of guns being drawn and cocked, she froze for a moment. Dare she hope?

With every ounce of strength left in her, she continued to kick and scream. The trunk lid popped open and bright light flooded in. Two tall highway patrolmen stood smiling over her, backlit by a show of lights that she could only assume were headlights. The tiny bulb in the lid of the trunk was all that illuminated their faces.

"You're safe now," one of them said.

"Are you okay, miss?" the other asked, extending his hand down to help her out as yet another siren wailed loudly in the background and a set of tires screeched to a sudden stop nearby.

Jenessa pushed mangled strands of hair off her face before reaching up to take the officer's hand, but the second she grabbed it and he tightened his grip around hers, pain shot through her bloody hand and she dropped back down.

"Excuse me, fellas," she heard Michael say, his voice could not have been more welcome. "I'm Detective Baxter."

The two towering patrolmen parted and Michael stepped in and scooped her out of the trunk.

Relief washed over her. She had never been so glad to see anyone in her life. Her heart rate began to calm as he cradled her in his arms, tears rolling down her cheeks.

"I was scared to death."

"You're safe now." He smiled down at her and pressed his lips to her forehead.

One of the patrolmen bent down and picked something up off the asphalt. He held it out to her. "Is this baby yours?"

Jenessa felt heat bloom on her cheeks. She tried to snag the bra out of his hand but he pulled it back. Michael's eyes rounded in curiosity.

"Sorry, but we'll need to bag it and tag it as evidence, eh Detective?" the patrolman said.

"What the—" came another familiar voice, just over Michael's shoulder.

"Logan?" she gasped. What was he doing there?

Then Provenza's head popped up too. "Glad to see you're okay."

"Are you really okay?" Logan asked, his voice filled with concern, his eyes with familiar affection.

Not a moment too soon an ambulance rolled up, lights flashing, its siren winding down.

"Your ride is here." Michael spun away from Logan and the circle of men, carrying her off to it. "I thought I'd lost you."

She gazed up into his soft brown eyes, alluring pools of dark chocolate, filled with so much emotion they glistened. She put a hand to his cheek and urged his face down to hers.

He needed no further encouragement and he kissed her tenderly. "I love you, you know."

"I know." She smiled up at him, then snuggled against his chest.

"I don't know what I'd do if I had lost you." He set

her on the back step of the ambulance as soon as the EMTs opened the doors. "Check her out, would you?"

"A few Band-Aids on my hand and I'll be good as new."

One of the paramedics began cleaning the blood from her hand to check the wounds.

"I'll ride with you to the hospital," Michael told Jenessa as the EMTs attended to her.

"I don't need to go to the hospital," she argued, wanting to dig further into the story of what David Makovsky had done and why, before too much time passed. "Tell him, guys," she said to the paramedics, hoping they would back her up.

One of the EMTs cradled her injured hand. "A couple of those cuts look fairly deep. I'll tape them, but they might need stitches," he said, "and you have a pretty good knot on the side of your head. You might want to have a doctor look at it to make sure you don't have a concussion."

She lifted her eyes to Michael. "But we've got to find Ashley Brandon."

"Daphne's assistant?"

"David Makovsky's stepdaughter, I believe."

"We're going to the hospital first," he ordered the paramedics, giving them a hand motion that told them to head out. "Put a rush on it."

Michael climbed into the ambulance and took Jenessa's good hand to help her to her feet. "We can talk on the way."

"Have it your way." Once inside the ambulance, she settled onto the gurney and continued to hold Michael's hand as he perched on the side bench. She wasn't happy, but it was clear Michael had already made up his mind.

As the ambulance siren blared and they sped toward town, pent-up anxiety vibrated through her nervous system. Making a stop at the hospital was going to take too much time. One of the killers could be getting away while she was receiving attention from the ER doctors that she was sure she didn't need.

"Now, tell me what you found out," Michael said.

Jenessa relayed to him what Drew Stone had told her while they were locked in the basement together. She was pretty sure David Makovsky was the one who plotted Suzanne Tremont's murder in retaliation for his wife's death in the bombing.

"How would he have had access to Daphne's bottle of juice?" Michael asked.

"That's where Ashley comes in."

"But why now? It's been fifteen years."

"That's why it's important to find Ashley." Jenessa gave his hand a squeeze for emphasis. "We've got a lot of questions for that girl."

Michael chuckled. "Even after what you've been through, you're ever the reporter."

"I can't help it."

"No, it was a compliment." He kissed the back of her hand.

"Listen, Michael. You need to get a look at Makovsky's phone records, find out if he received a call from, or made a call to, Ashley this morning, around eleven o'clock." Jenessa explained what Drew had said about the suspicious telephone conversation he had overheard.

Michael phoned Detective Provenza, putting it on

speaker, and filled him in on what Jenessa had told him. "We'll need to get a warrant to search Makovsky's records."

"I don't think we'll have any trouble getting a judge to sign it since we've just arrested the man for kidnapping and suspicion of murder," Provenza replied. "I have his phone right here with his belongings."

"Hey, can you have a car waiting for me at the hospital?"

"I'll take care of it," Provenza assured him.

"Thanks, Boss."

In the emergency room, Jenessa received a few stitches in her hand and the doctor determined she had suffered a mild concussion, ordering Michael to keep an eye on her for the next twelve hours.

Jenessa grinned at Michael. "Guess you're stuck with me."

By the time Jenessa and Michael walked out of the emergency room, Detective Provenza had procured the court order and perused the suspect's phone records. "Looks like Makovsky did receive a call about eleven o'clock, but it was from a burner phone—untraceable."

"What's that number?" Michael asked as they paused inside of the hospital's vestibule. Covering the phone with one hand, he whispered to Jenessa, "You got something to write on?"

She nodded and grabbed the pen from his breast pocket. "What is it?"

Provenza read off the number and Michael repeated it to her. Jenessa wrote the number on the palm of her hand.

Michael threw her a curious frown.

"Sorry, no paper," she shrugged as she whispered back.

"And I'll need Ashley Brandon's address," Michael said to his partner. "It should be in the file from our interview on the first day of the investigation."

Jenessa raised her forearm, poised to write the address.

"One three six five Magnolia Street, apartment three." Michael's gaze traveled along Jenessa's arm as she wrote, and an incredulous grin spread across his lips. "Got it."

"What?" she asked innocently.

"Thanks for the info, Boss. We'll keep in touch." He clicked his phone off and slipped it in his jacket pocket.

When they exited the hospital, Officer Luke was leaning on an unmarked police car, dangling keys from one of his fingers.

"Thanks, Cuz," Michael said, grabbing the keys from him. "Now," he said, turning to Jenessa, "let's get moving and hope she's still there."

"You're welcome," Luke called out as Michael and Jenessa climbed into the car.

As they approached Ashley's address, up ahead was a yellow cab parked at the curb, its lights on, and judging by the small trail of vapor rising from its tail pipe and disappearing into the cool night air, the motor was still running. Michael pulled to the curb a couple of car lengths behind the taxi and watched.

Ashley walked to the cab, dragging a large black suitcase with wheels and lugging a bulging carry-on bag over her shoulder, which she dropped to the ground when she reached the cab.

Jenessa gasped. "She's making a run for it." She started for the door handle.

"Stop." Michael put his hand out in front of her chest to hold her back. "Let's not spook her. Let me approach first and talk to her, then you can casually stroll by and do your thing."

She nodded her agreement, her gaze still on the suspect, adding a shooing gesture with her hand, telling him to go.

"I'm going, I'm going," he retorted.

"I'll sneak around to the sidewalk as soon as you're gone."

The cab driver opened the trunk and lifted the hefty piece of luggage, appearing to struggle a little as he wrestled it into the trunk. By the time he reached for her carry-on bag, Michael had stepped beside Ashley.

"Going somewhere, Miss Brandon?"

"Oh!" She startled. "You scared me." She blew out a breath, her eyes nervously dancing around. "Uh, yes, I'm going home."

"Home?"

"Where my family is." She seemed to recover quickly. "You may have heard, my boss died, so I'm out of a job."

"Your family?" he asked coyly, rubbing his chin. "I'd heard your mother is deceased and your dad lives here in Hidden Valley."

"Uh, well…" Ashley's gaze moved toward the sound of footsteps approaching.

"Hello, Ashley, Detective Baxter," Jenessa said, planting herself beside Michael, trying to act as if she had just happened upon them as she was out for a walk. "Enjoying the night air?"

Ashley's eyes lifted skyward for a moment. "Well...sure, we were just chatting." Ashley appeared a bit flustered by Jenessa's unexpected presence.

A sizable diamond solitaire hung from a fine silver chain. It was draped around Ashley's neck, framed by the collar of her blouse. "Oh wow," Jenessa exclaimed, "that's a beautiful necklace you're wearing."

Ashley's hand flew over the dazzling stone as if she was instinctively trying to hide it. "It's not real." Her gaze dropped briefly to the ground, then with a faint smile she lifted her eyes nervously back to Jenessa. "It's one of those cubic zirconium ones."

"It sure fooled me." Jenessa cast Michael a quick glance. Had he also realized it was likely Daphne's missing necklace? She returned her gaze to meet Ashley's, giving her a light pat on the arm. "It's stunning all the same."

"Thank you." Ashley's expression brightened at the compliment, then shifted to concern as she noticed the white gauze bandages wrapped around Jenessa's hand. Her gaze lifted as Jenessa pushed her hair back from her face, exposing a nasty black and blue bruise along the side of Jenessa's temple. "Are you okay, Miss Jones?"

"As a matter of fact—" she began to say, interrupted by the cab driver clearing his throat loudly as he stood beside his car, apparently wanting to get going.

"I'd love to stay and hear all about it—really," she pitched a quick glance at the man, "but I have a bus to catch, so I need to run. It was nice chatting—"

"A bus to catch?" Jenessa interrupted, acting

surprised. "Where you going?"

Before Ashley could speak, Michael answered for her. "I'm afraid she won't be going anywhere."

Ashley's eyebrows wrinkled in surprise. "Why not?"

The young woman's voice sounded innocent enough, but was it simply an act?

As Michael kept the conversation going, explaining how there were new developments in the Daphne Stone case and he needed to take her in for questioning, Jenessa slyly reached into his pocket and pulled his phone out. She punched a series of numbers into it.

A phone began to ring, the tone seeming to come from Ashley's purse. She dug around in her handbag and pulled out a small inexpensive-looking black phone and checked it. "I don't recognize the number. They'll just have to leave me a message."

Jenessa surreptitiously raised the palm of her hand to Michael, exposing what she had previously penned. "The number," she whispered.

A glint of recognition flashed through Michael's eyes. He grabbed hold of the unwitting young woman by the wrist. "I have a message for you."

With a cock of her head, Ashley frowned curiously.

"Ashley Brandon, you are under arrest for the murder of Dr. Daphne Stone."

CHAPTER 34

"UNDER ARREST?" Ashley gasped, her eyes wide. "Detective, you're making a terrible mistake."

"You have the right to remain silent," Michael began, then read her the rest of her rights as he cuffed her hands behind her back.

"I'm telling you," Ashley pleaded, "you have the wrong person. I had nothing to do with Dr. Stone's death."

Michael took Ashley by the arm and began to walk her to his car. "How about Suzanne Tremont's death?"

"Who?" Ashley asked innocently.

"Oh, girl, you are so busted," Jenessa said. "You might as well come clean. They already have your dad in custody."

Ashley's eyes narrowed. "Stepdad," she corrected.

~*~

After getting Ashley Brandon booked and a lawyer summoned to confer with her, Michael took Jenessa to get a cup of coffee. They waited in his office for the attorney to show up and meet with her client. Detective Provenza promised to let them know when Michael was needed.

In time, he and Jenessa entered the observation room. Provenza was standing at the two-way mirror, arms crossed, watching Ashley Brandon talk with her court-appointed attorney. He glanced over at her and his partner when they came in. With a pen and pad from Michael's office, Jenessa moved beside Detective Provenza. "Hello, Miss Jones. Good to see you're okay, but you shouldn't be in here."

Jenessa flashed him an impish grin. "Doctor's orders."

Provenza's brows lowered. "How's that?"

"The ER doc said I have a mild concussion and Michael has to keep constant watch over me for the next twelve hours."

"That's what he said," Michael said with a nod.

"Hmm." Provenza pinched his lips together. "You have been through quite an ordeal, I'll give you that."

"Hardest thing I've ever had to do."

"Good thing you're tough," Provenza said.

"And smart," Michael added, flashing her a proud grin. "Flagged down help with her bra."

"Oh really," Provenza chuckled. "I wondered why that thing was bagged and tagged."

"Just doing my job, boys," she replied with a little

smirk, crossing her arms protectively over her chest, uncomfortable with still being braless "So tell me," she pressed on to shift the focus in another direction, "why did Ashley and her stepfather wait fifteen years to get revenge on Suzanne Tremont?"

"According to David Makovsky—who is singing like a canary, by the way, once we told him that we had Ashley and she's agreed to testify against him—they didn't know where the woman was," Provenza replied. "And they still wouldn't have known, except that last year Dr. Stone gave a psychology seminar at Ashley's college."

"Ashley had already agreed to testify?" she asked.

"Well, no," Provenza muttered, "but it was just a matter of time, and Makovsky didn't need to know that."

"I see," Jenessa said, "just one of your interrogation tactics."

"Exactly."

"Go on," Jenessa urged.

"Ashley happened to see the unusual bowtie-shaped birthmark at the base of Dr. Stone's neck," Provenza continued. "Makovsky had talked about it over the years, so when Ashley saw it on Dr. Stone, she started researching her online, checking old photos of Suzanne against recent ones of Dr. Stone."

"That must be when they figured out Daphne was Suzanne," Michael remarked.

"Good point," Jenessa agreed, scribbling furiously on her notepad. "So that's when they decided to kill her?"

Provenza's gaze dropped briefly to her pad. "Whoa," he said, waving a hand at her. "This is an ongoing investigation. You can't be printing any of this."

"I need to get all the facts straight for my story."

"Besides, Boss, this is pretty much a done deal," Michael injected. "Ms. Brandon's already made a deal with the DA, right?"

Jenessa jumped right on that tidbit of information. "What kind of deal?"

"All right," Provenza relented. "But I don't want to see anything that says you got your information from anyone in the police department."

Jenessa bobbed her head at him. "Absolutely."

"She has agreed to testify against Makovsky in exchange for a lighter sentence." Provenza glanced toward the mirror, where the two women continued to converse. "She said she told her stepdad about what she'd found, and he was the one who hatched the plan and pushed her to help him."

"How?" Jenessa asked.

"She'd heard him rant against Suzanne Tremont since she was a kid," Provenza said, "so he convinced her it was time they made her pay for what she did to her mother."

Jenessa paused from her note taking. "What about kidnapping Drew Stone? And me?"

"According to Ashley," Provenza said, "that wasn't part of the plan. They had to improvise because Mr. Stone had overheard her talking about what they'd done, and then you showed up, snooping around his house."

"Well, yes, I was snooping around...for my story."

"See there," Provenza poked his index finger at her, "if you hadn't been sticking your nose where it didn't belong...well, you know the rest."

"That's what investigative reporters do, George," she smiled, "we investigate—same as you."

"Well," Provenza retorted, "not exactly the same."

"What's going to happen to Drew Stone?" she asked.

Provenza rubbed a hand over his jaw. "He's at the hospital at the moment, with a patrolman posted outside his room. Last I heard, his attorney was there with him."

"I can't even imagine what it was like for him," she replied, "knowing the woman you loved was going to die soon and was asking you to put an end to her suffering."

"Painful as it was, it's still against the law," Michael said with a rawness in his voice that told her he understood.

"So why didn't Makovsky just leave me tied up with Drew?"

"From what Ms. Brandon gave us," Provenza said, "it was because when he went back to grab some stuff and check on you two, you had gotten yourself untied. He was afraid you'd do it again and they wouldn't have time to get far enough away before you alerted the police. He panicked and took you to buy more time."

"So they were in communication? Brandon and Makovsky?" Michael asked.

"Yes, by cell phone," Provenza replied.

Michael draped an arm around Jenessa's shoulders. "Was he planning to kill her?"

"She didn't think so," Provenza glanced toward the two-way mirror, "but you never know when these things can go sideways."

Jenessa grinned at the elder detective. "Then it's a good thing I was wearing my lucky leopard bra, George."

~*~

Michael pushed open the gate that led to his parents' backyard, letting Jake and Jenessa go through first. He had been there earlier in the day, helping his folks get the place ready for the party, while Josie kept Jake otherwise occupied.

When Michael and Jake were leaving their house, Josie was still packing up her belongings. She and Michael had had a serious conversation when he had gotten home the night before. Fortunately, Jake had been fast asleep.

Michael had made it clear she could no longer stay at his house, even if it meant he had to foot the bill for her to stay in a hotel temporarily, until she decided where to go from there. Though she'd begged him to let her stay, reminding him she was out of money with no immediate prospects for work, he told her she still had to go.

"If you're that broke," he'd said, "maybe you should look for a job in Hidden Valley."

That suggestion did not elicit a positive response, only a seething scowl.

Josie had tried to use their son as a ploy to tug at Michael's heartstrings. "Surely you would never separate Jake from his mother," she'd cried.

He'd recalled Provenza's sage advice to *give her the boot*.

"You're welcome to see Jake as often as you like," he'd shot back. After all, she was his mother and he would never deprive his son of seeing her. "But you're not going to live here and we're not going to be getting back together."

When using Jake didn't work, she'd attempted romantic advances, but Michael fended them off with a renewed resolve. He'd made sure it was abundantly clear that he was not changing his mind.

Josie had pouted and sulked for the rest of the evening. In the morning, she'd moped around the house, paying little attention to her son.

Michael got Jake ready for the party, making sure he had his swimsuit, towel, and a change of clothes.

"Josie, we're leaving," Michael had told her. "Need a ride?"

"No, go on without me. I called Logan."

And that's how she'd decided it was going to be. Not that Michael had been surprised.

~*~

"Thank you for inviting me to Jake's party," Jenessa said to Michael's mom. She had brought a brightly wrapped birthday gift for him.

"My pleasure, honey." She gave Jenessa a sideways hug. "Here, let me take that from you."

"Can I help you with anything?" Jenessa offered.

Michael's mom smiled and shook her head. "I think we've got it all under control. You just go and enjoy yourself, dear." She plucked the present from Jenessa's hands and headed for the gift table to add it to Jake's growing bounty.

The Indian summer had stretched into the end of September and graced the afternoon with warm temperatures and a cloudless blue sky. The water in the swimming pool sparkled in the bright sunlight, looking cool and inviting.

Several bouquets of helium balloons in various vibrant colors were strategically placed around the yard, and streamers cascaded from beam to beam in the pergola that shaded the expansive patio. The back of the charming, white single-story house had a pair of french doors set off by three wide, red-brick steps down to the concrete patio.

Soon the yard was overrun with excited children and their parents, squeals of delight and the sound of splashing water filling the air. Michael's dad manned the gas grill under one end of the pergola and a long table was set up beside it, dressed in a Teenage Mutant Ninja Turtles tablecloth with matching paper plates and cups.

Hamburger and hotdog buns were laid out, as well as an abundance of condiments and full-to-the-brim bowls of chips and dips. The crowning glory was the huge platter of cupcakes Ramey had brought, each with a fondant cut-out of one of the turtle characters on top of the dark green frosting, covered with a drizzle of bright green sugary slime.

Ramey and Charles McAllister stood beneath a neatly trimmed tree near the edge of the patio, watching his son bounce a couple of times on the diving board before going into the pool, headfirst.

With a Ninja Turtles paper cup full of fruity punch in one hand, Jenessa made her way over to talk to them.

"I'd give it a nine-point-seven."

"Beg your pardon?" Charles asked, drawing his gaze away from his son.

"Charlie's dive," Jenessa replied to her boss.

"Oh yeah." Charles chuckled.

"Hello, Jenessa." Ramey gave her friend a quick squeeze.

"He's pretty good," Jenessa said, glancing in Charlie's direction. "Did you teach him that?"

"No," Charles said, "he took swim lessons the last few summers."

"I'm going to go and get some punch," Ramey said. "You want any, Charles?"

"I'll go and get it," Charles offered.

"No, you stay and chat with Jenessa. I'll be right back." She spun away and was off.

With Ramey gone, this was her chance to probe Charles about his son. "That boy of yours is going to be a heartbreaker," Jenessa said, then took a small sip of punch.

"What do you mean?"

"He's a good-looking young man. Did he get that blond hair from his mother?"

"No, Calista had dark hair."

Jenessa eyed Charles's hair, which was a medium brown. "So where did the blond hair come from?" *Logan maybe?* "The milk man?" She laughed.

"What?" Charles asked before realizing she was joking. "No."

"Was Charlie adopted?" *There, she had said it.*

"Adopted? What would make you ask that?"

319

"Oh, I don't know," she lied. "I'm gathering information for an article I've been thinking of doing on adopted kids and their need to connect with their birth parents."

"Sounds interesting," he said, his gaze floating back to the swimming pool. "But no, Charlie was not adopted."

"Sorry, I just wondered because his hair is so light compared to yours and he has green eyes. Yours are brown."

"My hair was light as a child too, turned dark in my teens," Charles said, his gaze sliding back to Jenessa. "My mother has green eyes. That could be where he got them."

Ramey returned with a cup of punch in each hand. "Charles?" She handed one to him. "What were you two talking about?"

"Jenessa thinks Charlie was adopted," Charles said with a chuckle.

Ramey shot Jenessa a look of surprise at her boldness. "What did you tell her?"

"That he's not, of course."

"Hey, look who's here," Ramey said, nodding in the direction of the gate. "There's Logan and Josie."

Jenessa turned to see. Logan had hold of Josie's hand, her long dark waves spilling over her shoulders. Something about seeing those two together didn't sit right with Jenessa, but she hadn't been able to pinpoint why. Was it because Logan was supposed to be in love

with her, not Josie? Or was it his possible involvement in Jake's life if he and Josie were to get serious? Would that interfere with her mother-like relationship with Jake? Her emotions were a jumble as the questions kept whirling in her head.

Suddenly she thought of Charlie. Jenessa turned and looked at the boy as he climbed out of the pool. He looked so much like Logan. Too bad she was wrong about his having been adopted.

~*~

Michael had come to relieve his father from the barbecuing duties, but his father refused to give them up.

"Okay then, but it looks like we're running out of chips and tomatoes, Pops. I'm going to go inside and get some more, then you can take a break."

"I'll be here when you get back," his dad replied.

As Michael reached for the doorknob, Jenessa joined him.

"Hey, babe," he said. "Enjoying the party?" He opened the door for her.

"I am, but I was looking for the bathroom." She stepped inside and he followed.

Standing in the family room, he gestured toward the hallway. "Right down the hall to your left, but wait." He grabbed her hand before she set off. "I'm sorry I haven't been able to spend much time with you this afternoon. I need to help my folks, after all, this is my son's party."

"No problem, I understand. It's given me a chance to visit with Ramey and Charles. But I want you to know I'm happy to help out."

"No need." He tugged her close and kissed her, her lips sending a warmth spreading through him. When he let go, he was sure his eyes were smiling from the pleasure of it. "Thanks for just being here."

She tossed him a flirty grin and headed down the hallway.

While Michael was busy in the kitchen, Josie came into the house. "Michael?" she called out.

"In the kitchen," he responded.

~*~

Having quickly finished her business, Jenessa proceeded down the hall toward the family room, seeing Josie pass by on her way to the kitchen. The woman was ravishing as always, and apparently unaware of Jenessa's presence.

Jenessa hung back in the hallway, curious about their conversation. She felt a little guilty for eavesdropping, but her feet refused to move.

"Michael," Josie's sultry voice came, "I just got a call from my agent. I'm so excited—a casting director in Hollywood wants me for a juicy supporting role in a new movie." Her voice rose with elation. "Can you believe it?"

No reply came from Michael. Jenessa could only assume he was glaring at her, speechless.

"Say something," Josie pressed.

"What do you want me to say?"

"Something. Anything."

"I'm not surprised," he said flatly.

"So that's how you're going to play it?" She sounded irritated he wasn't happy for her. "I've got to run, Michael. Could you say good-bye to Jakey for me? Explain I had to leave suddenly and I'll call him later."

"You can't do that to him. At least say good-bye and give him a hug, Josie."

"In front of all his friends? You know he'll start crying and kids will tease him at school because of it."

"You'll be breaking the little guy's heart if you don't at least say good-bye. Bring him in the house and do it in private."

"No, really, look at the time. I need to get going. Logan is taking me to the airport."

"Why am I not surprised?"

And so the arguing continued.

Jenessa had heard enough. She quietly stepped outside, hopefully undetected, finding Logan waiting at the bottom of the steps, leaning against one of the pergola's supports. "Hello, Logan."

He straightened at seeing her. "Hey, Jenessa." A delighted smile spread across his face. "I was hoping I'd get a chance to talk to you."

"You were? Why?"

"After your ordeal last night, I've been wondering how you were." He leaned in and looked closely at the bruise on the side of her face. "You did a pretty good job of covering that thing up." He gently lifted her bandaged hand. "I hope Baxter is taking good care of you."

His tender touch sent a tingle dancing up her arm. She couldn't afford to have Michael see Logan holding her hand again, so she pulled it back. "Yes, he is."

"He'd better be."

"What about you? I hear Josie is leaving. Are you okay?"

"I'm fine."

"You sure?"

"Let's just say I'm not heartbroken." Logan crossed his arms and leaned a shoulder against the post. "Don't get me wrong, I like Josie. She was fun and really easy on the eyes, kind of a celebrity too, but it was nothing serious, just someone to pass the time with."

Something in her heart lifted at the thought they were not serious.

"I have to give other women a try, to fill the void, you know?"

"Fill the void?" Jenessa asked, wishing she hadn't.

"That you left in my heart…but so far none of them have stacked up to you."

Their eyes met and neither said a word, the moment pregnant with emotion.

"Before I forget," Logan said, breaking the silence, "there's something I wanted to tell you. I have some good news and some bad news."

"Oh really." Did she want to know?

"The good news is that my father's legal ploy to get out of jail has been denied."

She exhaled a sigh of relief, knowing Grey Alexander would make her life hell if given the opportunity. "What's the bad news?" She held her breath.

"The bad news is that he vowed he will never give up the fight."

"I'm not surprised to hear that." That was typical Grey Alexander. "Let's talk about something else, if you don't mind."

"Like what?"

"Well," she almost didn't want to broach the subject, but if anyone could help find their son, it would be Grey Alexander. "Is there any leverage you can use with your father to find out who adopted our baby?"

"Wow. That was out of left field."

"Not really," she said. "I think about him often."

"This might surprise you, Jenessa, but I've been curious too, especially in the last few years."

"You have?" she gasped.

"Well you don't have to sound that shocked." He breathed a laugh. "I'm not heartless. I just didn't want to disrupt the child's life. I know that if I had adopted a baby, I wouldn't want the birth parents butting in and upsetting the kid."

"I don't want to disrupt his life. I just want to see him, see what he looks like, know who's raising him, find out if he's happy. I want confirmation that I did the right thing in giving him away."

Logan shook his head slowly. "You just have to trust that you did the right thing, because you will probably never know."

"Can you at least ask your father who adopted our son?"

"Why do you think he would know?"

"Do you really believe the all-powerful Grey Alexander would let just anyone raise his grandson? His heir to the Alexander fortune?"

"Hey, that's my fortune you're talking about. Besides, I'm sure I'll be giving him more grandchildren someday."

Now that statement did surprise her.

Before Jenessa could respond to Logan's

astonishing declaration, Josie walked through the french doors and down the steps, her violet eyes glistening from the argument she'd just left. "I'm ready to go," she said to Logan, pushing her dark tresses back over one shoulder.

"Mommy! Mommy!" Jake hollered as he came running to Josie, dripping wet from having just gotten out of the pool. "Watch me dive!"

Josie crouched down to his level. "Sorry, baby, but something important has come up and I have to leave for a while." She gave him a quick, awkward hug, apparently trying not to get soaked. "Now go back and have fun with your friends, birthday boy. We'll talk later, okay?"

The excited countenance fell from his angelic face, replaced by an unmistakable expression of sheer disappointment. Jake pushed his lips into a little pout and expelled a defeated, "Okay." He turned and stalked back to the pool, his little shoulders drooping.

Such anger rose in Jenessa's heart that tears began to mist her eyes. She blinked them back, feeling her spine stiffening and her hands balling into fists. She wanted to throttle the woman.

Logan must have sensed her fury for he put a calming hand on Jenessa's shoulder.

She shrugged it off. "Poor Jake. He just wanted to show you his dive, Josie."

"I simply don't have the time right now," she replied to Jenessa with a look that said she didn't appreciate the girlfriend butting in. "Hollywood won't wait." Josie's attention quickly shifted. "Logan, we need to go."

"Sure, I understand," Jenessa replied with as much sweetness as she could muster. "And don't you worry, Josie, I will take good care of your son."

Josie's head whipped back in Jenessa's direction, arching a perfect eyebrow, pursing her luscious lips. "My husband too?"

"Ex-husband," Jenessa shot back, "with the emphasis most certainly on the ex."

Josie's intense eyes briefly rounded at the remark before they narrowed with fury. "Then you're welcome to him." She spun away and marched off.

Logan followed close behind, casting Jenessa a rueful look over his shoulder as they slipped around the corner of the house.

~*~

Michael traversed the red-brick steps to the patio, one hand grasping a couple bags of chips, the other a plate of sliced tomatoes. Jenessa turned at the sound as he set the food on the table.

She laced her arms around his waist. "Josie's gone. Are you okay?"

"I am now," he replied, his voice serious, his lips drawing into a tight-lipped smile.

Michael could never tell Jenessa how close he had come to taking Josie back for Jake's sake. But he'd thought back over his life—just him and Jake—they were happy and Jake was thriving, without Josie.

In the end, it was the thought that Jenessa would turn to Logan if he took Josie back that helped him make the final decision. It would be daily torture, regularly running into the woman he loved, watching her live her life with another man, especially knowing that he'd had the chance to be with her and didn't take it.

Besides, wouldn't Jake be far better off with his dad and Jenessa in a happy relationship than his mother and father in a contentious one? Eventually, Josie would probably end up heading off to greener pastures once more.

"Josie got an offer for a movie deal and she's off to Hollywood again, leaving me to explain it to our son. It breaks my heart."

Jenessa pulled back. "Her leaving?"

"No, her leaving Jake without the decency to explain it to him herself." Michael looked in the direction of where Logan and Josie had gone out. "Maybe she'll come back a little more often if she and Logan become an item."

"They're not."

"Not what?"

"An item. They're just friends."

"How do you know?"

"He told me—she's not the girl for him. He wants someone more like—"

"Like you?" Michael pulled her close. "But he can't have you. You're already taken."

She looked up into his face, her smile warm and wide. This woman filled his heart. He leaned down and gave her a brief kiss, her lips so soft and inviting. He wanted more of her. If only they were alone, he would show her how he really felt about her.

Did she feel the same? Did he have her whole heart? Or did a part of it still belong to Logan Alexander?

She leaned her head on his chest and hugged him hard. "I love you, Michael Baxter."

THE END

Thank you so much for reading my book,
The Stone House Secret.
I hope you enjoyed it very much.

Debra Burroughs

The highest compliment an author can get is to
receive a great review, especially
if the review is posted on Amazon.com.

Debra@DebraBurroughs.com

www.DebraBurroughsBooks.com

ABOUT THE AUTHOR

Debra Burroughs writes with intensity and power. Her characters are rich and her stories of romance, suspense and mystery are highly entertaining. She can often be found sitting in front of her computer in her home in the Pacific Northwest, dreaming up new stories and developing interesting characters for her next book.

If you are looking for stories that will touch your heart and leave you wanting more, dive into one of her captivating books.

www.DebraBurroughsBooks.com

Made in the USA
Middletown, DE
18 June 2021